FACEMAN

A HULL GANGLAND COMING OF AGE STORY

CHRIS SPECK

Flat City Press 2024

Photos by Specky

'Sometimes you have to spit in your hands and raise the black flag.'
Templeton 'Faceman' Peck
The A-Team

ISBN-13: 978-1-7393308-9-7

PROLOGUE
Hull
Present Day

Our Dave can't sleep. It's fairly usual these days. Alone, he lays awake in the front bedroom of his big terrace on Westbourne Ave and watches the shapes that the branches make on the ceiling in the moonlight. He gets up for a wee but doesn't put the light on. He lays down again. He checks his phone. The doctor at the medical centre down the road prescribed him pills to help him drop off but Our Dave doesn't trust them. Pills make you sick. Outside it's windy and the branches sway in the darkness, there's the sound of a wheelie bin falling over and far away the call of a dog fox. There's nothing worrying Our Dave specifically, nothing more than normal. He has people he looks after, the drivers at the taxi office on Chants Ave, the houses he owns dotted around the city, the smuggling business that he controls that brings spirits in from Europe. If he worried about everything that could go wrong, he wouldn't have got any sleep for the last forty years. He doesn't know why he can't sleep these days.

There's a big bang, it sounds like another wheelie bin getting blown over by the wind. Our Dave gets up and goes to the window overlooking the street. The blinds are open, he likes to wake up with the light even though Hazel never did. The road outside is deserted and at peace. This is Westbourne Avenue, Hull, one of the posher streets but run down in some places. It's a contradiction, like this whole town. This street is late nineteenth century Victorian with houses built for the middle classes of the day, there are huge ten bedroomed properties with big ornate gardens and enormous halls, some kept in the original state, others chopped up into flats. Our Dave's property is one of the more modest houses with three bedrooms and a long garden with a shed at the end. He bought it with Hazel back in 1985 when you could afford a house on a working wage. It was a good street back then and it's a good street now.

Our Dave looks at himself in the mirror in the moonlight from over the roofs of the houses opposite. He's just over six foot and thin with strong arms and hairs peeping out of the white vest that he sleeps in. He wonders how he got to be so old, genuinely. He sees elderly fellas walking down Chanterlands Ave with their grey wispy hair and paper-thin skin and realises that he's much the same. It was just a minute ago that he moved in here with Hazel, and she made him carry her down the drive and through the front door. He thinks back to those days more and more now. Where has all the time gone? He does not know quite how he ended up here so old and with so much responsibility, and lonely as well. This is what not being able to sleep does to your head. He'll be fine in the morning. Maybe.

Our Dave turns to go back to bed, but before he does, he hears a creak on the stairs. It's not loud. He knows the floorboards near the top need replacing because they squeak whenever he walks up them, he was thinking the next owner could fix that problem. He probably doesn't have too many years left here. He frowns. There's another creak from the landing and he gets the sense suddenly that another person is in the house. His heart begins to pump as he stands there at the window in just his boxer shorts and vest. His stomach turns over. The hairs on his arms stand up. There's another creak and the wind whips up outside blowing over another one of the wheelie bins on the street. He thinks he sees the door moving. Our Dave's right hand goes to a fist by his side.

In the past, Our Dave has done things he is not proud of. Back in the seventies he was paid to sort people out, that's why he had that shotgun buried under his shed at Ragland Street allotment, and his business these days is not just the daytime taxi office on Chanterlands Avenue with the three drivers, but also, the wholesale smuggling of spirits into Hull through the docks. It's a criminal enterprise. Our Dave is a criminal, he'll give you a smile and a wave if you see him down the street, he'll buy you a pint if you see him in the St Johns, he helps those in this city who can't help themselves and he does it with a glad heart, but for what he has done and for what he does, he should be in jail.

This could be anyone creaking across the landing of his three bedroomed semi on Westbourne Ave, it could be a business rival, or a faceless goon paid to get rid of him, it could even be a run of the mill Hull burglar. A black glove pushes open the door slowly and a shape slinks into the room, nearly squatting and moving deathly slow. The figure is wearing a leather jacket and a balaclava, in one of his black surgeon's gloves is a matt grey pistol, a silenced Beretta M9A4. He aims at the bed where Our Dave ought to be sound asleep.

Our Dave has to act now.

He has to get this man in the balaclava first.

You get a sense of things when you get older. You start to see patterns emerging. You can guess what a person is going to say by their face. The seasons come and go quicker than they ever did. You can't move like you used to, but you know the tricks.

Our Dave has never been much of a fighter although he did his fair share of it when he was younger. He used his height and his intelligence, as well as the world around him to his benefit. You can slam someone's head in a car door, you can use the butt of a sawn-off shotgun to clobber a person on the chin – you don't have to rely on your fist. This is why Our Dave grabs the heavy brass clock from the bedside table as he moves, it was a wedding present from Hazel's mother to them both in 1984, and it was old back then. It hasn't worked for years. As soon as Our Dave lifts it, the gunman is aware he is not in bed, and in another heartbeat, he'll know that there is someone standing in the window looking down upon him in the darkness. Our Dave flings the clock across the bedroom and then makes a run down the end of the bed towards him. The gunman adjusts his position, and the matt grey pistol aims at the movement in the darkness, he pulls the trigger and there's the hiss of a bullet, and the sound of glass cracking as it goes through the windowpane behind. At almost the same moment, the weight of the bronze clock crashes into the man's neck just above his chest. Our Dave is on the gunman with a heavy right hook to his head, he feels the wool of the balaclava under his knuckles as he connects and falls on top of him. The gun clatters to the bedroom floor and the two men struggle. Our Dave is not the man he was even ten years ago, he doesn't have the supple movement to be able to swing punches like he did, so instead, he tries to get his hands around the man's throat.

The gunman is not an amateur. He's been paid very well to do this job, he stalked the house for a week before he did anything at all, he picked the lock to the back door yesterday evening while Our Dave was out so he knew how to do it. He's looked at the house floorplan because next door was for sale a few years ago and the details are still on the web. He does this sort of thing a lot, so he's prepared and even though he's never been to this town before, he knows the streets already and has a car parked round the corner for a quick getaway. He's here to kill Our Dave even if he doesn't know his name or why, he just does what he has to do for the money. It's nothing personal, of course, the hitman can't just give up because this old man has got a bit of spirit. You have to see a job through to the end, even if it gets messy along the way.

Our Dave's rough joiner's hands go round the throat as he grits his teeth. The gunman wriggles his hips to get a better position and then punches up with the flat of his hand into Dave's chin. The old man falls backwards onto the floor of his bedroom.

Some jobs are messy never mind how much you plan.

In the darkness, the gunman checks around the floor for the pistol, he doesn't want to have to strangle the old man, the bullet will do a much better job. The Beretta is on the landing just outside the door and he bends down to pick it up. The heavy brass clock must have broken his collar bone, and it hurts as he draws in breath, he stoops to collect the weapon.

Our Dave manages to get to his wobbly feet. He's been taught to do a job properly as well, you can't leave something half done and just expect it to sort itself out. Our Dave steps through the bedroom door and shoves the gunman hard so he falls into the banister. If Hazel were alive, she would have made him fix the wood a long time ago along with the creaky floorboards, Our Dave has got the skills, he was first a joiner fitting ships out on St Andrew's Dock in the seventies. Every time he comes up the stairs, he can still hear his wife lightly nagging at him to get it fixed, it's why he hasn't done the job yet, if he did, he wouldn't feel her there. This is why the gunman falls through the wood of the banister that has come loose from the wall at the far end. He collapses over it and into the big space down towards the hall below, it's a ten-foot drop, and he goes face first. The gunman's head smacks the bottom step and he breaks his neck, the rest of his body thuds to the floor like a sack of spuds.

It's happened so quickly.

Our Dave puts the landing light on and goes down the stairs in his bare feet. The gunman is a crumpled-up mess at the bottom of the steps still wearing his balaclava. Our Dave's heart thuds in his chest. He pushes the body onto his back with his foot and looks down at the black leather jacket and the surgeon's gloves on the hands.

This is new. Nobody has ever tried to bump Our Dave off like this before. He looks up to the broken banister and then down to the motionless man in black below. There were plenty of people in the past who would have wanted to get rid of him, but not these days. He's careful who he deals with and nice with it. Our Dave stoops to collect the matt black Beretta pistol, it's heavy and well looked after, he turns it over in his hands. It's been a while since he's held a gun and he's got a feeling that it might come in useful. In the cupboard under the stairs, Our Dave keeps his tool bag, it's the one he carries when he does odd jobs for people. He makes sure the safety catch is on and slips the gun down among the spanners and loose screwdrivers – just until he can think of a better place to hide it.

The moonlight shines through the windows around the door and Our Dave can hear the wind rattling the trees outside. He stands looking down over the lifeless gunman on the wooden floor.

If there is anyone who knows how to get rid of a dead body in this town, it's Our Dave.

CHAPTER ONE
Face

Gradually, and over many years, Tom Williams has developed a middle-aged gut, man tits and a sagging arse. He's got a round face, thick black glasses and a patchy brown beard with hair of the same colour that grows down over his ears. He sometimes wears a dark tweed suit jacket with suede elbow patches and dealer boots that have seen much better days.

Tom works at the university teaching law, and this is why he can afford a house on Westbourne Avenue. In actual fact, the pay is a lot worse than it used to be because of inflation and without his pretty short haired wife, Tom would struggle to get the mortgage these days. The job sounds much harder than it is. Tom is good at remembering things and he's a geek when it comes to law. You don't teach all the time and so Tom can go in hungover most days, he buys cases of wine from an online company that delivers weekly, and he wanders down to Princes Avenue at the weekend to drink in the German beer house where the people are friendly and non-judgmental. It's kind of the only place he feels at home these days. You wouldn't notice right away, but Tom has got a messed up and scarred face.

In 1988, when he was six, Tom's grandfather and he had a car crash. Just the two of them. It was half five on a Sunday afternoon as he delivered little Tom back to his parents, the old man had been sipping whiskey since twelve. He managed to drive his Jaguar off the flyover at the bottom of Hessle Road. The car landed on its roof; it was engulfed in a fireball. Before he retired, Tom's grandfather was a skipper on the trawlers. He used to say he would have been a pirate if he wasn't a trawlerman. He didn't survive, but young Tom did after he spent many weeks in intensive care. The burns are extensive, they are all over his face and his neck, down his back and along his arms; even his chest and stomach are ridged with scars. That's why Tom has the beard and the hair, along with the glasses. You might think you'd be the first to say something funny or profound to him about the way he looks, but you wouldn't be, there is nothing comedic or rude that hasn't been said to him before. He would rather hide if he can. He would rather be normal.

It's early Saturday morning and Tom has just collected a case of six bottles of wine from the delivery driver. There's a satisfying clink as he sets the cardboard down on the floor in the porch. He's noticed a big glazier's van outside Our Dave's house opposite and he wants to see what's happened. In that jacket with the patches on the elbows, Tom walks across the road to see the old man, they live opposite each other, and they are friends – kind of. Two men in overalls, one inside and one on a ladder are switching out a pane of glass from the upper window. Our Dave stands outside with a mug of tea in his hand.

"What's happened?" asks Tom.

"A bird flew into the window and cracked it." Tom looks up. The old piece of glass has already been taken out. He would never guess it was actually a bullet hole. Tom likes Our Dave in the way that most people do. He's always up for a natter and he's friendly enough in a round about sort of a way.

"It'll cost a bit," says Tom.

"Aye, I should say it will," answers Our Dave. He knows the man who runs the glazier company, and it won't cost him a thing. "How's you?"

"All good," says Tom. Our Dave looks the man up and down without doing so. He smells faintly of last night's wine; his hair is greasy, and the thick glasses cover the melted wax-like scars of varying colours on his face.

"I saw your daughter on her skateboard yesterday afternoon on the Marina. She's got some bottle, she has, she was making some big jumps." Our Dave was in one of the posh offices down there on a spot of business and the smooth steps are full of skaters and sometimes the sweet smell of weed.

"She's a he now, Dave," says Tom. Our Dave raises an eyebrow slightly. "His name's Alex. He identifies as male."

"I see." Our Dave is not going to pass any judgement. He may be old in some ways, but he knows that the world changes, in fact that's the only thing you can be sure of.

"The misses finds it hard to get her head around," says Tom. "She'll need time, I guess." Tom's wife is attractive with a short dark pixie cut and well applied make-up, she's liberal enough, but feels like she might be losing her daughter somehow.

"Well, she does look like a lad," says Our Dave. Alex wears very baggy, low-riding dirty jeans, huge t-shirts and a beanie hat over the thick matted blond hair.

"Best let them get on with it," says Tom. "I'm sure you got up to a few things when you were young, Our Dave." The older man smiles and nods. When he was young Our Dave did what he was supposed to do and didn't question it, he drank bitter, played football and got a job as a joiner. You didn't get to choose. The glaziers have carried the new pane up the ladder and are beginning to fit it into place.

"Sorry to pry, Dave, but is everything ok?" asks Tom. Our Dave looks at him suddenly and his brow knits in an uncharacteristic frown.

"Yeah, why?"

"You look a bit pale, and your eyes are red." Our Dave tries on a smile.

"I'm fine, kid." Tom here may look like he's a floppy haired scatty brained lecturer, but he notices things about the world that other folk wouldn't. Nobody else would see that Dave's eyes are bloodshot and that his left hand is shaking slightly. It was Tom here who saw the ambulance outside Our Dave's house eighteen months back and Tom who knocked on his door to see if Hazel and he were okay. It was Tom who checked through the electoral register with his students during a public information class and saw that only Our Dave was registered at his address. Tom visited the government website out of curiosity and found out that Our Dave's wife Hazel was dead. Cancer. He has not mentioned it. He is too middle-class to do so.

Our Dave doesn't like to lie, especially not to good people, but he told Tom that Hazel had gone to visit her ill sister in Exmouth and that was why he hadn't seen her for a while. It's good to have nice neighbours and all that, but Tom is a bit too keen to be pals. Dave guesses that his wife is horrible to him, and he doesn't have any friends at all – like lots of blokes.

"Is Hazel still down south?" asks Tom. He's gone along with Our Dave's lie. It's no business of his what's happened, but he likes the old man, he wants to help if he can.

"Aye," he doesn't add any more detail.

"You must be missing her." The mask drops for a split second, half a heartbeat even, and Our Dave finds his eyes projecting the part of him that he needs to keep hidden. This is the bit that says she is gone and is never ever coming back. It flashes just for a fraction of a second like a distant lighthouse far away in the fog on a bitter cold night, and then it's gone.

"It's good to have the house to myself," says Our Dave. Tom's face looks back at him level and serious. Perhaps he noticed it in Our Dave's eyes.

"If you ever need anyone to talk to, Our Dave, then I'm always free on a Saturday, especially now Alex's off with his mates."

"I've got loads of stuff on, Tom." He hasn't.

"The taxi office? There's never anyone in there."

"I've got to catch up on paperwork."

"Really? What kind?"

"Inland revenue stuff."

"I'm very good at that." Tom really is. Our Dave scrambles for a lie to tell this earnest and well-meaning man who lives across the road. Ordinarily someone like Tom here would never phase Our Dave, but the experience of the masked gunman the night before has shaken him emotionally somehow, and dragging the body to his car and then driving it up to Cleveland Street incinerator to burn it has been hard on him physically. The gunman was a big lad. He had to wait until five in the morning for the change of shift between workers till he got the nod to back his grey Ford Galaxy into the car park and unload.

"I've got issues with the council too, business rates and carparking outside the office – bits and bobs I just need to sort out." As soon as Our Dave says this, he knows he's made an error. It's easy to forget when you look at Tom, but he does lecture law up at the university and he has done for nearly twenty years. He understands the law, and the chance to help someone out does not come often. When he first moved into the house opposite some eight years ago it was Our Dave who came over and introduced himself, he found himself plumbing in the dishwasher and the washing machine and since then, he has jump started Tom's estate car, leant him tools and it's Our Dave who keeps the spare key to his house in a pot on the kitchen windowsill. He can see Tom's eyes sparkle. This is something he can help with.

"I'm free tonight," says Tom. "I'll come round and have a look." This is the kind of thing Our Dave would say, as if you haven't got a choice.

"I don't really have it all organized," says Our Dave and it's at the office." If Tom sets one foot inside the house, he will know Hazel has not been around for months.

"I'll meet you there. What time?" Our Dave is being backed into a corner.

"Seven?"

"I'll bring some wine."

"I don't drink it."

"This is good stuff, Our Dave, of course you'll drink it. I

owe you, and you'd be doing me a favour by letting me help out." Our Dave is sure he has said this kind of thing himself before.

"Okay." Tom smiles and his eyes twinkle under his thick rimmed glasses. He pats Our Dave on the shoulder and makes his way across the road to his house leaving the glaziers to finish fitting the window.

Tom is pleased with himself because he will have to stay sober until he meets Our Dave at seven. In recent times, Saturday has been a day for Tom to get lightly plastered in the afternoon developing into full on pissed up by the evening, and then absolutely battered into the early morning. It wasn't always like this, once upon a time Tom had little Alex to look after on Saturday night and until Christmas past, he did just that, he would do homemade chicken kebabs and they'd watch a film or play video games. It's his wife's night off, officially and she goes for cocktails with the girls or for a night away in York or Leeds, or wherever else she goes.

Tom liked spending time with his daughter and up until six months ago, he thought he knew her. Since she turned sixteen she has grown up. He has to remember to call her he. It's not that he doesn't want to, it's hard for his brain to make the switch after so many years. So, since late last year, Tom has been relieved of his childcare duties. Alex goes out with his skater friends, his wife toddles off for drinks at a friend's house round the corner, and he sits in the kitchen with a glass of red wine after he's been in the pub all afternoon.

In September last year one of Inma's friends moved back to Egypt and couldn't take her cat with her, it's a fat English Shorthair with a fluffy blue crisp coat and light-yellow eyes. It's called Galal, and Inma claims it only understands Arabic. Tom turned to Google translate to find out that the name means 'wheel'. Seems fitting. It hates Tom and he's learned to keep away from it, the beast scratches and claws him, dashes from the room when he enters and whines at the back door to come in, then whines to go out. Like his wife, Galal has a disregard for Tom, she is dismissive of any attempt at warmth, rude in the way she stares at him and fickle with what she wants him to do.

In the loft of the big, terraced house on Westbourne Ave, Tom's wife stores the dresses she sells online. Tom has a desk in the corner that he calls his office. Inma is doing well with her clothing business, she's been running it for many years now and there are coats, shoes, long and short knitted skirts, some hung up in rows on rails and others packed in carboard boxes. She buys them wholesale from Thailand or India or Indonesia, and then flogs them on her website or social media. She's half Spanish with a black pixie haircut, back in the day when Tom met her, she was eighteen stone, after she had Alex, even bigger.

Over the years she has worked on herself, at first, she started eating less and healthier and then began the gym, it took a long time for her to get where she is now, there was surgery too to remove the excess skin from her stomach and back. Tom, on the other hand, was probably at his best when they first met, he was a successful lecturer at the university, better paid than he is today and with a wide circle of friends. Childcare and the pressures of work were an excuse for him to retreat into himself. Tom's life seems to have faded as Inma's has taken off. She takes videos of herself in the outfits and posts them on Insta, she mimes to songs too and does make-up tutorials, she's popular. If you were to look at the family from outside, you'd think what a successful lot they are with their big house on Westbourne Ave and the spacious garden with a big shed at the bottom painted green. Of course, that's what they are – successful.

In the kitchen Inma is writing information on the big calendar that they have next to the American style fridge freezer. She's dressed in big jeans and a cream crop top that shows off her flat stomach, something she would never have been confident or thin enough to wear twenty years ago. She has false black nails and smooth hands that move as she writes the details. She's ready for her Saturday night out.

"That fence has come down again," she says. She means that a square panel has blown over in the wind and snapped. Her tone is accusatory, as if it's Tom's fault. The fact that it will take him weeks to get it fixed will irk her.

"I saw," he says. "I'll wait for the windy weather to blow over and I'll get another one."

"It means those kids from next door will come rooting through our garden. Last time they churned up the grass playing football, and their mother doesn't give a toss." Much to Inma's dismay, the house next door was taken over by a developer last year and the big semi was carved up into three flats. An Iranian mother and her two teen sons have moved in downstairs, there's a hippy couple on the second floor and a man who has a big motorbike in the attic room. It's not that she doesn't like foreigners, she just doesn't want the street to lose the character and charm that it has, cutting these big houses up into flats is greedy. The Iranian boys are in year ten and eleven at the secondary up the road and have wide, fearful brown eyes. They like football and their mother shouts at them a lot.

"It's my father's birthday on the fifth," she says. "I'm going to have them round here." She means the in-laws, and the house will have to be spotless for this. Tom nods as he stands in the doorway to the kitchen. He will drink his way through that one.

"Alex's gone out then, I see," he says.

"Yes, I've told her to be back by seven."

"You mean him?" Inma looks up at Tom and her eyes are perfect ovals accentuated by the eyeliner, her nostrils are flared.

"She's a girl. We've talked about this."

"I thought you accepted it."

"To her face, yes. She's still my daughter even if she's got greasy hair and baggy trousers. It's a phase she's going through. You'll see." Inma stops writing on the calendar and stands back.

"I'll be out at seven," says Tom.

"Where?" Inma manages to seem both surprised and disgusted by this.

"I said I'd help Our Dave out."

"Who's that?"

"The old man across the street." Inma frowns. Tom adds more detail: "The fella who fixed our washing machine when we first moved in, he fitted the fence at the back end of the garden for us as well. He runs the taxi office opposite the chip shop." Inma's face softens.

"He's not an old man," she says in Our Dave's defence. If she can take issue with what Tom says, she will.

"He's older than we are."

"What does he need help with?"

"A legal issue."

"What time will you be back?"

"I don't know."

"It's my night off, it always has been. Every other night of the week I'm here and available, just not Saturdays. You'll have to cancel."

"Alex is sixteen, he'll be fine without me here."

"Where are you going?"

"Avenue Cars, the taxi office on Chants Ave." Inma takes her handbag from the kitchen table and puts it over her shoulder. She smells of perfumed spice, it's rich and sweet at the same time. Tom likes her pixie cut, he likes her calm dark eyes and olive skin too.

"You'll be back at eight then," she says in a level, commanding voice.

"Maybe."

"Don't be a cock, Tom, you're no good at it."

"I'll just be out and if Alex gets back before me, she'll be fine. She's sixteen."

"You mean 'he'?"

Imna walks towards him standing in the doorway of the expensive kitchen. They paid extra during the refurb for underfloor heating and Tom can feel the warmth under his feet. She is a few inches smaller than he is and her eyes are smooth and brown, he can see the curve of her neck and smell the perfume. She's absolutely perfect, more so even because she doesn't want anything to do with him.

"Alex's not here now," says Tom and he tries to make his eyes smoulder. Imna sneers, these days she doesn't even conceal her facial emotions. She is disgusted by him somehow.

"What do you mean?"

"We could pop upstairs." She looks down at the floor. She is his wife. She did say yes when he asked her to marry him all those years ago on a Greek yacht, but this is disgusting in some way, as if, just because he is allowed to and they live together, he can make this kind of proposition.

"I'm late already," says Inma as she brushes past him. Her heels tap down the long hallway to the front door, she opens up and slams it shut behind her so the letterbox rattles.

However disgusted Inma was with the suggestion of sex, Tom is more so. They have not had any intimate contact for as long as he can remember, and he is desperate, on a physical level as well as emotionally for the closeness that they used to share. Every advance he makes is spurned - in the mornings under the covers he tries to cuddle up, in the evenings he sits down next to her on the big brown sofa. Slowly and in desperation, his own low reserve of self-worth is ebbing away out of him but so painfully moderate is the leak, that Tom does not even feel it leaving him. He does not resent her. Who would want to be with him anyway, he thinks.

In the silent hallway, Tom looks at his reflection in the big ornate mirror from the expensive furniture superstore out of town. He takes off his glasses and brushes away his curtain style long hair so he can see his features and his big beard. They don't adequately cover the burns he has on his face. He has just got worse while Inma has begun to shine. At school the kids called him Face. It was a simple play on words, like the way they called the perpetually miserable bus driver Happy. His skin is a mess and these thick glasses and long hair hide the obvious.

Tom is an intelligent man, he breezed through his law degree and the exams for the bar, he was to be made a partner for a firm before he started teaching. Now, he's an expert in European law, he has a knowledge and sense of history, he used to be invited, at times, to travel down to those more affluent universities where he guest lectured. He is used to dealing with complex issues and this is why Tom looks down at the case of wine he brought in earlier – the drink stops his mind spinning and gives him peace, so he thinks. There is nothing else to do on a Saturday night with Alex gone and his wife out. Tom will just have one large glass before he goes to visit Our Dave.

Tom is in the middle of a drinking session that has lasted daily since well before lockdown. He thinks he's fine. The one beautiful thing about being a drunk is that you don't realise you are one until you stop.

CHAPTER TWO
Kasia and Friday

Saturday nights are not as busy as they were back in the day, but the Dairycoates Inn just off Hessle Road, is emptier than it should be. Leatherhead seems to have gone away for good and the pub has taken on a sanitised feel.

Years ago, it had that lived in sense, the leather seats around the outside of the lounge needed recovering and the carpets were worn out, but the beer was good, at least, and there was always a friendly smile from the bar lady. Ever since Kasia took over eight months ago, things have gone uphill and downhill at the same time. The beer is still good, and the seats have all been refurbished, the carpet has been replaced with a wood effect floor and there are spotlights in the ceiling that make it feel like a hospital.

This used to be a pub for working men to drink in, but Kasia has put the prices up in line with what she thinks the place is worth and because her overheads have risen as well. Leatherhead would never have done that, as horrible as she was, the fat old cow would have taken a profit hit to look after these old fellas who reminded her of her granddad or her uncles. The drinkers that once gave the place the veneer of being legitimate have drifted off over the last few months, some to the Halfway Hotel on Hessle Road itself and others just stay at home with cans and the TV. Kasia still has her main business, of course, that's running better than ever before.

In 1959 a chemist named Paul Janssen synthesized Fentanyl and the drug was authorized for use just under ten years later in medical settings. It's a hundred times more powerful than morphine. Kasia's heroin comes in off the docks and she has her men cut and mix it down with this fentanyl that will make a gram into three grams, and then it gets sold out the backdoor of the pub or by her dealers. That part of the game is tailing off as well, there are ways to make highs which are infinitely cheaper and less risky in terms of the law. She has a Vietnamese lad on board now who knows how to cook drugs up in the lab she has above the cold storage unit near the old St Andrew's Dock. Europeans have been making stuff which is called spice on the streets for years now, it's worse than heroin easily. Kasia still has the iron framed shop bike that she rides to the pub in the morning, the plastic flowers around the basket still get polished after every ride, and nobody in the pretty wide world would ever believe that thin, red headed Kasia with her long proud nose commands a drug empire that covers all of Hull and the surrounding areas.

Kasia still rents the little three-bedroomed semi at the top of Woodcock Street. It's half a mile from the pub. She's lived there since before Leatherhead employed her as a cleaner, and there's no reason to change. Understand that Kasia does not need all the money she makes from the pub and the other business, but it gives her security. Her grandmother grew up under the wing of the communist block back in Poland, and she instilled in Kasia the need to make sure that you have enough for whatever problems might arise in the future. Money will not make you happy, she used to say, but it helps.

At the little kitchen table, Kasia sits opposite her daughter. Her name is Alicja. The blonde girl is working on her homework with a bright coloured pencil. She is in year three at the primary school round the corner, Kasia can see how bright she is already, she can also see the wayward traits that her father had. When she first came to the UK, Kasia was not alone. Alicja's father was called Pawel. She planned to marry him with his blonde hair and crooked teeth because he had a good heart, but it didn't quite work out like that. They took jobs in factories off Hessle Road, and earned good money, and they were free from the old country, for a time but it was easier for Pawel to score weed in the UK, and he earned enough to buy a big gaming PC that he set up in the bedroom. In six months, Kasia had lost him to cannabis smoke and the distant rattle of gunfire on Call of Duty. She was pregnant already and when she told him, he was more alarmed than happy. Kasia wanted it to work, and she wanted him to change. He tried as well, and he was a good and sweet father to Alicja until she was nearly four, but Pawel never did manage to stop smoking weed completely and he never got a better job than the one he started out with in the fish factory.

Two years ago, Kasia decided to get rid of him, it wasn't anything like what she did to Leatherhead. She just told him that if he didn't leave, she would run away with Alicja, and he would never see his daughter again. This was a prospect Pawel couldn't bear, so he left. He used to phone every week, now it's every two weeks, Kasia never lets him speak to his daughter anyway; she bins all the cards, toys and letters that he sends too. As soon as he moved out, she accused him of domestic violence and after the criminal proceedings Pawel was issued with a restraining order. He started to care for his daughter too late in Kasia's eyes. As far as she's aware, little Alicja's father is down in London working on a building site. This is how she likes it. Alicja knows he is gone and that he's never coming back. She asks about him less than she used to.

"I've finished," says the blonde girl as she puts the pencil down. She has wide blue eyes like her father.

"We speak Polish in this house," says Kasia.

"I'm not very good at it," she answers in Polish. She turned eight the month before and her accent is perfect along with her diction and grammar.

"You're good at anything you set your mind to," says Kasia. "Is that all your homework done?"

"Yes," answers Alicja.

"Excellent." There's no emotion to the word. Kasia promised her daughter they could go round the corner to Hessle Road, and she would buy her a reading book from the supermarket there if she finished all of her homework now. There are no food or drink treats in this house.

They put on their coats, go out the front door and walk down Hawthorne Ave to Hessle Road. Opposite are industrial buildings, one is a gardening place and the other sells tiles. This is a working street, people come here because the businesses are cheap. If you want somewhere pretty, then you'd be better off somewhere else. They pass the big gym on the corner and then the closed down Lithuanian shop. Here on Hessle Road proper, lots of the little businesses are boarded up; weeds grow out the guttering along the rooves and rotten shutters are down in front of the big windows. Once upon a time this was a rich street, trawlers landed fish off the docks, and everyone profited from it in one way or another. Nowadays the big supermarkets have hoovered up all the trade and the little independent shops have collapsed under the pressure.

Kasia and Alicja walk side by side and in silence. They each have duffel coats done up to their necks albeit of different sizes. Kasia has sensible Dr Marten copies. Alicja wears trainers that are good for her ankles. At the pedestrian crossing, they wait for the lights to change although there's space enough for them to cross between the cars. It's best to do things properly. As they walk down towards the big supermarket, a man with a bald head and a puffer jacket catches Kasia's eye. He looks away quickly because he knows who she is. Others down this street wouldn't. It suits Kasia just fine that British people think Poles are hardworking and organized, they are in some ways, but in truth they're warm and rude and brave and sweet, just the same as most folk. It's Kasia that's the cold fish, not where she comes from.

Inside, the two walk to the back of the supermarket to the homeware section where they keep the books and the electronics. It's not so busy because it's evening. On the aisle with the kitchenware there are pans and pots, knives and ironing boards and right at the end, Kasia and Alicja see a couple. She's petite with long straight hair and blue eyes and he's taller with a wispy beard, chiselled chin and a long overcoat with sensible shoes. They stand close to each other as they look at the crockery and there is electricity coming from these two – it's in the way they stand together without being joined. As Kasia gets nearer, she sees the blonde girl turn to the man, she gives him a great and wide smile that is all teeth and eyes, and he smiles back. They have shared some sort of joke, and they lean in, she puts her hands around him and they hug just as Kasia and Alicja pass by. It's sweet.

In the next aisle that's full of books, Alicja is curious.

"What was wrong with those two?" she asks. "Why did they hug?"

"They'll be in love," says Kasia. She knows not to lie to children.

"What does that mean?"

"It means they trust each other, and they want the best for each other." Alicja's clever blue eyes narrow, she knows what love means, she was just testing her mother.

"Why aren't you in love?" she asks.

"It's a special thing," answers Kasia. "It comes fleeting, and it leaves quickly." She is not sure why she's answering such a question without thinking, that's not like her at all. "If it happens to you then you're lucky, you have to hold onto it."

"Were you in love with my father?"

"Yes," there is no pause in Kasia's answer.

"Are you in love with him now?"

"No, but don't go thinking that doesn't make you special, Alicja. I love you more than I do anyone." Again, there is no emotion to Kasia's voice as she says these words, they are just facts like the earth goes round the sun and day follows night. She loves her daughter.

"Do you think you'll be in love again?" Kasia has never considered this.

"If it happened to me again," she says. "I wouldn't let it go so easily. I'd fight for it. I'd fight for it like I'd fight for you."

It's pretty easy to drink a bottle of wine. Tom can do it in three glasses. You'll often hear folk say that the first is the best one all night, but with Tom, the first is just to quench his thirst and start the buzz. On the second glass he tastes the rich notes of smoked applewood or whatever it says on the bottle, and at the end of the third, he is calmed greatly. Don't go thinking that a bottle of wine will get you drunk either, for Tom, it's just a warm up to the rest of the evening so that when he walks along Westbourne Ave up to Chanterlands with his long coat buttoned up against the late February air, he does not stagger at all.

The street is gearing up for a Saturday night; a gang of eight or so kids in hoodies on various mountain bikes pass stinking of weed, two lady joggers in pink flash by, a car slows down to go over the speed bumps with the windows open and music blaring, a Just Eat delivery bike with a square blue backpack whizzes by on the path. Westbourne Ave is home to all sorts. There are houses along here built in 1882 boasting eight bedrooms with an expensive Land Rover parked in the drive, a little further down the big terraces have been turned into flats that are home to asylum seekers. Posh folks make guacamole in their kitchens and drink expensive white wine while three doors down, two lads who sell weed, have made a bucket bong with an empty cider bottle and are playing fortnight on an old PS4. Tom feels at home down this street, for while he is a lecturer at the university there's still the maverick in him, so he likes to think. It doesn't take him long to walk up to where he said he'd meet Our Dave – Avenue Cars.

Back in the day when he got taxis, Tom would always use this office, these days he push bikes up to work and walks to the pub on Princes Ave. If he does go into town to get the train anywhere, he gets the bus. He goes round the back of Avenue Cars to the little car park and taps on the door. It takes a minute for Our Dave to step through the galley kitchen and open up.

"Come in," he says. Tom unhooks his rucksack from his shoulders. Our Dave can hear the clink from within as the man unzips it and draws out a smooth bottle of red wine.

"It's Italian month at the wine club," he says. "This is a chianti; it really is good. Have you got any glasses?" Our Dave does the kind of smile that's not a smile at Tom, he can see the man has had a drink already and senses the loneliness that comes off him. It's the desperation to have someone to drink with.

"I thought we'd sort the business out before all that," says Our Dave. He really does need some legal help and if he can get Tom to do it before he's off his face it will be better.

"Ah yes. I'll have a look at the paperwork first, shall I?" Our Dave nods and shows him through to the back office and the big round table.

Once upon a time, the back room would be ablaze with action at this time on a Saturday. There'd be a lass on the phones taking calls and bookings, drivers coming in and out for pick-ups and punters waiting in the front room for cabs to take them off into the city. It's dead these days. Who'd have thought it? First nobody has enough money to drink and next, the younger generation are teetotal.

Our Dave sits down at the round table and puts on his reading glasses. He's gathered the documents he needs Tom to look at in a yellow folder, it's legalese from the council concerning carparking at the front of the taxi office. Tom sits down next to him and brushes the long hair away from his face, Our Dave can see the burn marks on his cheeks and down his chin. As his brown eyes consider the written words on the papers, Tom becomes the lawyer he is. It takes him ten minutes to read the documents Our Dave has set out for him, and he does so carefully. Unlike the man who walked into Avenue Cars a few minutes before, he is level-headed and realistic, educated and to the point, the confidence is reassuring. It takes Tom another ten minutes to draft a letter on Our Dave's laptop to the council explaining the man's position and asking for clarification on a number of points. In half an hour he's done what the posh lawyers in town would charge a day to do. Our Dave has made Tom a coffee which he sets down on a coaster next to him now he's finished. The activity has sobered Tom up a little, so he has a headache and once it's clear the business of law is concluded, he slips back into the dickhead he thinks he is. Our Dave can see that this is an act, perhaps it's not a conscious one.

"I brought us some wine remember," says Tom.

"I don't drink the stuff," answers Our Dave. "It messes with my guts."

"This is top quality Italian, Dave. Have you got any glasses?"

"How much do I owe you?" he asks. Tom frowns.

"Nothing. You've done me a few favours before, I'm happy to help you." Tom didn't expect his night to finish so quickly. He was looking forward to company,

"Well, I've got to get on," says Our Dave meaning their business is done. He is sorry he can't oblige this man with his scars and the glasses and beard to cover them over, but wine really does mess with his guts and Our Dave isn't as good as talking shite and getting drunk as he used to be. Tom stands up and packs his wine back into his rucksack.

"Another time, maybe," he says.

"Aye," answers Our Dave but he doesn't mean it.

Back in his house on Westbourne Ave, Tom opens the same bottle of wine he was going to drink with Our Dave. He eats crisps sandwiches and stares out into the garden. The cat runs away from him when he goes to sit in the front room. He tries to watch TV but he's too drunk. He babbles at the walls around him. The oblivion is not as good as he thought it would be. It never is.

Alex gets back home about twelve and leans his skateboard

against the wall quietly. He's not worried that he'll get caught. His mum will still be out, and his father will be asleep, pissed. He walks down the hallway, and the lights are all still on. The long wooden banister has been ripped out of the wall with force, and one end lays on the bottom step. His father falls about when he's this drunk on a Saturday night. Alex will pretend he did not notice this.

Upstairs, the light is still on also in the master bedroom, and there is Tom, passed out, fully clothed on the double bed. Alex didn't do much skateboarding; he and two friends walked all the way up to the Quadrant Estate near Cottingham to score some weed and then drank a bottle of whiskey sours on the way back – he is crossfaded and tired more than off his head. Alex has seen his father like this before. He walks a few steps closer to check that the man is alive and breathing, then, he turns the light out and closes the door.

Inma returns about half one, takes off her boots at the bottom of the stairs and goes up. She passes the ripped off banister with a huff and then upstairs, sees the same thing as Alex did in the darkness – a six-foot man with a big beard laid diagonally across the bed asleep, only now he is snoring. His shirt has come up so she can see his flabby, hairy belly as he lays there with the moonlight across him. Inma has had a drink of course, but she's not drunk, she snarls in silent disgust at the man she married. The woman backs out of the room and closes the door, she stomps across the landing of the big house in her bare feet and taps on what she still believes is her daughter's room.

"Come in," says Alex. Inma opens the door and puts her head around the wood. Alex is in bed with his knees up to his chest and a phone in his lap. He removes an earbud as he looks at his mum. "What is it?" asks Alex, as if something has happened.

"What time did you get in?"

"About half nine."

"Was your father here?"

"Yeah."

"How drunk?" Alex likes his dad, and he has already lied anyway.

"Not very."

"Have you seen the state of him?" Alex has, but will not say this to his mother. She has a temper. She says it's because of her Spanish blood.

"No."

"He's passed out, again, and the banister's been pulled off the wall – did you notice that?"

"No." Inma's eyes narrow in hatred.

"This can't go on, Alex," she says. "I can't take this, week in, week out." Alex gives her a thin smile. At least in a year or two, when he's done his A levels Alex will be out of this house and then his mother and father can shout and bicker on in peace.

Tom has a hangover most days, except on weekends when he is more often than not still drunk. His head pounds as he walks to the bathroom where he locks himself in and takes down his trousers to sit down on the toilet. He looks at the time on his watch. It's just after six. He is still wearing his shoes. Tom holds his head in his hands as he feels his brain throb, it takes a minute to piece together what happened. Like every Saturday night – nothing happened, he just got drunk.

He walks down the stairs and sees the banister that has come off the wall. In the kitchen he surveys the damage from the night before, there are three empty wine bottles on the big farmhouse table. One of them has a little left in the bottom so Tom picks it up and drains the last few drops – it is Sunday, he reasons, and he doesn't have to drive anywhere. He boils the kettle and looks out the kitchen window at the garden in the light fog of a February morning as the water rumbles.

You don't set out to become a drunk, and even when you

are one, you still don't think you are. The world is full of booze: characters sip whiskey in movies, late night radio presenters read out texts from listeners who are settling down with a glass of red, billboards advertise the stuff, it's hardwired into the bible, there are pubs dedicated to it on every street corner in every city and village up and down the country. It's normal. Tom rubs his eyes. The spiderwebs glisten in the mist across the fence on the decking – he is still drunk. The only excuse you need for drinking is the fact that you exist. He makes himself a cup of black coffee in a Haltemprice 10k mug that Inma got for a run last year.

Tom is an intelligent man, he likes to multitask, that's why, in his office up at the university, the radio is permanently on while he works, he is answering emails while he researches, grading papers while he writes, each task done at mini breaks from the other, and the more complex the task, the better. When Tom's brain is taken up with other things, he feels free, it's why he's so good at his lecturing job and the research too, and yet, when he walks through the front door here after riding his bicycle home, he feels the intense pressure of normality on him. He has to just sit and relax or watch TV or read a novel – the booze that he drinks is like an off switch, so he thinks, but it is killing him slowly and his brain too. He swallows as he picks up the coffee cup and the truth swirls around his brain just behind his eyes but does not come to the surface.

He'll get that banister fixed before Inma wakes up. Then he'll have a shower and be fresh as a daisy for the rest of the day, well, just until early evening when, depending on what Inma is up to, he'll stroll down to the little German beer house on Princes Avenue for a pint before tea – it is Sunday after all. He'll pop across to see Our Dave and borrow his tool kit and everything will be well. If he can get on with the job, he'll make Inma poached eggs on toast for when she wakes up.

Our Dave is loading the boot of his grey Ford Galaxy with

boxes. Tom walks across the road. It's just before seven and Westbourne Ave is quiet. The mist is still heavy in the air.

"You busy?" asks Tom.

"Just delivering some stuff for someone. Did you have a heavy one?" asks Our Dave.

"Not really," says Tom. You can see in his red eyes that he did. "Can I borrow your toolkit, like I did last week, I pulled the banister off the wall, and I need to screw it back in place?"

"Aye," says Our Dave. He lifts one more big pot into the back of the car and closes the boot. "I'll grab it for you."

"I'll bring it back as soon as I'm done."

"It can wait till tomorrow, Tom. I've got someone to see in Leeds." He goes inside the house to the cupboard under the stairs and grabs the yellow tool bag that he takes with him to do odd jobs. It'll have everything that Tom needs and he's borrowed it before. Ordinarily, Our Dave does not miss details, he can't afford to in the business that he's in and any evidence he leaves must be swept away and cleaned up, this means accounts, computer data, video evidence; folks must be paid for their silence and compliance, the truck drivers who smuggle in booze must be trustworthy, the customs officials who turn a blind eye must be reliable. He cannot miss a single hair. The events of the other night have shaken him somewhat, or maybe he's getting old. The thing is, that everyone makes mistakes, that's the only thing you can be absolutely sure of.

Our Dave hands the yellow bag to Tom in the street in the early morning, and the still drunk man with the beard and long hair smiles as he takes it and walks back towards his front door. Tom sets the bag down at the bottom of the stairs and examines the broken banister – it's come out of the wall plug, he'll just need to screw it back in. He unzips the yellow bag and pulls open the material to reveal the tools within, then reaches down to rummage about for a screwdriver. His hand touches something unexpected, and his fingers go around the handle. At the bottom of the stairs and still reeling from the wine from the night before, mild mannered drunk and law lecturer Tom Williams holds the Beretta pistol up to his face in wonder and fear.

Here is destiny.

At about the same time, Our Dave is just speeding up to join the M62 towards Leeds. Like Tom, he feels his stomach churn. He remembers he left the Baretta pistol in that bag. He won't be back till late tonight, so he'll have to get it tomorrow and hope Tom hasn't found it.

If he has, Our Dave will have to become a little more serious with the man than he ever hoped he would have to.

CHAPTER THREE
Sunday

After he fixed the banister back to the wall, Tom went straight across to Our Dave's house to return the tool bag – the man wasn't in. He's decided to pretend he never saw the matt black Beretta pistol with the safety on. You wouldn't want to leave it outside Our Dave's house for anyone to find, so Tom takes the bag home and puts it in the cupboard under the stairs. It's best not to think about it.

Tom cleans up the kitchen and as he sips green tea, he feels the drink leaving his system. Sunday is kind of bleak and scary. Work looms on Monday, and the hangover is crueller as the day wears into the late morning. He feels his heart pounding in his chest and his stomach stings, his head aches. Tom does not complain, this is all his fault after all. He'll have a drink later and all will be forgotten.

Imna comes down at around half ten in her summer dressing gown. She doesn't speak to him as she makes coffee and then sits at the kitchen table with her white tablet.

"Good night, was it?" he asks. She looks up at him and her brown eyes are cold.

"It was ok. I see you had a bit to drink."

"I had a glass of wine." She swipes the page on the tablet. She is not interested, and it is obvious. Only married people could get away with this, Inma is not naturally mean and disinterested, quite the opposite. She's bubbly and emotionally aware but the relationship with Tom has deteriorated to such a level that she feels herself being actively rude. It doesn't happen quickly, and is the result of a hundred thousand little let downs over the years – Tom didn't call her when he said, he came home late and left her with the baby, he didn't do the dishes, he leaves his dirty socks on the bedroom floor, he smells, he drinks too much, he tries to kiss her, he asks too many questions, he looks dreadful with that beard and his greasy hair. Week after week, day in and day out, each little now forgotten misdemeanour has compounded to form a weight of utter hatred. Inma is not the woman she was when she married him, she has lost a lot of weight over the years, the dress business is going well, her Instagram account is blossoming, sales are good, she has friends along this avenue in their expensive houses who dress well and whose husbands are not drunks or some who do not have husbands at all. All this is through her hard work.

"I went to see Our Dave," says Tom. He sits down opposite. Inma continues to look at her screen. If she ignores him, he will stop talking. "I helped him out with some legal stuff. He's a lovely bloke, he leant me his tool bag this morning. The banister came off again." She types something onto the screen as if he is not there. "I thought we could go for a coffee later, maybe take Alex with us." She does not respond. "Would you like to go out later?" It's pathetic for him to have to repeat himself. She looks up.

"I'm busy." Inma is angry with him.

"What's wrong?"

"You."

"What do you mean?" She sets the tablet down. It's here. She did not expect this moment to arrive so soon, but it has to come out of her.

"I'm sick of you, Tom. I don't want to be around you anymore. I'm sick of your drinking."

"Weren't you drunk?"

"I had a couple." They look at each other, these two, across the farmhouse table in their big kitchen on Westbourne Avenue with the late morning sun breaking through the mist. Inma is tired. She had a white wine spritzer, two sex on the beach cocktails and a bottle of cider. "I can't carry on like this." Tom nods. He wipes his face and down his long beard. Failure is familiar territory; it is what he has learnt to understand. Tom isn't really a Hull lad, he comes from the leafy town of Hessle which has a different local authority but is part of the same city in reality. He has a cruel older brother and a working-class father who resented his posher sons, his mother was a bossy primary school teacher with a loud voice and exacting instructions – it's natural for Tom to be a failure, he has been considered one all his life. Tom may be a lawyer and a lecturer, and he may have a big house and a pretty wife but Julian is a barrister in London. Before he died, Tom's father reminded him often that his success was down to the opportunities afforded to him – 'if I'd have had your chances when I was young, then who knows where I'd be now'. Even in success, Tom is a failure too. So, these frosty exchanges with Inma are normal for him, the withering stares and huffs are standard behaviour that he expects somehow.

"I think we have to consider that we may not be right for each other, Tom," she says. "I'm going to sleep in the spare room tonight as well. I need some space to think." Tom looks down at his brown, past their best dealer boots that he is still wearing from the night before.

"Okay," he says. "I'm still thinking about my dad."

"It was a year ago, Tom. You said you hated him anyway." She is cruel to him. He is so easy to hurt.

"I did hate him, but he was my dad." Tom knows this is an excuse. He does not grieve about the old man at all. They had no relationship, and in the shed at the bottom of the garden, he keeps all the old man's paintings along the walls like a gallery, one on top of another looking out into the darkness. He has his old chair there as well and bottles of whiskey the old bastard couldn't drink before he died. There's even a box of cigars.

"I've got work to do this afternoon, so I'll be in the loft."

"What have I done?" he asks.

"I'm not the woman I was, Tom. I'm different. I'm growing. Things change. I'm changing as well." She gets up and collects her coffee from the table.

"Where does that leave us?" asks Tom.

"I just don't know." The crueller she is to him, the more he fancies her. She still has some of the eye make-up from the night before and her short black pixie cut is messed up but looks good for it. Her bare feet have the toenails painted purple.

"It might be over between us," she says. Tom looks out the window at the long garden, over the decking and to the shed at the bottom.

"I know," he says.

In the loft, Inma's phone buzzes in the pocket of her dressing gown. She takes it out and smiles at the message. This is a secret she keeps only to herself. She has reasoned that it is not her fault. Tom is such a drunk and a jerk that she has been pushed this way, she has been without meaningful love for so long that it has grown in another place, like a wildflower between thorns and nettles. In her heart she knows it is wrong. This is the man she visits sometimes; he is a chiropractor from Chanterlands Avenue who fixed her back problems two years ago. It is wrong. He is well built and toned with smooth skin, strong arm muscles and a bright white smile under dark hair. They are making plans to be together. His name is Deano. She has been made to do it. It's not her fault at all. It's all Tom. If he were a better man, she would not be carrying on this way. She would not be texting the chiropractor a message with her nimble thumb across the touchscreen:

"Tomorrow morning," she writes, "ten o'clock."

It's Monday afternoon. Tom is hungover but not so you'd notice. At the university, he sits at one end of a round table with his head of department looking back at him over the top of her colourless spectacles. The room is in half a mess with piles of papers on the floor and open folders on the desk. There's the smell of cheap perfume mixed with fags and a

Moroccan tapestry hanging on the wall. Like Tom, his boss has been here a long time, she is in her mid-fifties with long brown hair that is greying at the roots and a dress sense that is shabby without being actually dirty.

"Things are changing, Tom," she says. He nods. Isn't that the truth. Her name is Lucy. "I mean we just aren't getting the funding or the number of students that we used to."

"I know." He's been called in here for a chat. He doesn't know what it's about.

"Looks like we're going to have to lose a few people."

"Really? Who?" She takes off her colourless glasses to look at him with her slightly bloodshot eyes. Lucy will have had a bottle of wine last night as well, she smokes too, so her face is wrinkled and looks older than it should.

"They've asked me to take redundancy, Tom."

"Oh," he answers, and is relieved.

"They're going to ask you to take redundancy too."

"Why?"

"We're dinosaurs, Tom, you and me. We don't do enough research. You stopped contributing to journals years ago. You don't do any lecturing on the circuit anymore. They want young blood, people with energy and fire."

"I've been here twenty years. What about experience?"

"What about it?"

"Doesn't that count for anything?"

"Not really. It's not hard to teach, is it? Not these students anyway. If you were working in a secondary school then you'd get paid danger money. It's the end of the road for me and you. At least you can go back to being a solicitor, I'm too old for all that." Lucy does not look any more defeated or depressed than usual.

"What if I say no?"

"You'll get pushed if you don't jump." Tom swallows.

"How long?"

"The end of the year."

"June?"

"You'll get a redundancy package like me."

"I'll appeal."

"Go ahead. They'll get you in the end."

"What for?"

"You smell like a brewery most days, Tom. I'm not saying it's wrong, but it would be used against you, not by me of course." He takes a deep breath and looks at Lucy's yellow finger ends as she holds her glasses. It is falling apart quickly.

"So that's it then? That was my career?"

"I guess so."

"I'm forty-four."

"You're not past it yet, Tom. You'll have to do some work, but you can learn to be something else." Lucy has been a good boss over the last fifteen or so years, she is not too demanding, has a sense of humour and realises that university management is not as clever as it thinks it is.

"It's just a shock, that's all."

"Why don't you take the rest of the day off? Go for a drive somewhere. Have a walk. Let it sink in." Tom hangs his head in defeat. "I'll give you the best references I can. So will the senior management team. It might be good for you to have a change." Tom looks up to her and sighs.

At half three he is sitting at the bar in the Queen's on the roundabout at the end of Princes Ave. He drank the first Guiness in pretty much one go and will take the next few more slowly. As he sits there looking at himself in the reflection of the mirror behind the bottles of spirits, he remembers something – he's got a gun in a tool bag in the cupboard under the stairs.

Our Dave has tried to call Tom many times. He must have an old number. He knocked at the door after eight in the morning so as not to wake anyone, but Inma answered and explained that Tom had already left for work.

This is a potentially difficult situation. Our Dave does not know how to play it. He knows Tom is a pleasant and harmless drunk sort, but you can never predict how people will react when faced with something that is obviously criminal. What if Tom takes it to the police? How will Our Dave explain this away? If he doesn't do either of these things, then he will have to come up with a reasonable explanation as to why he has a matt black Beretta pistol in his tool bag. It's worse that Tom is a lecturer in law, for he will know the ins and out of what he is legally meant to do in such a situation.

Our Dave sits at the wheel of his grey Ford Galaxy without starting the engine and thinks about the problem. It might be for the best that Tom goes to the police, Our Dave might as well just tell them the absolute truth about what he does. He'll explain about the booze smuggling business and that he was attacked in his own home. He'll tell about how he burned the body in the incinerator as he has done many times before with other cadavers and that he pays the workers there to turn a blind eye and to wipe the CCTV video evidence too. However, there are complications. There are the three drivers who depend on him for work at the taxi office, there are the lads he bribes to let the shipments go through the docks, then there are the chaps at the incinerator who think he's burning old carpets or booze that he can't get rid of. If Our Dave goes down, then so do they. He rubs his face with one of his big hands. He'll handle it, he'll talk to Tom, and they'll work it out, somehow.

Tom arrives at his garden the back way. He has had five pints as well as a bag of chips on the walk home, and tells himself he's not drunk because he can walk straight. These big houses on Westbourne Ave have long gardens that lead to alleyways that the locals call ten-foots. Tom has a big padlock on the latch that he unlocks. There's someone he needs to see here. He pushes open the big wooden gate and it scrapes along the ground on the other side. Tom is going to the shed at the bottom of his garden here. He's going to see his old man.

The old yale lock creaks as the thin metal door of the shed swings open. He closes it behind him, and his eyes adjust to the darkness within. Little shafts of light break through the thin corrugated iron roof and there's the smell of must and the unmistakable stink of his father. The old man is still here.

The near side of the shed is full of junk, old doors and broken garden chairs, plastic urns and a stack system stereo from the eighties. This is his father's stuff. Along the side of the shed wall and against the back are his father's paintings. They loom out of the darkness as he gets used to the light, there are paintings of trawlers and faces, flowers and windmills all standing on top of each other and facing out into the gloom.

A year or so past, the man died on the eleventh floor of the hospital from a lung infection, he was eighty-five. Tom's mum passed away years before and it was Tom's job to clean out the house up at Hessle. In the garage the old man had his art studio and there was forty years work of mess in there, hundreds and hundreds of paintings and drawings, thick books of sketches and drawers crammed with acrylic paint, brushes left in corners to rot and there was the smell of turpentine and fags. It took Tom weeks to clean it out and although he couldn't keep all the pictures, he kept enough at his brother's request. He brought his old man's armchair into the shed in the hope he could sell it, but nobody wants the thing.

Tom goes over to the stack of three car tyres on top of each other and reaches down into the middle. Here he keeps an opened bottle of whiskey that his father did not manage to drink during his lifetime. There are others behind his chair. Tom pulls it out and unscrews the top with a spin as he sits down on the tyres. It will be some sort of supermarket brand, his father did everything as cheap as he could. Tom takes a slug from the bottle. The whiskey is bitter and nasty.

"Are you there, Dad?" he asks into the darkness. He knows the old man is, somehow, the smell of him is still all over the chair and the dark shapes on the painting crowd him. "I thought I'd come and say hello. I lost my job today, and it looks like I'm going to lose Inma too." He makes his father's words up himself.

"You haven't tried hard enough, Tom." These may or may not have been what the old man would say, it is Tom creating them out of the thin air of memories. "You've had everything given to you, son. You grew up in a cracking little town and you went to a good school, you had chances."

Tom takes another pull on the whiskey. It stings his throat. He remembers his father's white beard and his long eyebrows, the flat cap he wore to cover his bald head and the mucky shirts all speckled with paint. He was working class, and even though he and Tom's mother did well for themselves, the old man still clung to the identity that he grew up with. He was a poor, simple lad from Hessle Road whose father was the skipper of a trawler before he was a drunk and lost all his money, and well before he lost control of his Jaguar and drove it off the flyover, with Tom in the passenger seat. Tom's father has a monopoly on suffering because he grew up skint and poor unlike his rich, middle-class sons.

"How did you go and lose the job?" The imaginary voice has a trace of sarcasm on it.

"They're restructuring, they're letting me go."

"What will you do now then?"

"Join a firm. I haven't practiced for a long while, but I'm sure I'll pick it up again."

"You'll have to give up all that piss you drink."

"I know." Tom says this too much.

"You've to lose weight as well." Tom looks down and sees his belly stretching the buttons across his stomach. "And what will you do about Inma?"

"What can I do if she wants to leave me?"

"You'll have to stand up for yourself, Tom, don't be a doormat all your life. Your mum mothered you too much, she did. I know it. I should have stepped in like I did with your brother Julian. I should have stepped in and said, 'let him make his own mistakes, June', but I didn't. Look at Julian now, off in London with a good career and two strapping lads. Look at you. Your daughter's not even sure what bloody sex she is." Tom sighs and looks at the supermarket whiskey bottle. He does this to himself.

"When I was a young lad, Tom," continues the old man, "there wasn't time for all this drinking and fannying around, you had to work and get a job, you needed money."

"I'm doing the best I can," says Tom into the darkness.

"You've always been a loser, you have, Kid, I knew how you'd turn out. I blame your mother. I blame myself as well. You had it too easy." Tom's memory is cruel. His father was worse than this in real life for he was less verbose, he could crush whatever you said with his eyes or just by his silence as he sat there in his chair with his hands all gnarly and old with long fingernails that he couldn't be arsed to cut.

"I've got a gun in the house," says Tom.

"What did you tell me that for?"

"I might do myself in." His father scoffs.

"And you'd leave everyone else to clean up your mess. What would it do to your Alex? How would it look for Inma too? You'd never go through with it anyway, you're too bloody soft. Look at you, with your beard and that stupid floppy haircut, you look like someone from the nineteen seventies."

Nobody is nastier to you than yourself. Tom's mother and father were not any worse than anyone else, his brother Julian was a bully and thug, but it was Tom who did all the heavy lifting in terms of self-abuse. It was Tom who saw hatred in his father's eyes when it was not there, and his mother's angry shouts always seemed to be directed at him. As an adult, Tom is a professional at being horrible to himself; he can even put words into the mouth of a ghost.

"Your granddad said you needed a good slap round the face. A good solid one to knock all the shite out of you and fire you up, and if your eyes didn't blaze in hatred back, then I should do it again." Tom heard his grandfather say these words as a six-year-old when they visited his terraced house on Tyne Street off Hessle Road. It stank of fags and mould and there were newspapers all over the floor. He heard the old man explain it to his father and the memory sticks in his head because it scared the hell out of him. "He said he wished he'd done the same to me." The ghost of his father is blurred. Tom takes another gulp of the cheap whiskey, and it burns all the way down his chest.

"What am I to do?" he whispers.

"Stop being you," comes the reply.

"What do you mean?"

"You've done shite at being Tom Williams so far, be someone else for a change."

"I don't know who I'd be."

"Be like your brother, be like me, be your grandfather."

"Julian is an arsehole; you are as well. Granddad told me he would have been a pirate if he wasn't a skipper. He said he did what he liked, and he liked what he did. You said he was a bastard."

"Aye, he was, a powerful bastard, Tom, a dreadful selfish man, but he did what he wanted. He made money on the trawlers, and he drank, and he went with women, and he fought, and he lost the lot, but he did what he liked, you had to respect him for that."

"Sounds like a load of bollocks to me, father."

"Does it? You're arguing with yourself, lad. You need to put Tom Williams in the wheelie bin, son, get rid of him and I don't mean by bloody shooting yourself with Our Dave's gun. I mean you'll have to change." Tom takes another glug of the whiskey and some of it dribbles down the side of his mouth. He is becoming drunk. At least his father is honest with him, and so Tom can be honest with himself. There is sense in the advice from an old ghost. He cannot continue to live like this.

"I'll change," he says to the empty armchair, and suddenly he is aware of himself sitting on the stack of car tyres in the gloom with the paintings looking down on him. The old man is gone, for the time being.

Tom gets up, staggers to the armchair and sits down. It has been a hard and heavy drinking few days.

He needs a rest.

CHAPTER FOUR
Kasia, again

This is the Dairycoates Inn just off Hessle Road. It's Monday night. The rush of traffic on the flyover outside has died down but there aren't many drinkers in the bar downstairs. Kasia has added quality German Flensburger to the pumps alongside the bitters and generic lagers, but the punters here don't want what they don't know. She mustn't get too clever, she reminds herself, it doesn't matter what she thinks drinkers would like, it's what they want to drink that counts – this pub is the front for the drug business after all.

In the sleek kitchen upstairs, Kasia sits at the table with her thin laptop open in front of her. She is perched on a stool and wears a sensible jumper and tight jeans above non-brand trainers that are comfortable but not trendy. Her hair is scraped back into a tight ponytail and she has no makeup on, she could be a thin, bland Eastern European girl relaxing after a long day at a factory job.

A woman in a cycling jacket enters the room up the stairs from the pub below. She has big shoulders and smooth blue eyes with bits of her blonde hair spilling out from under her cycling helmet. She sets the square blue delivery backpack down on the floor. This is Laura, pronounced in the European way, she's Lithuanian, from Klaipeda on the coast, but she has lived in Hull longer than she lived in her own country – Hull is her city now. She has high cheek bones and is pretty when she does herself up. Laura might be in her mid-forties.

"Well?" asks Kasia.

"It's all delivered."

"Good," she answers. Laura is her team leader. She works at one of the fish factories normally but does jobs for Kasia from time to time. Laura was Lithuanian special forces ten years ago and has skills that you wouldn't think she has. She's trustworthy. Kasia compensates her well, and Laura has just moved into one of the new build houses at Kingswood north of Hull. When she's not on her bike, Laura also has a brand-new electric hatchback, all paid for, that she would not be able to afford on her factory wage. She operates as a link between those in the cold store unit that Kasia has just off the docks and Kasia herself. There's a computer lab there, next to the cold room, where the Vietnamese tech wizard cooks things up for her and 3D prints things they can't buy.

"I got a message from the scrap dealership," says Laura. Kasia cocks her head. "They're looking at the problem."

"It's been a few weeks; it should have been sorted by now."

"They're looking into it."

"Did you transfer the money?"

"Not me. The Vietnamese in the lab sent it on the web. All secure." Kasia nods. They speak in code, it's easier that way because they both know what they are referring to. The scrap dealership is a company that gets rid of people who are bothering Kasia. She's used them once before for a link she had down in Peterborough, he handled some of the distribution and got a bit too cocky and clever. She doesn't know the details but heard that he fell off the roof of a multistorey car park. Of course, Kasia would rather handle these things herself, but Peterborough is a long way and she doesn't know the town; there are so many things that could go wrong. It's much better to pay a professional company to get things like that sorted – Kasia has hired people before for jobs she can't do, she had the outside of the pub painted last year and has had the roof completely retiled. The Vietnamese lad would have used the dark web to transfer the money so it's untraceable. That's the way Kasia needs it to be.

"Is that everything?" she asks.

"Yes, thank you, Laura," she says. The woman picks up her square, bright blue delivery bag and swings it onto her shoulder as she goes down the stairs.

Kasia looks out of the window at the dusk sky turning dark

over the horizon and the lights from Asda in the mid distance. It's not that she dislikes Our Dave, it's just that he knows too much about her. If he were to be arrested then he could easily implicate her, and Kasia is too deep into this to let anything go wrong. She has to make sure that she and Alicja are totally secure from all angles, that means there can't be any business friends, there'll be no deals made and even old truces will have to be torn up. It can't be that difficult to get rid of one old man. Kasia thinks about the last time Our Dave visited her and sat on the stool at the end of the table, he was well-meaning and sweet. She closes the laptop. There's no room for sentimentality in this business, Leatherhead taught her that.

Alicja comes into the kitchen from the spare bedroom. She studies at the pub after school while Kasia works on the laptop. The blonde girl is wearing her primary school uniform with a blue jumper and a grey skirt underneath with white socks.

"Will you get married, mother?" she asks. Kasia narrows her eyes. Her daughter's Polish is not nearly as good as it should be.

"Who have you been talking to?" she asks.

"I read a book."

"What book?" Alicja shows the little paperback to her mother. It's in Polish at least.

"It's about a mermaid." Kasia slides off her stool.

"What about a mermaid?"

"She's lonely. She finds a prince and she falls in love with him." Kasia does not tolerate foolish talk, but this is her daughter, so she'll allow it. She walks to the line of coat hooks and pulls down Alicja's yellow jacket.

"Why did that make you ask if I would get married?"

"You're lonely."

"I'm not."

"You don't have anyone."

"I have you."

"One day I'll grow up. I might leave you like my father left you." She is as bright as the noon sun this one.

"Yes, you will go your own way like your father, but I'm not lonely. I have this pub to run. I have things to do."

"You still need a husband like the mermaid in this book. She's got friends but she wants to be in love."

"You'll learn about love in time to come, Alicja," says Kasia. She means the fumbling in the back of cars and the heavy drunken kisses she's shared behind bars in the summertime. "It's not like you read in books."

"What is it like, then?" Kasia thinks back to the warm man she arrived in the UK with, and the smooth muscles on his arms with his deep laugh and blonde hair. Her stomach grumbles when she does so. Desire and hope are still inside her, somewhere.

"It feels warm, and you feel safe." She holds the coat for Alicja to slip her arms into the sleeves.

"Will you find someone to love?" asks the little girl. Kasia turns the girl around and zips up her coat. They look each other in the eyes, mother to daughter.

"Maybe I will," says Kasia but she doesn't think this is true. Words cost nothing after all.

Tom calls in sick on Tuesday morning, it's after ten o'clock. He leaves a message on the human resources answering machine and he doesn't have to put on feeling dreadful because he genuinely does. He woke up in his father's chair in the shed in the early morning, went out the gate, fitted the padlock back on, then walked down the ten foot and round to Westbourne Ave proper and to his front door. He let himself in and slept on the couch.

In the kitchen he looks at the big garden stretching out towards the shed where he stayed the night before. His phone buzzes, it's Imna:

'I'm going to stay at my mum's for the rest of the week. Alex says she's staying there with you.' Tom answers quickly.

'You mean he's staying with me?' There's no answer back. It's the kind of dickhead answer he would expect himself to give.

There's a knock on the front door. Tom walks down the big hall to answer it. There's the tall figure of Our Dave standing outside the door in the cold February sunlight.

"Now then," says Tom. In this town, this is a common greeting. He expects a polite and friendly answer in return.

"I need my tool bag, Tom," says the tall man. He is not wearing his customary smile and there is an air of something dark about him with his checked shirt tucked into his jeans and his rolled-up sleeves. Tom is not thinking straight.

"I found a gun in the bag, Dave," he says. The man walks into the porch and closes the door behind him with a slam. Tom steps back. He is suddenly afraid.

"No, you didn't, Tom. There's nothing like that in there, it's just tools, screwdrivers and spanners and whatnot." Tom licks his dry lips.

"I'll get it for you, shall I?"

"Aye. I need it for a job I'm doing down on Belvoir Street." Tom takes a few steps backwards down the hall and then turns, goes past the stairs, and opens the cupboard under it. This is where the family keep shoes they don't always wear, there are coats hung up and the vacuum cleaner jammed in one of the corners. This is where Tom left the yellow toolkit that Our Dave lent him a few days before and in which he found a heavy matt black Beretta pistol. He goes to the place where he left it in the corner. It's not there. He scrabbles around the shoes and moves a rolled up sleeping bag out the way. It's still not there. He tosses aside a shopping bag with a beach blanket inside and moves the vacuum cleaner. It's still not there. Tom stands up and moves out the cupboard. Our Dave looks down on him and his face is level and serious.

"It was here yesterday," says Tom. "I tried to bring it back Sunday. I didn't want to leave it outside your front door with what was inside."

"What was inside?" Tom swallows. He never thought he'd be afraid of this man.

"It was just spanners and screwdrivers and whatnot, like you'd find in a normal toolkit."

"You better start looking for it, kid." Tom considers this big man in front of him. His eyes are earnest and the nostrils are flared. Our Dave is fairly certain that Tom is not a liar, but this is serious. If this information falls into the wrong hands, it would mean a great deal of suffering for lots of people.

"I wouldn't tell anyone, you know."

"About what?"

"What I found inside." Our Dave darkens further.

"It's much better, Tom, if you just pretend you didn't know. That's what you need to do. Find the bag, give it back to me and absolutely forget that it ever happened." Tom looks back up at Our Dave. He may be a drunk and a fool, but he can put pieces together so they fit nicely; he qualified as a solicitor before he started lecturing, he's good at sudoku, he can get the conundrum on Countdown straightaway.

"Like I'm supposed to pretend that your Hazel is dead?" Our Dave's eyes are bleak and lonely.

"Just like that, aye."

Tom does not know anything about Our Dave here. He isn't aware of the man's history or what he did in the late seventies and early eighties, he has no idea about the smuggling business or the money that passes through his rough joiner's hands. All Tom can see is a lonely older man whose wife died eighteen months ago, a man who can't bear to face the truth and so he has a gun in his tool bag somehow. Tom hits upon it as he stands there, Our Dave will want to put a bullet in his own head. Now he looks at the tall man, he can't believe he didn't realise this sooner, there is, after all, always someone having a harder time than you.

"I know what you need it for, Our Dave."

"Go on."

"Now Hazel is gone. It might be a way out." Our Dave grins at the stupidity of it and then his serious face returns.

"I need that bag, Tom." Our Dave's voice is low and calm. This is a simple, dark command with streel to the words.

The front door opens and slams shut again. Alex walks towards them with his skateboard. He breezes past into the kitchen.

"I see you're alive then, father," he says. "Mum thought you might be dead in a ditch when you didn't come home last night."

"She didn't message me," calls Tom after him.

"I don't think she was particularly bothered either way," comes the reply from the kitchen. Tom is not sure if this is some sort of joke.

"I had a yellow tool bag in the cupboard under the stairs here, have you seen it?"

"It's on the table in here," calls Alex. Tom and Our Dave move into the kitchen after the long-haired lad. There, on the farmhouse kitchen table is Our Dave's tool bag zipped up. Alex has opened the fridge and takes out a carton of milk. Both men are relieved.

"What's it doing there?" asks Tom.

"Mum moved it there."

"I thought you were at college."

"I was," says Alex. "I'm done for the day, I'm revising. Why aren't you at work?"

"I'm sick." Alex gets a bowl out the cupboard and sets it down on the kitchen counter. He's about to have cereal.

"I'll just grab my tool bag then," says Our Dave, any sense that there was any danger previously is gone, like a storm has passed over and the sky is now clear and bright. Tom steps into the tall man's way.

The change has to begin somewhere. Why not here? If Tom is going to have a go at being someone else, then he's going to have to start acting like someone else.

"I think you should leave it with me, Dave." Clouds darken the older man's brow.

"You do?"

"Yeah. Like I said a minute ago. I need it, still, and I'd keep it really safe. I mean I know some of those tools are important to you." He is grasping at lies. Our Dave glares down at him. "You've been a good friend to me, Dave. I mean it. That's why I need the tool bag. I just don't want you to do anything stupid, that's all.." Our Dave won't to say too much with young Alex filling his bowl full of muesli from the expensive supermarket.

"You'd be putting yourself in danger, Tom."

"I don't care. You do a lot for people round here. I'd be happy to help." In Tom's mind he is defending Our Dave, he has no clue at all about the intruder or what kind of a man his neighbour opposite is or has been. Tom thinks Our Dave is going to top himself, and he needs to do something right for once in his life, so he wants to protect the old man from himself.

Our Dave steps back and considers the situation for a moment. The offer of support is genuine. The coppers are highly unlikely to look for the gun here. Maybe this is the best place for it, and maybe, Tom is someone Our Dave can use as well. He's got skills for sure. Our Dave will have to take a risk with this one.

"You'd be careful with it."

"Of course." Our Dave swallows.

"Okay. Let's have a chat about it some other time, when you're free." Tom nods vigorously. Our Dave backs out the kitchen and walks down the corridor, they hear the front door close as he leaves.

The air shimmers for a moment in the kitchen as the emotion from the exchange dissipates. Tom sits down at the kitchen table and his heart is beating heavy in his chest. He is pleased with himself for a change.

"What was that about?" asks Alex as he stands at the counter eating cereal between words.

"Our Dave is having a hard time. He needs someone to talk to." The expensive muesli crunches between Alex's molars.

"You know mum's going to leave you?" He has that teenage honesty to him, as if nothing really matters and his parents mean even less than strangers.

"I know." Tom might as well be honest. "If I was her, Alex, I'd leave me as well."

"What are you going to do?"

"Carry on, I guess. I'll be here for you kid, as long as you need me." There's mistrust in Alex's eyes, as if he doesn't need this crumpled attempt at reassurance from a man with a thick, ragged beard and long brown hair to his neck.

"I won't be here much longer, Dad. When I'm done with college, I'll be gone." Tom nods. Alex is already more a grown up than he is.

"That will be the best thing for you, Alex."

"You'll be alright though?"

"An old pisshead like me? Of course." This is the first time Tom has referred to himself as such.

CHAPTER FIVE
Shave

It's Wednesday afternoon. Our Dave got a message from Bev that the taxi office was out of coffee so, on his way down Chanterlands Avenue, he's stopped at the cheap supermarket. There are a few to choose from down this street, one is totally overpriced, another more so, and then there is this one where Our Dave always goes. It's not just that it's nearer the office, there is someone he needs to see here.

Lilly looks different. She wears a blue tabard overall and has a yellow name badge pinned to her chest. Her jet-black hair is tied in a ponytail and she doesn't wear the false nails like she used to. At the till, she is bleeping through items for a stunted looking old lady and nattering away to her at the same time. She notices Our Dave come in the door and gives him a smile; her veneers are still brilliant white. Our Dave collects the coffee and a packet of biscuits and goes to the till. It's quiet at this time of the day. Lilly smiles at him again as she bleeps the coffee and picks up the custard creams.

"How are you, Dave?" she asks.

"Good. How's it working out here?"

"Okay." Lilly was an independent working girl a few months back and things happened to make her change jobs. Our Dave offered her work up at the taxi office, but she can't drive, and they don't need anyone to answer the phones. Her and Bev didn't get on either, which means they'll be firm friends at some point in the future. Lilly has worked here in the cheap supermarket for a few weeks, she likes it because it's simple, you turn up, work, and then you get paid. Nobody threatens her and she doesn't have to worry for her safety. Lilly has a gob on her, and she loves to talk.

"Two people have had their dogs nicked from outside the shop this week." Dave nods. You can't get a word in sometimes. "They use them for dog fighting. The big ones do the fighting. The little ones are just bait for them to practise on." Lilly loves the gossip. She soaks it up like a cloud and rains it down on anyone who'll listen.

"I'll keep my eyes open for anything." Our Dave knows most of what goes on down Chants Ave. Lilly looks at him for a minute with her big eyes, another customer has joined the queue behind Our Dave which means she won't have much time left to chatter.

"How's Gaz?" she asks in a whisper. She wanted to ask this all along.

"All good. He's up in Scotland again." Lilly looks pleased.

"Is he still with that lass?" Our Dave nods.

"Aye. She's gone with him. Looks like it's serious." Lilly gives one of those forced smiles to show she is happy, even though she isn't.

"You will say hello to him when you see him, won't you, Dave?"

"Aye, I will."

"Say I was asking after him." Our Dave takes his change and is glad this lass is doing ok.

He goes over the road and round the back through the car park then through the kitchen door. This is Avenue Cars, a taxi office on Chanterlands Avenue, Hull. It's just after half past one. Bev stands outside the backdoor smoking her vape, it glows orange when she takes a puff. She gives Our Dave a smile as he walks to the door.

"A bit late for you isn't it, Dave?" She says this because Our Dave is usually here before anyone else in the morning, and today he wasn't.

"I had something to sort out." Bev is a blonde lass in her early fifties, but she's aged well so her Tinder profile looks good and she gets a lot of interest, even if she never checks. "How's it been?" he asks.

"All good. Dilva has had to go off to pick up her son from the school, but Liz is here." Dilva is a Kurdish woman who started work at Avenue Cars a few months ago. She ferries the foreign kids to school and she speaks Kurdish, Farsi and her Arabic is good as well. Like Bev here, Our Dave gave her a chance, and he was proved right. Bev considers Our Dave as he is about to go through the door.

"Have you not been feeling yourself?"

"I'm fine, you know me."

"I do, a bit too well, Our Dave. You look like you haven't slept." He stops. Bev is razor sharp. You can't lie to her because she will see it, so you have to tell her a version of the truth.

"I've been having stomach troubles, Bev. You don't get to my age without something going wrong."

"If anything's worrying you, I'm here to listen. I can't promise I'll do anything, but you can talk and I'll nod my head." Bev means well. She knows that Our Dave won't tell her what's wrong with him, that's just how men his age are around here.

"I'll be fine, Bev." Last year they had trouble. It all got sorted in the end, but Bev did shoot a man in the back office here. She thinks about it sometimes, about the noise and the mess.

The night is black outside, and Tom hasn't closed the blinds in the kitchen, fairy lights along the bushes outside illuminate the decking. Tom sits in the spacious kitchen in front of his laptop at the farmhouse table, he is sipping a glass of red wine, he promises himself he will take it easy tonight so he might only drink the rest of the bottle. Most people have a bottle a night, anyway, so he's heard, maybe.

Inma returned half an hour before. She is upstairs packing a suitcase. Tom feels bleak but okay. He tries to look at the laptop screen, but his eyes are swimming, and it is hard to concentrate. He hears her coming down the stairs into the kitchen, she drags a wheelie suitcase behind her and it trundles on the orange terracotta tiles below her feet. She stands looking down at her husband, Inma is dressed in a black padded Gillet and a white jumper underneath, she's got no makeup on but her black pixie cut is well brushed. Tom still fancies her.

"I'm going to my mother's," she says. Tom nods. He knows this. "Where were you last night?"

"I fell asleep in an armchair." He is not lying. Inma looks disgusted by him, as always.

"If you carry on like this, Tom, you'll be dead in a few years." She does not know how right she is. He picks up his glass of wine and takes a sip.

"Is that it then?" he asks.

"I guess. Don't you even want to fight for us?" Inma actually doesn't really want him to beg her, but a bit of remorse at the situation would be good for her ego.

"I don't know what to say, honestly. I think it's probably best for you to go."

"It's been twenty-two years, Tom. Is that all you can say?" Inma has been waiting to say this in anticipation of him coming out with something horrible. It doesn't quite fit, but she wants to use the sentence.

"I don't think I can change your mind. It's good for you to get away from me. You can start new. If I could get away from myself, I think I probably would." It's in these moments that she remembers why she loved him, he is self-aware and funny, self-deprecating and warm with it.

It's not easy for her but she has a life to step into already, partly with that smooth skinned chiropractor from Chanterlands Avenue and partly with the freedom she will get to travel and take pictures for Instagram. Alex is old enough now. Inma can do this. She does feel bad for him sitting there looking up at her with his big beard and floppy hair covering the burns on his face, but she's tried to help him. The state he is in is Tom's fault.

"I've lost my way," he says. "I don't quite know where. If you'll stay, maybe you can help me find out where I've gone wrong. We've been together so long." Inma knew this would come eventually. Tom said that he wouldn't try to change her mind, but he can't seem to help himself.

"I'm sorry Tom, we've grown too far apart in all this. You'll have to find your own way." He nods.

"We had some good times," he says.

"Yes, we had some good times," she repeats, although right now she can't recall any of them. She's anxious to complete this breakup. "You'll be okay," she says. She is not sure if this is true.

"I will," he answers, "and you will be as well. You'll be happy." Inma smiles. She thought she would cry, that's why she didn't wear any makeup, as it turns out there aren't any tears at all.

"Goodbye Tom. I'll be in touch about the rest of the stuff and the finances as well."

"Good luck," he says. Inma walks to the door and looks over her shoulder at the man she married twenty years previous. When she walks out of this house, it will all be done. Her stomach gurgles as she taps down the hall to the front door. Tom finishes his wine in one gulp and sets the glass down. He closes the laptop. It's another slap in the face. He's off for a pint.

"I'm just slipping to the pub," Tom calls up the stairs, and there's a grunt from Alex in his bedroom. Tom won't be late, and he'll lock the door anyway. He takes his denim jacket off the peg on the coat hook, puts it on and gets a look at himself in the mirror as he does – there's the big beard, the long greasy hair and the red eyes under his thick black glasses. He'll just go for the one – it is a Tuesday after all and so a pint is well deserved. He closes the door behind him, and the letter box clatters against itself.

It's not too cold as he makes his way down the path and

out into Westbourne Ave proper but there's a light drizzle. He's heading for the Queen's, it's not as chatty as the German beer house at the other end of Princes Ave but still friendly. He'll be able to have four or five pints without getting bothered by anyone. Tom can feel the glass of red wine working its way into his brain and around his body. Drinking is an easy thing to slip into, the world that he learned about in the noughties is geared towards it. It's not like you're on your own either – there are buildings that serve nothing but booze, characters in your favourite movie drink it, your mum does too, like everyone else. If it's calamity or celebration, you have a drink. If you are bored or excited, you take a drink. You drink in terror or hope. It is the only constant.

Tom goes out of Westbourne Ave and crosses the road. He walks alongside the green railings of Pearson Park on his right, and the part of him that feels pain and sees sense, the bit that is funny and warm, that part shrivels a little more as the wine takes effect. You can wallpaper over the cracks of your life with drink, and the hangovers might be bad, but they stop you seeing the real picture of your existence as it is. It must be five years since Tom has had even a day off the drink and that was only when he ploughed his face into the pavement on Newland Avenue after falling off his bike. He is lost to the booze.

As he walks, the big oaks in the park sway in the dark breeze above and there's a tiny voice inside him calling out on the distant wind:

"How do you become someone else? What if you're tired of being yourself?" Tom has always been steady, clever, a bit of a dickhead but you know where you are with him, poor Tom with the burns all over his face. As he walks alongside the darkness of the park, he hears a real voice call from behind him.

"Ey mate?" It's a gravelly Hull voice and Tom stops and turns. A man in blue tracksuit bottoms and a dirty cagoul with the hood up staggers towards him. "Have you got any spare change?" Tom shakes his head – he really hasn't, he pays for everything on his card. As the man approaches Tom can see his rotten bottom row of black teeth and the off-kilter gait – he's not so different from Tom, he just uses a different drug and has gone a bit further down that road. He could be from the homeless refuge up the road.

"I'm skint," says Tom. He is not afraid of people like this. Perhaps he should be.

"I'm not asking for much mate," rasps the man, "just a couple of quid." His voice has the quality of steel being dragged along concrete and he does not seem threatening, more desperate. Tom has stopped at the little path that leads into the park. It's silent in the late February drizzle and darkness. Princes Avenue in front is deserted too, anyone with any sense is at home waiting for the summer. The man with his hood up staggers nearer and Tom can see a snarl form on his face. This isn't so innocent. There are footsteps behind Tom suddenly, and a hand yanks at his denim jacket to pull him down the path into the park. His head spirals and his eyes blink. His heart rate rises. There's a gang of them.

More rough hands grab and spin Tom round then shove him forward, so he stumbles against the green railings inside the park itself. This is why Inma doesn't want Alex walking home alone here at night. Some people are desperate, and others are just bastards looking for someone to kick in. Tom blinks up and sees the figures moving towards him out of the darkness – he has been beaten up before of course, but never when he was this sober. He finds sense and self-preservation rising in his chest.

"Give us your phone, pal and I won't cut your throat," it's the gravel voice of the hooded staggering man again, it sounds at once tired but utterly genuine. There appear to be three others. Tom is too shocked to move immediately as they come closer to him, he's bruised his shoulder on the railings and the needles of rain make tiny lines in the yellow from the streetlight a few yards behind the trees.

Tom's hair and long beard are wet, he's lost his thick black glasses. The man in the hood moves nearer still and puts his face right up close so Tom can smell his rotten breath and see the stains on his Diadora tracksuit collars. He should reach into his pocket and pull out his phone to give to these men along with his wallet. Tom should be much more frightened than he is given that he's only had a glass of red wine, his heart should be beating much faster because he's an academic and a swot, he went to a lower middle class school where he enjoyed the Shakespeare plays they made him read, he's got books on art, he understands Latin phrases, he can get a quarter of the general knowledge questions correct on Mastermind. Tom's grandfather told him that he would have been a pirate if he wasn't a trawler skipper. Perhaps what Tom is about to do next is in his blood.

He makes a run for it into the darkness of the park behind him. The men give chase. Tom knows this is a bad idea as he races onto the slippery grass toward the children's play area in the darkness. He can't help himself. It must be ten years since he last broke into a sprint.

Pearson Park would never get built these days. It opened in 1861 and the land was donated by a wealthy ship owner named Zachariah Pearson. He probably wouldn't have expected the park to turn out like it has. It's not the biggest one in the city, but it has a Victorian hothouse, it's a replacement for the original. There's a statue of Prince Albert in the middle and one of a young Victoria some way off. In recent years the council erected a colourful bandstand in the little flower garden. Kids come here to kick a football about, there's a little bowling green at the Beverley Road end, eastern European types drink cans in the summer on the park benches next to the duck pond, the ornamental gateway to the entrance was restored in 2019, there's a cast iron drinking fountain behind the hothouse from 1861. There's a lot you'd miss here, like there's a lot you'd miss in this city.

Tom is out of breath within ten yards as he runs into the darkness of Pearson Park. He slips on the grass in the drizzle but doesn't fall, and he can hear the voices of the men behind him as they give chase. He wheezes, and ploughs on, surprised at how fast he can go. Tom powers up a little hill towards a curious tower just before the kid's play area. This is the cupola. It's a small dome that sits atop columns up stone steps with an elaborate lead point stretching into the sky. Until 1912, this sat upon the top of Hull Town Hall; when the building was demolished, they moved the cupola to a new home in the park as some sort of folly. It's too late for Tom to see the mesh fencing that protects it in the darkness, and he crashes headlong into the wires, confused.

The men are upon him in the darkness. Against the protective fencing, they turn him round and deliver punches into his stomach, one of them claws at his face as another rummages through his pockets for his phone and his wallet. The men are not out to kill him, this violence is only the means to getting his money. The one with the stagger who called to Tom earlier has just found a new source of medicine out the back door of the Dairycoates Inn just off Hessle Road – the heroin is dynamite, and he has heard it's been cut with what they call the zombie maker, fentanyl.

The cable ties that hold the wire fence together behind Tom come apart under the force of the attack, and he falls through the space to the cupola behind him, his back lands on the little steps and his head hits the stone with a clunk. He looks up.

The drizzle is getting stronger and one of the men has followed him through the gap in the fence, it's the little one who scratched his face, and he stands over him looking down. All Tom can see is the wide grin under his hood in the darkness – the man grabs the dome of the cupola for stability and lifts his boot ready to stamp down onto Tom's face. There's no need for the man to do this – they already have Tom's wallet and his phone, injuring him further won't do them any good and it could turn an honest mugging into a murder.

Tom looks up into the darkness of the raining night sky above, his hair is wet over his face, his back stings from the fall on the stone, his fat stomach strains at the buttons on his shirt. He is at once defeated. It's not just these men who have chased him down and robbed him on Pearson Park – it's the wretchedness of everything. What's the point in Tom? What's the point in any of this, it will only be more drinks in pubs, more bottles of wine, watching as his wife packs up the house around him and leaves, Alex growing older and seeing his old man degenerate into more of a drunk.

Tom has had enough of this.

He didn't close his eyes when his grandfather drove through the barriers on the Hessle Road flyover at eighty miles an hour. He wasn't afraid then and he isn't now. He's learned to be a bleeder and a geek, but that's not what he is inside, not at all. Tom's a bit like his grandfather and before the rat man above can bring his boot heel down on his face, Tom has rolled to the side and is standing up; his out of shape legs complain and his hair sticks to his face. He runs at the rat man and they both crash into the wire mesh fencing before falling into the wet grass and mud. It's all huffing and rolling as Tom tries to belt him. The man is smaller and has more fighting experience too, his skag head lifestyle means he's skinny and fit, so he wriggles out from under Tom in the darkness and the rain. The man's associates call to him a few yards off. They are leaving.

"Come on, Browny," rasps the man with the stagger from a few yards away. Browny gets to his feet next to where Tom groans on his back. Like a lot of the rat men in this city, a great deal of evil has been done to Browny here, he doesn't often get to pay anyone back for it, so, he boots Tom in the head with a thud before he disappears off into the darkness.

Tom manages to sit up. He's dizzy and his jaw stings. His trousers are muddy, and he has scuffed his hands and back on the cupola next to him. He stands up and the late winter rain starts up heavier. He doesn't feel as bad as he should because this defeat is unlike the others - he didn't just let this happen to him. This is the way it has to be from now on.

Tom's granddad did say he needed a good smack in the face. He said it might do him some good. Tom feels like the boot that connected with his jaw has knocked a piece of him into place.

At the front door Tom fumbles with his key in the lock and lets himself in. He staggers down the hall and calls up the stairs.

"Alex," he yells. There's a muffled reply. He repeats the call. "I need you to come down here." He waits at the bottom of the stairs for his son to come out onto the landing.

"What is it?" Alex calls.

"Have you still got that shaver you use for the side of your hair?"

"You mean the clippers? Yeah," he's not sure why his father is asking. "Why?"

"I need your help." Alex begins down the stairs and sees that his father is in a state. He isn't wearing his glasses, he's wet through, and he's bleeding from his bottom lip where Browny kicked him with his fake Timberland boot. The bruise will probably come out later. Alex has seen him looking worse to be honest.

"What's happened?"

"I got mugged." Tom makes it sound matter of fact. "I tried to run but they caught up with me."

"Do you need me to call the police?"

"No. I want you to get those clippers."

"What for?"

"I need to get this beard off my face and this hair too. I'm done hiding." Alex nods. He likes his dad and he's worried about the old fella as well sometimes.

"You want me to cut your hair?"

"Aye, right now if you can." Alex goes back to his room to find the clippers and while he's rummaging through his drawers, he thinks about his old man standing in the hallway, piss wet through with his face bleeding down his shirt. His mother has just left, for good, and so his father is bound to go off the rails. Who can blame him?

An hour later Tom looks at his clean-shaven face in the hall mirror. There's a bruise on his cheek where the mugger kicked him, and his eyes look watery and sober. It's the first time he's seen his jaw line for many years and the burn scars on his skin are angry and red. His face looks like a complicated street map of a busy city centre with little alleys off the main roads. Alex also did his hair, he cut off big chunks with the kitchen scissors and gave his dad a number four all over. Tom looks like a convict.

"Are you happy with it?" asks Alex from the other end of the hall.

"I am," says Tom although he's not sure if he is. "There's no point in covering it up anymore. I don't care." He is not sure if this is true either. Alex leans on the wall as he looks at his dad – a year or so ago, the young man made the decision about who he was, and it was not as easy or as trendy as people think. He went from dresses and ponytails to sensible shoes and oversized charity shop shirts. He sees his father in a different light. "They used to call me Face at school, or Roadmap or Brad Pitt," says Tom. These names hurt him. They still do.

"When did you grow the beard?" asks Alex. He has never seen his father without it. He looks younger and fresher too.

The skin is an absolute mess, especially over his lips and left cheek, your eyes are drawn to it when you look at him.

"When I left school. Your mother wanted me to shave it off, she said the burns would look cool."

"Why didn't you?"

"I did, and then she told me to grow it back again." Tom gives Alex an honest smile. "You can say what you like about your mum, but she knows what looks good and what doesn't."

"That's your opinion. What are you going to do?"

"About what?"

"About mum."

"There's nothing I can do. If she wants to leave, how can I stop her?" It's a rhetorical question. "A wise person once said that you've only got control over your own actions."

"Have you been drinking?" asks Alex. It's unusual for his father to say something profound that makes sense.

"I've had a glass."

"Did they hurt you, the muggers, I mean?" Tom gives him a grin.

"Kind of. They chased me up to the cupola, they pushed me through the fence, and I cracked my head on the steps. They got my phone and my wallet as well."

"Shouldn't you tell someone?"

"I'll get the card stopped. They can have the phone. It doesn't do me any good scrolling the bastard thing night and day." Without knowing it, the robbers on Pearson Park, who will have already sold his phone for a thirty quid bag of something, have done Tom a real favour.

"Are you going to drink anymore?" He means tonight.

"I don't think so," he answers. Alex does not realise how much his father needs his support. "Shall I make us a cup of cocoa?"

Alex nods and gives him a smile.

CHAPTER SIX
Changes

In 2019, Paul Sarel bought a large diesel van in red from Barry at Richmond Street Garage. It was a Mercedes and had two hundred and thirty-five thousand miles on the clock, Barry got it from the fruit and veg man off Walton Street market who was upgrading. Paul bought it cheap and turned it into a camper with a stove, a little chimney, and a double bed inside, then, he drove it down to Portugal and lived on the road from April to October 2019. Things didn't go as planned, life is hard on the road and so, Paul drove it back up to Hull, and because he didn't have anywhere to live, he parked it up in the New Adelphi car park, right at the back.

The Adelphi is a run-down music venue on a terraced street off Newland Avenue, capacity 250 at the absolute max, and it attracts local musicians and legendary pop stars on the way to the top. It gives out good vibes. Paul lived in the van for a time and used the toilets of the Adelphi to brush his teeth. The weeds and brambles began to grow up around the back of the red van and the back tyres went flat then so did the front ones. Paul took over managing the Adelphi itself because he was there so much, and then he moved in upstairs.

The van stayed. The windscreen developed a green mould on the outside and rust collected on the hubcaps, the little chimney fell off and the brambles grew through the undercarriage and into the driver's side door. In October 2022, Anita Divali was touring with a Canadian folk singer and playing the drums, Hull was the last stop on the calendar and the female guitarist was going on to Manchester to get a flight home, so she didn't need the band. Anita has a thin, brindle lurcher dog called Clive and she noticed the van after the gig while she smoked outside. She didn't have anywhere else to go. It took a chat with Paul the manager and that night, she and Clive slept in the back. That's how it was.

Anita was a wild one in days gone by. She was brought up in a strict Indian family where her father drove a taxi and they fixed old TVs and video recorders on the side to sell on. She was all set to get married when she was sixteen. Anita couldn't live that kind of life, and she wasn't going to get married like her mother wanted. She took to drinking heavy and moved out. She lived rough on Birmingham and then London streets where you have to be off your head to get any rest. She learned to play drums in a squat and fell in love with a heroin addict who taught her yoga. She got his dog when he died. She'd never call a dog Clive. She misses him – the heroin addict, she still has the dog.

Anita spends the winter doing the van up. She's lived in squats and on the road all her life so she knows how to look after herself just fine, and, if anyone should think about robbing the Adelphi or the van, then Clive will go off on a barking fit to scare them away. Anita digs up all the brambles that have grown through the metal, she adds insulation against the cold, cleans the glass and resprays the outside red because she is resourceful and hardworking. She takes a job behind the bar of the Adelphi, and like anyone who is friendly and brave, she slots right in between setting up the drum kit and pulling pints, chatting to the bands that are about to play and then mopping the floor when they've done. Clive is happy here, Anita feels settled so that when Paul Sarel gets an upgrade for his mobile phone he gives his old one to Anita and she gets a contract.

The van gets cold and lonely at night. She doesn't drink anymore so she snuggles up to Clive for warmth and wonders, under the three military blankets with her clothes on, if there might be something more life could offer her. She is wise and open to change, open to possibilities too. In the darkness of the van, she takes out that mobile phone and fires up the screen with a crack in it. She finds the app she's heard of, the one where you find someone, not for a quick bang, but for something more than that. She uploads a picture of her smiling and another of her cuddling Clive in the front seat of a van that hasn't moved for five years.

What can it hurt?

In 2005 Joanne married a Welshman she met while she was at university here in Hull. She is from Upper Poppleton, just outside York and studied English literature for three years. She likes the city as most students do, and when you start to feel at home you don't want to leave. She met the Welshman at the Piper Club on Newland Avenue, and they were together a long while after. When she finished uni she trained as a teacher and the Welshman got a job at the council in planning. Joanne had a baby girl and by the time she was six, the Welshman wasn't interested in either of them; he left to join the army. Joanne stayed on in the house they bought on Bricknell Ave near the primary school and became a teacher in the secondary up the road where she teaches ethics to sixth formers and English up to GCSE.

Years ago, and after she'd split up with the Welshman, she was followed on the way back from Spiders nightclub. Whoever it was, chased her across the wrought iron bridges and through the industrial estates till, by chance, she flagged down a taxi. The event gave her sleepless nights so the counsellor she spoke to suggested she took up a martial art – not to actually hurt anyone but to give her confidence to know that she could if the need be.

On Saturday mornings, in the scout hut of the primary school next door there's a mixed karate club, so she took her daughter. Joanne is good at it and when her daughter stopped going at fourteen, she carried on. The big sensei with long black hair in a ponytail invites her to the adult sessions on a Monday night and she enjoys the rough and tumble with bigger lads who hit hard. She finds time for herself in the training and calm in the complex katas and three step moves.

Joanne runs Parkrun on Saturday morning, she has a six pack and long dark beautiful hair. Her teeth are straight and white because she looks after them and she has the rosy glow of health and well-being about her. Her daughter has moved away to university in Leeds already and so the house has a sanitary, cold feel to it.

In 2022 when her mother moves into a care home, she sits at the old woman's side and holds her frail hand. She looks down into the watery eyes and promises she will find a man, a good man who can be a companion to her, just like dad. It's at the back of her mind for a year and a half until a friend tells her about an app that she used to get a date.

One night after she's pulled her shoulder muscle at karate she can't sleep. She sits at the kitchen table scrolling social media and sees an advert with a woman and a man holding hands and smiling. She clicks on the app and downloads it. Before long, she's uploaded pictures: one of her on the beach in Kos last year, another as she is sprinting at Parkrun, another zoomed in on her in a dress at a wedding five years ago. She clicks the button and watches the circle on the screen as it whirs round to upload the data. She's a grown woman, a black belt at Wado karate, she can control a classroom full of rowdy, knobhead teenagers.

What can it hurt?

Kasia lays beside her daughter and gets the little girl to read. Alicja's choice was the mermaid book, her Polish is not perfect, but Kasia did not say anything, and she just enjoyed the story. In all these years she has not considered the idea of true love like she hears in the fairytale. Reading makes Alicja tired, and it doesn't take long for her eyes to begin to close. Kasia takes the book and slips off the bed without noise. She dims the light as she leaves.

In the kitchen, Kasia opens a bottle of beer that she took from the pub and pours it into a clean glass from the cupboard. She takes it to the kitchen table and sits down in front of the laptop. She knows that she should not be working at this time of night but she is curious about something.

She heard the bar lady she employs at the Dairycoates Inn talking to a customer this afternoon. The blonde woman explained very clearly that she had met her husband on the internet via a dating app. She had not been looking for a one night stand or a bit of fun, but the steady steel of a lifelong partner, the woman listed a string of essential demands that she had wanted, the ability to drive, an interest in fitness, a non-smoker or drinker as well as someone with a steady job. Kasia listened to her speak. If she wants a specialist piece of equipment for the kitchen or for the pub she doesn't go to the shops in the high street, she will look for it online. Why wouldn't this be the case for a partner? She can specify what kind of a man: he will be lean, older though, at least in his forties with an education, and shrewd too. He will be her equal, but she will keep any information about what she does from him. She will be yet the cleaner who looks after the Dairycoates Inn just off Hessle Road. They will go for coffee and then bike rides along the riverbank in the sunshine, he will meet Alicja and she will approve. They will make dinner together on Saturday nights and sit next to each other on the couch. He will make her smile and she will make him happy.

Kasia takes a sip on the beer and her clever fingers go at speed across the keyboard of the laptop. It takes just a minute to download the program and log in. She creates a fake male profile and spends ten minutes looking at her competition before she realises that there is no way to know if they are successful or not. It doesn't look like rocket science anyway.

She looks through the photos she has of herself on her phone as she takes another sip on the beer, there is nothing flattering if she is honest with herself. She looks through Facebook and finds a photographer called Serjei who is Latvian but speaks Russian, Kasia writes him a message and gets a quick reply. She explains she needs a series of photos for a dating site in clear, standard Russian, and he responds with a fee and some suggestions. Kasia offers him more if he can do the shots tomorrow. He agrees.

Kasia isn't going to just throw some photographs and a description onto this website, she'll have to approach it with caution and preparation. She will have to present the best of herself because she expects the best results. She closes the laptop and the house at the top of Woodcock Street is cold and quiet. She looks at the couch at one side of the front room opposite the flat screen TV that she almost never turns on. Her stomach flutters as she thinks about a man she cannot yet imagine being there. She is successful, she has made sacrifices to get where she is today, she has done things she could regret if they were not for the greater good of her and Alicja. She is going to go on these internet applications, as many of them as is needed until she finds the man she wants.

What can it hurt?

Tom did not sleep well. There are all sorts of stories about alcoholics who don't get a drink, about how their bodies writhe with itches and their brains fire with hallucinations. Tom's heart feels like it is beating out of his chest, so he goes downstairs to the kitchen and finds the bottle of wine he opened before his wife left him. He pours himself a glass and looks at the liquid there, like red poison staring back at him in the weak, pale glow of the kitchen spotlights.

He sees the future. It is a bleeding, green liver inside his chest, the yellow skin on his face and the madness within his eyes. Tom would drink this. The man who stands in the kitchen in his bare feet is not so much Tom anymore, so, in the spirit of this, he's not going to drink it. He tips the contents into the sink and looks at himself in the reflection of the window above the sink. Without his beard he is younger and more earnest, without the hair there is nowhere to hide. He only needs the glasses for reading, so he's ditched them for walking around. He is glad of this. He is Tom, but different. The rest of this night will be hard, he is already sweating, and his heart is pounding.

Upstairs in the bedroom he sweats into the sheets and his skin tingles and itches, unseen creatures crawl over his legs and ants test his chest. He rasps and scratches his face where he feels the scars that he's not touched for so many years along his cheek and above his lip. Tom knows the symptoms of alcohol withdrawal, he has read claims there are hallucination and tremors, even seizures in the most severe cases. In the past this has given him the excuse to have another drink.

He lays on his back in the double bed and thinks how lucky he is not to have his phone with him, how lucky too that Inma is not curled up asleep by his side. He gets up to wee, looks out of the window into the darkness, lays down, then feels himself cresting high on a wave and crashing back down again. Tom touches the bruise on his face where the thug kicked him earlier. Inside his chest, he dreams that his liver is swollen and huge, green, and rancid and ready to explode with poison. Tom knows all the million terrible things that can happen to a man such as he who has drunk heavy and deep for so many years – his stomach and digestive system will be shot, he has an increased risk of cancer, he could have a stroke and his mental health will have suffered also. He rolls and twists in the bedsheets and in the morning when the weak sun peeps through the blinds that he did not close the night before, he sees his face pale in the mirror in the bathroom. He is alive.

If he can do one night, he can do two. He brushes his teeth. He has been here before. This is the naivety of someone trying to give up the drink for the first time, It's not a chesty cough. As soon as Tom feels better and a little bored a day or so later, the booze will call to him.

It's just whether he will go to it or not.

CHAPTER SEVEN
Friends and a drink with Bev

It's half nine in the morning at the taxi office and Our Dave sits at the round table with a cup of coffee. The girls are out on jobs. The events of the other evening with the gunman are fresh in his mind. It's not so much getting finished off that bothers him, more how that would leave everyone else. Hazel used to say that he needed to delegate more, but it was always easier just to work the business himself. So, now, here he is with a booze smuggling network, bank accounts, properties and not another person knows how it's all put together. When someone does finally put a bullet in the back of his neck, that will be the end of it too, the authorities will have to unpick all the properties he owns and figure out all the different accounts. He sets his phone down on the table. That's what happens when you try to do things on your own for too long – you end up alone.

There's a business-like double knock at the back door of the taxi office. It's too bright to be the postman. It might be someone here to finish the job.

"Come in," he calls. He watches the handle turn and a figure comes through the back door of the kitchen and into the office wearing a long dark coat. Our Dave looks up to the beardless face and does not recognise the shaved head. The man has a yellow tool bag in one hand.

"Tom?"

"I've brought your tool bag back," he says. "I didn't want to leave it on your step." Tom sets it on the table with a clink.

"You shouldn't have brought it here either," says Our Dave.

"Well, I know that you wanted it back. You might need to do something with it. I don't want it in my house."

"Have a seat." Tom pulls out a chair. "What do you think I want with it?"

"To kill yourself." Our Dave looks back at him. He has to play this one carefully. Tom looks pale and washed out and his eyes are red around the edges. His jaw has a purple bruise from where he got kicked the night before.

"What happened to your hair and the beard?"

"I got Alex to cut it all off. Inma left me last night."

"For good?"

"I think so." Our Dave frowns in concern.

"Maybe she just needs a bit of time."

"Maybe. I'd leave me if I was her, Our Dave." Tom has said this a few times now. He's getting sick of it.

"You look like shite." Our Dave is just stating a fact. Without the beard and the hair, you can see Tom's emotions and his eyes. Something about this man has changed, not just the way he looks. If he's prepared to bring back the gun, then he might be prepared to go to the authorities with it too. Our Dave needs to get him onside, quickly.

"I got mugged on the way to the pub," says Tom. "They got my wallet and my phone. One of them belted me."

"Did you call the coppers?"

"What good would they do?"

"Maybe I could help you out, Tom? Who were they?"

"Druggie types, Our Dave. I'm just gonna leave it. They did me a favour to be honest. I needed a bit of sense kicking into me."

"Are you not meant to be at work?"

"I'm off sick, so I thought I'd bring the bag back."

"Is it still in there?"

"The gun? Yes, it is." Tom wears his litigation poker face. "What is it to you?" Our Dave thinks quickly. There is potential danger here, for he does not know if he can trust Tom at all. The old man leans forward. He's not a natural liar, but he has to reel Tom in somehow. If the man goes to the police with the weapon, it would open a huge can of worms.

"Someone left the gun. You get all sorts in the taxi game.

It's more trouble if I go to the police with it. You know, Tom, it might be better if you kept it after all. Just to be safe." There's a sense of the mysterious in the man from across the street and it's enticing to someone who has taught law for the last twenty years. Our Dave does not like to lie to good people, again, but this is only a slightly different version of the truth.

"You'll have to tell someone, Our Dave."

"About what?"

"About everything, your wife's death, what's in the bag. If you don't it might come back round and bite you on the arse."

"What would you know about keeping secrets, Tom?" Our Dave is not accusing the man or trying to belittle him. It's a straightforward question.

"I drink." Our Dave nods, he already figured. "I drink every day. I'm a shit husband as well. I think my wife is having an affair." He swallows as he says this. Now he's started he might as well carry on. "I'm about to lose my job. I'm a coward and a dickhead most of the time. I don't know why I'm telling you all this. I came here to help you. I thought we could talk, or something. I thought we could talk about Hazel." Our Dave does not have to hide the pain just below the surface. Maybe that Baretta would be the perfect way to sort this out, it's best out of his hands.

"So, you'll keep the gun?"

"What makes you think I'm trustworthy, Our Dave? I'm half pissed at the best of times."

"You learn to judge people in my business."

"The taxi business?"

"Something like that. You get a sense of folk." If Our Dave is really going to be able to trust Tom, then he's going to have to get him mixed up in something so he can't back out without difficulty. It's self-preservation at best. "Do you know how to do a will?"

"A will and testament? Haven't you got one?"

"I do mean that, and I haven't got one no." Tom licks his

lips where there used to be the hairs of a beard.

"They're very easy to draw up, Dave, as long as there aren't any complicated clauses. I wouldn't charge." Our Dave nods and smiles.

"What makes you think she's having an affair?"

"Condoms in her handbag. I had the snip years ago. She hates me more than normal. She looks prettier than ever; she disappears for hours on end at night."

"You don't sound too upset."

"How could I be, the state I'm in."

"You're just going to have to get yourself out of the state then. How long are you off work?" Our Dave has a way of switching between subjects, it makes the difficult questions easier to answer because they catch you off guard.

"This week. Looks like I'm going to get the boot though. I really don't know why I'm telling you all this, Our Dave, you're just the bloke across the street whose gun I'm looking after." Tom knows that sarcastic humour well enough, but he doesn't get much of an opportunity to use it.

"Life has a funny way of bringing people together, you know, especially people who need something from each other."

"What do you need from me?"

"Apart from that gun, I need a few things sorting, my will for a start, something's happened to make me think about what will be after I'm gone. There are other bits and bobs too. Contracts for the drivers here need updating, and then there's the council business you helped me with the other night." Tom nods. This is all straightforward stuff.

"What do I get from you?" he asks. He can't see it.

"You need friends, Tom. That's what you haven't got, and in actual fact, they're in heavy supply on this street if you know where to look and what to do." Tom wrinkles his nose at this.

"I've got friends," he says. Our Dave nods in agreement but doesn't answer. They both know that the older man is right. Tom does not have any friends; this is glaringly obvious. Like lots of men, he traded all of those that he used to hang around with for his job, his wife and his kid, it's not uncommon. It's one of the reasons middle class men like him are so lonely as they get older.

"Maybe we could start this afternoon," says Our Dave. "You can go home and drop the bag, then come back with your computer. I'll dig up some of the papers I need to sort the will. How does that sound?" Tom gives a sigh and stands up from the chair, he looks down at the yellow tool bag that has the Baretta in the bottom somewhere.

"I guess it'll give me something to do," he answers. He collects the bag then turns around to go out of the office.

"Maybe we could look after each other," says Our Dave after him. It's not meant in an underworld way. This is Chanterlands Avenue, Hull, there's no hidden agenda of extortion or money lending. Our Dave really does need someone, and so does this desperate man with a disfigured face. "We could help each other out."

"I'd like that, Our Dave," says Tom. "I'm in a bad way."

"Me too," Men don't speak to each other like this round here. It's all deadpan sarcasm, proud chests, drinks and football. Our Dave and Tom are strange men to be friends, even associates, perhaps it's why this seems to work.

"I'll put the bag back under the stairs," says Tom.

"Make sure you don't blow your head off." This is more the kind of talk they are both used to.

It's not yet spring on Chanterlands Avenue. February is just coming to an end and Christmas seems like ages away. At this time of year Steve from the cycle shop goes on his annual holiday and the retired previous owner, a lowland Scott from just outside Dundee takes over for a few weeks. The letting agency on the corner of Perth Street is waiting desperately for spring proper when people decide to move. Mustafa from the

Kurdish barber has just booked three tickets for his family to fly to Sulaymaniyah from Manchester at six hundred quid each – which is good.

Tom has never walked down here at this time of day, and without the worry of work hanging over him, he sees things that the unobservant might miss. There's a parking warden hidden in the alley of the Yellow Spade plant shop having a cig with his eyes on the street ahead, an old man stands at the bus stop with his hands in his pockets and his face shaking against the half cold. Tom walks past the Avenues Pub and the betting office with two pizza shops opposite, he passes the boarded-up off-licence on the corner and walks down Westbourne Avenue. This is his street, but he doesn't know as many people on it as he should, he's been too busy with work and his family to get to know anyone other than a bottle of expensive red.

Our Dave is right. Tom doesn't have any friends. Like lots of men his age he thinks his family and wife are enough for him to deal with and it's only needy sorts who go off and play chess at a club or go running with other men dressed in Lycra. Tom knows the cool kids in the German beer house on Princes Avenue even if they don't know him, he stands listening to the bands when they have the street festival there. Like always, he is pretending to be something he's not. He feels his freshly shaven face. There's no need to do that anymore, like the ghost of his father said, he's failed at being Tom so he might as well be someone else.

It's just working out who that other person is going to be.

It's been a steady week so far. Our Dave and Bev are in the galley kitchen at Avenue Cars. Tom has been there most of the week sorting legal stuff out but now it's just the two of them.

"I'm not doing it, Our Dave," says Bev. "I'm not doing it and that's final. I've made my mind up." They stand a few yards away from each other and look in different directions. Our Dave examines the deserted car park. Bev stares into the empty office. It's late Thursday afternoon. They know each other a little too well.

"I mean you'd just be going out for a drink with him. Nothing else."

"What for? I'm not interested in him, Dave. I'm not looking for anything." She is a little angry she has been asked. "What am I meant to do?" This is rhetorical. Our Dave holds his hand up in defence.

"You could just give him some advice, that's all."

"Advice about what?"

"Getting back out there after a break up, standing up for yourself, I don't know… how to use them dating apps on your phone. Will you be having a drink tomorrow night?" He knows that she will be. Now Chloe has gone off to university in Newcastle, there's no point in staying in. Bev has joined West Hull Fitmums, it's a running club that meet outside Pearson Park at seven on Friday and Wednesday nights. Bev does the four-mile group and has a glass of wine afterwards.

"I'm done with fellas, Our Dave."

"It wouldn't be a date though; he's done a lot for us this last week." Our Dave means Tom. He's spent the last few days at the taxi office setting things in order. Everyone now has a will and testament and he's been over some of the tax affairs of the drivers. Turns out there is quite a bit of money to be saved when you look at it with keen eyes. Tom has been charming somewhat and defeated just the same.

Our Dave turns to look at Bev and she to him. She's been different since Chloe has gone to university, weaker somehow but more open as well. She swallows. She has not been out with a man since the episode with the Dutchman. Our Dave paid for a ticket for her to fly out to meet him, and he was sweet enough, but just like the rest of the men she's met overall and only after one thing, even over all those miles. It wasn't the love affair she thought it would be. He had dirty fingernails, he didn't close his mouth when he ate and even though he wore expensive aftershave, Bev could still smell his body odour under it.

"Will you go out with him, just for one drink?" Bev narrows her eyes at Our Dave.

"It'll be just one drink." she whispers. Tom is younger than she is, and she really is doing this as a favour. Our Dave has told her that the man's wife just walked out on him. She kind of gets why, it's not the burns on his face, it's more the shrinking confidence when he's not talking about the law, as if he's ashamed to be there. Bev guesses that he'll be a needy sort, worried about hurting anyone's feelings and afraid to show his own. A bit like her first husband who could only communicate when he was pissed up. Tom is a lawyer however, and a lecturer too and like Our Dave said, he has done a bit for her this week, the tax advice alone will save her a grand a year. She is coming round to the idea.

"You're a good lass, Bev," he says.

"I wish I was," she answers.

This is the Avenues Pub. It's Friday night. Tom is at the bar and Bev is just behind him. This isn't a date and so Bev doesn't have to pretend to be anything, she's asked for a half of cider. Tom orders a Guiness.

"Shall we sit down?" he asks. Bev nods. She was never going to ask him to come here, so, while he was filling in some paperwork for Our Dave over at the office, she struck up a conversation. Men are really easy to manipulate. She just dropped a few hints and he suggested coming here. They take a seat opposite each other at a little square table near the windows and away from the few drinkers at the bar.

"Our Dave says your wife left you." Bev isn't the sort to mess around.

"She did. It'd been coming a long time. Are you married?"

Tom knows that she is not. Unlike her, Tom will dance around a subject before he gets to the point.

"I walked out on him more than ten years ago." Tom nods and takes a sip on his drink.

"How did that work out?"

"Pretty good for the most part."

"Is there anyone special?" Again, Tom knows there isn't. He's heard Bev tell the two other drivers that she's finished with men for good this time.

"No. When did she leave you?" It's embarrassing for Tom.

"A week ago."

"How you going on?"

"Ok. This is my first drink since Sunday. I shaved my beard off. I went for a run down Westbourne Ave this morning. It nearly killed me." Bev nods. He has the self-depreciating humour that she likes, and he pronounces his words like a TV newsreader. "Did Dave ask you to do this?" Tom doesn't look as smart as he is.

"Yes. He said you needed a bit of advice." Tom looks out the window as he thinks.

"He's a good old lad."

"He is." Tom takes a big gulp of his pint and it's half gone already. He is ready to change if he has to. Bev glugs down her half of cider.

"How long will it take?" he asks.

"To give you some advice?" Tom nods. "A couple more drinks," she says.

"I'll slip to the bar."

Bev has had her heart broken on many occasions. The first time there were floods of tears, that's not the case now. These days it always goes the same way. You meet someone, you like them, and they like you, then something rotten happens and it's over. Repeat.

Bev starts with the basics. Clear out your wardrobe. Chuck away all the shite you don't want and never use. Get a haircut.

Tom has already done this. Find a friend and spend time with them – Tom is trying to do this as he sits in the pub. Eat well. Try to do some exercise. Try to imagine that there is nothing wrong with you. Get back on the scene as quick as you can – it's like falling off a horse, you have to get yourself up, dust yourself off and get right back on. Tom counters this by saying how he heard Bev, many times, comment that she is finished with men. She swallows another half of cider and explains without mawkish sentiment how many times it has gone wrong for her. Bev's clear blue eyes are ringed by dark mascara and there is sincerity in her words.

On Bev's instruction, Tom downloads a dating app on his replacement phone and, after two and a half pints, Bev takes over. She is an expert at this. She changes the filters on his profile photos, takes a new one of him there in the pub and then enhances it so he does not look too bad. She pumps in a bio. 'I lecture law. I have burns on my face. I don't eat ready salted crisps.' Tom wrinkles his nose when he reads it. Bev sets the parameters into the app, and then copies the bio, she downloads other apps that do the same thing and pastes his profile onto there. It takes her ten minutes.

"I'm not sure about the bio," says Tom. Bev has warmed to him. He is modest and honest. She's not sure how needy he actually is given how well he has taken losing his wife. "Don't you think the bio is a bit funny?" asks Tom again. Bev shakes her head.

"Funny first, big cock second," she says. Bev is serious when she says this. Tom doesn't know how to react. This blonde woman is unlike his estranged wife in so many ways, she is warm, brave, and open, she's lived through bad times and come out with a smile on her face. Tom likes her. She hands Tom back his phone with the dating apps all updated and ready to go.

"So I just start swiping now, do I?"

"Not yet. You wait twenty-four hours. Then you can."

"You're an expert."

"Kind of. I did it for years. If you do get chatting to anyone, have a phone conversation first if you can, that way you can work out of they're a nutter without seeing them in the flesh. Make sure you do the coffee date – no more than twenty minutes and have an excuse so you can leave if they get weird on you. After you meet, if they're not right for you, message them and say. Ghosting is for arseholes." Tom nods. "Don't get your hopes up, either. There'll be loads of people on there who don't want to meet up at all, it's just kind of a game for their ego." Bev sighs. All this is hard won from experience and tonnes of dates.

"I'm not sure I'm ready for it all," says Tom.

"Why not? Are you still in love with your ex?"

"Maybe."

"Then you're not. Don't confuse being used to someone with being in love with them. It's what you're used to. Try someone different. You might like them."

"I don't know if I'm confident enough." Tom does a sigh.

"I never said it would work. Maybe there's nobody out there who's even interested. It isn't going to be a success, it's just some pictures on a phone. What can it hurt?" Bev's blue eyes look back up at him.

"Did it hurt you?"

"In the end, but it wasn't the app. It was my decisions." Bev is self-aware and she tells the truth, even if nobody wants to hear it. This is different from the world that Tom lives in. The people that he hangs around with sugar coat problems and provide constructive criticism rather than honesty. "You be careful," says Bev, "and it'll just be whatever you make of it." Tom nods.

"What can it hurt?"

CHAPTER EIGHT
A walk with Our Dave

Tom walks down Westbourne Ave in the sleepy mist of Sunday afternoon. There's a crisp end of winter cold in the air. An earnest jogger staggers past. A man walking a Westie dog crosses the road. Tom notices a van turn up the street, it's one of those new electric ones, it's a BMW Transporter with a sleek design and a brand-new sky blue paint job. Tom looked at the same kind on Autotrader last summer – they cost a packet. In the front seat are two squared jawed types wearing dark glasses and light blue overalls. They look like goons from an A-Team episode. He turns and watches the van drive up the street and for some reason, he gets a funny feeling in his legs.

Opposite the Food Hub takeaway is Eighty Days Beer House. Tom has done a lot of drinking in here. At capacity it can fit forty drinkers inside and another twenty or so outside. The décor is shabby chic without any of the chic, but there is a certain Berlin charm to the place with the chairs that don't match the tables, the candles jammed into cognac bottles and the toilet upstairs that is covered in graffiti. It attracts all sorts. Richard Tong takes in his little border terrier called Woody. The architect couple, who are both called Phil take in their whippet on Sunday afternoons. They show reruns of indoor league pub game tournaments from the eighties on a tiny old-fashioned colour TV high up in the corner in the daytime. You can be yourself there, whoever you are, and all Merv the owner needs you to do is keep drinking.

Eighty Days is just far enough for Tom to walk. Our Dave plays dominos there on Sunday afternoon and he's asked Tom to come along and although the old man hasn't paid Tom anything for any of his services, somehow, this feels like work. It's been nine days since Tom last had a drink - the longest amount of time for probably twenty years. It was last Friday that he and Bev had a couple in the Avenues Pub, and she fixed up his dating profiles along with giving some advice. When he got home, he turned them all off and drank a pint of water with an Alka-Seltzer. The next morning, at seven o'clock when he woke up, he ran the length of Westbourne Ave in the crisp March air, and when he got to Chanterlands Ave, he ran back home again. According to mapometer.com, a distance of 1.2 miles. It hurt like hell.

Without the drink, he started to feel better on Tuesday morning, the itching stopped on Wednesday, and he started to notice things a bit more on Thursday. Now Tom feels his knees creak in the morning, he senses the light coming through the big oak trees in the late afternoon, he wakes up with erections, he tastes coffee and feels the effect of it. Life is not easy, and he is not nearly over his addiction but for the time being, it is at bay.

His life is changing. He took Bev's advice and cleaned out his wardrobe to fill three bin-liners of clothes and books and general tat. Alex grabbed the clothes he liked and they took the rest to the Dove House Hospice shop where Tom bought a leather jacket for fifty quid that makes him look younger. He and Alex have been talking a lot more, and just like the booze covers up those things that you don't want to see, so it covers up those things you might have missed. Late at night Tom learns, Alex paints watercolour characters in a sketch book while he watches YouTube, he's got much better on a skateboard and feels settled in the person he has become. He's looking forward to leaving school and finding out about the world – all this was going on right under Tom's nose and he did not see. He is warmed that he now does. It is sweeter than any full-bodied red.

Tom stops outside the German Beer house and peers in through the big windows. There's Our Dave sitting at one of the low tables chatting with a red faced man who looks like he's been drinking for the last few hours. He sees Tom, grabs his jacket from a chair and steps outside to greet him.

"Are we going somewhere?" asks Tom.

"Aye," says Our Dave. "I've to do my Sunday visits."

They walk side by side down Princes Avenue and then right into Duesbery Street. Our Dave has long strides. He's taller than Tom and goes at a fair rate when walking despite his age. Tom is dressed in a ratty tweed teacher's jacket with leather arm patches, and Our Dave with his hands in his jean pockets as he walks, has a bomber jacket over one of his checked shirts.

"Where we going?" asks Tom.

"Down to the river, like I do every Sunday at this time. There's a car showroom opposite the old factory there. I usually have a cup of coffee and then walk back. Takes about an hour."

"Is there something you need me to do there? I mean in a legal profession; I can pop back and collect my laptop."

"I just thought you might like a walk." Our Dave has been alone for much longer than anyone realises. The key to success is keeping busy. At this time of year just before spring, his allotment behind Newland Ave is not worth bothering with, so he spends the weekends on visits and odd jobs. Our Dave could easily just sit in the front room of his house on Westbourne Ave looking at the wallpaper that Hazel put up a few years earlier. He's felt himself being dragged down that road already, so he must keep up the pretence that he is a busy a needed man – which of course he is. He also needs to keep Tom close to him, as well as appraise him of his business interests. The more he knows and is involved in, the less likely he will be able to say anything to the authorities.

"Just a walk?" asks Tom.

"It's good to keep busy." Our Dave looks down at him as they stride along Duesbery Steet towards the old railway line footpath behind the houses. "Especially in our situation." Our

Dave is conscious that somehow this man knows more about him than he would like.

At Beverely Road there's the remnants of the old station there with big platforms covered in weeds and graffiti, in summer drunks gather here but in the cold months it's warmer to stay at home. Tom and Our Dave cross the normally busy road past the Station Inn and go along the old railway line behind the back of the houses towards the run-down industry of Bankside and the river Hull. The bike and pedestrian track is studded with weeds growing through the tarmac and there's rubbish along the fence.

Ordinarily, Our Dave makes this journey alone every Sunday, he's become a creature of routine, it's security. As they walk together in silence, the older man is aware that Tom has entered into his confidence more than anyone else for the last few years, even more than those he looks after and works with. Our Dave has tried to talk to people before but like men of his generation, the only emotion he is allowed to show is light to medium sarcasm. He realises they have been walking in silence and this doesn't seem to bother Tom.

"How's it been without your misses?" Our Dave asks.

"Strange but okay. I'm learning to cook a bit more."

"How do you find it?" Our Dave swallows. He knows what Tom is referring to.

"What do you mean?" This is his defence.

"I mean with Hazel gone down south to visit her sister," Tom is playing along with the charade.

"I've always been able to look after myself, Tom. Hazel taught me to cook years ago." He feels a lump in his throat when he says this. The track turns again, they have passed a little housing estate, and the old bike path narrows as it joins a road opposite a swing bridge over the river Hull. They stop. To the right and looming over the wide fast-flowing water, is the old Spillers Mill. There's a vast red bricked factory building that looms over the river, it's been a wreck since the early eighties and every window, all the way up to the top high in the sky, is smashed. It looks like somewhere you could breed zombies in a dystopian future. Our Dave sets off towards it.

"It's not the most picturesque part of town." says Tom.

"It's got character," answers Our Dave. There's nothing pretty about this little industrial area that clings to the banks of the river Hull. There are run-down cafes, plastic factories, HGV training centres; someone has fly tipped a leather sofa on the waste ground before the river and there's the smell of the cocoa factory from up the road. On weekdays, you can see workmen dressed in dayglo jackets with safety boots, but at this time on a Sunday, it's deserted and eerie.

"Just down here's a car showroom. I come at weekends to make sure it's all okay."

"You own it? It's not on the books."

"A lot of things aren't written down, Tom." On the left, opposite the muddy river are twenty or so cars of various styles in a wide fenced off carpark. It's all closed up today. In the far corner is an old metal shipping container with the word 'Reception' painted red on a piece of cardboard pinned on the side. Our Dave unlocks the padlock and pulls open one of the wire gates. He makes his way through the car lot between a lime green sparkling mini and a bright white BMW. Tom follows. He approaches the door to the metal container, and with the keys from his jacket pocket he opens up the door at the side.

"I've got someone who looks after it for me in the week," says Our Dave. He pulls open the door but doesn't go inside. Tom stares across at the cars and the deserted road in front with the old, smashed up mill building looking down on them from the other side of the river. It's desolate.

"Who buys a car from here?" asks Tom.

"Those who know," says Our Dave.

"Does that mean all these cars are nicked?"

"I wouldn't say that. We don't open on Sunday afternoon.

The guy who runs it for me goes down to the Whalebone for a few pints."

"Who else knows about this place, Dave?" asks Tom.

"Nobody at the taxi company. I took it over as a favour."

"You've got quite the empire."

"By accident, most of it, Tom. That's why I need your help."

Tom takes another look at the river and the run-down buildings behind the cars. It's as if he's in another city. They stand next to each other outside the container these two, it's so unlikely that they would even know each other, let alone be friends.

From round the corner comes the same posh sky-blue van that Tom saw earlier down Westbourne Ave. The one with the two goons with dark glasses who look like they're out of an eighties action TV show. He frowns.

"Funny that," he says.

"What is?" asks Our Dave.

"I saw that van down our street as I was walking to meet you earlier." Our Dave narrows his eyes as the sky-blue van turns into the car lot and the big, new tyres crunch on the tarmac. It stops.

Our Dave' stomach drops. You get a feeling when things aren't quite right, especially when you've been around these kinds of people as long as Our Dave has. The van is too new. It'll have been nicked from somewhere in Manchester or Sheffield. The men inside are wearing shades even though it's overcast March. Our Dave comes here every Sunday about this time after his game of dominoes. He'll have been watched. There was a man in his house two weeks passed who tried to kill him. The passenger and driver's door of the blue van open at about the same time. He is too old for this. Our Dave thought that by his age he'd be living in a caravan overlooking Hornsea beach, not watching two goons with automatic weapons getting out of a BMW transporter. The world slows down. He grabs Tom by the arm and yanks the man backward into the metal container that is the reception office for this used car lot, and he sees the look of horror on his scarred face.

Tom has not been drinking for a while, every other day he has been running the full length of Westbourne Ave and going a little bit further every time. He is a clever man. It hasn't taken him long to join all the disparate dots that he's seen over the last week. There's a gun in the tool bag that Our Dave lent him. The man has several businesses and properties all over the West Hull area. Tom has seen large payments go out of the accounts he's looked at. The taxi office doesn't make a lot of money, yet Our Dave's assets suggest he does.

As Our Dave pulls him into the darkness of the container office and closes the door, he puts it all together – Our Dave is into something that is not quite legal. Tom is surprised at the power of the man as he pulls him backwards onto the floor behind the desk. They fall and Tom lands on the older man with a crunch, he's about to protest when he hears the rattle of something like heavy rain spraying against the outside of the container. Like he understands that Our Dave is not just that nice man from across the road who runs the taxi office, he also understands the rat-a-tat noises against the metal are something else.

They're bullets.

It feels odd to lay there on top of Our Dave in the darkness as the container rattles and the bullets ping from the outside. The older man's arms are around his shoulders and Tom's head rests on his chest. It's as if they're lovers. Tom can smell Our Dave's aftershave and the mint chewing gum on his breath. Outside they hear the slam of doors and the van tyres squeaking on the gravel as they back up and drive away. Tom gets up and stands in the darkness of the metal container. He feels odd but not as afraid as he should be.

"Amateurs," says Our Dave from below. Tom holds out his hand and the man uses it to get to his feet. He can move quickly for an old fella. They stand opposite each other.

"How do you know?" asks Tom.

"If they'd known what they were doing, we'd be dead."

Tom swallows. He really needs a drink.

They didn't open the container door right away even though Our Dave explained the men in the blue van would have driven off and probably swapped cars a few miles away. They would have thought they committed a murder. Tom looked so pale that Our Dave promised he'd take him home rather than the Whalebone pub which was going to be his second stop on his Sunday visit.

This is where they are now. Tom is too much of a drinker to have a drinks cabinet, he always sinks everything he's got in one go, but there is whiskey in the shed where the ghost of his father sits in the empty armchair. Tom doesn't hear a peep from his old man as he picks out one of the full bottles from behind the chair. Back in the kitchen, he pours Our Dave a glass before he pours himself one. He is shaking. His legs tingle and his head is still spinning. This is a version of shock he reasons as he sits down at the kitchen table and takes a sip of the whiskey. Our Dave sits opposite. He collected a manila file from the safe at the car dealership office and he's looking through the contents. He takes a delicate sip on the glass of supermarket whiskey Tom poured him.

"What just happened?" asks Tom.

"We got a taxi. I know the driver so we didn't pay."

"I mean before that." Tom takes a glug on the brown liquid. If he were a normal person it would burn all the way down his throat, because he is Tom, it feels delicious in the way it rasps on his tongue and tingles to his stomach. Our Dave looks up from the papers. He might as well be straight.

"I think someone wants to finish me off, Tom," he says.

"You don't say." Tom isn't ordinarily sarcastic.

"That gun you have in the tool bag. Someone broke into

my house. He dropped that when he left. He put a bullet hole through my bedroom window." Tom remembers the glaziers from a few weeks before.

"You'll have to go to the police, Dave," he whispers.

"I can't," comes the reply. "Neither can you, now. You've already helped out too much. This has been coming a long while. You already know I don't just run a taxi office, Tom. You've seen more of my affairs than anyone has. It's the reason I want to get it all sorted, I mean the will and all the legal stuff. They'll get me in the end, and I just want everything to be right for when they do." Tom drinks the rest of his whiskey and pours himself another one. "I didn't mean to get you involved, Tom. I'm sorry." The whiskey is getting to work on the man with the scarred and burned face. Perhaps for the first time in his life, Tom feels like a grown up, like his expertise is needed and he is someone of value. The danger is intoxicating.

"Someone would have seen those men, Dave. There'll be cameras and evidence, there'll be a case against them. People don't drive round shooting in broad daylight. This is Hull, it isn't Moss Side in the nineties." Our Dave shakes his head.

"There are no cameras down that street, kid. There aren't any on the car lot either, why do you think we sell cars there? Why do you think they followed me? You said yourself you'd seen the van down this street." Tom nods at this but doesn't look at Dave as he thinks.

"They'll still be out there. They'll know they didn't get you." He is suddenly worried, not so much about himself but for Alex who might be upstairs.

"Like I said before, they're amateurs, otherwise we wouldn't be here. They won't know I'm alive for a few days."

"Who are they?"

"That's just it, Tom. It could be any number of people from the past, but these days, I'm not so sure."

"So they were hitmen?" It sounds ridiculous for him to say

this. Our Dave picks up his glass and sniffs the whiskey without answering the question or drinking. He sets it down.

"I've no idea how I've confided in you, Tom," says Our Dave. He looks different somehow from the friendly, almost carefree man that you might see wandering down Chanterlands Ave.

"You haven't told me anything."

"I know. You seem to have worked it out."

"What have I worked out?"

"You tell me."

"I think you've got some sort of enterprise that generates money that you need to launder. You do it through a series of businesses and properties around this city. It's well thought out. It looks like it works, but I can't see where the money comes from." Tom reaches over to collect the whiskey bottle he just poured them both a drink from, he wants to pour himself another. Our Dave holds up his finger to stop him.

"Would you mind, Tom? I need you to be clear for me, just for a few minutes only. I need your intelligence." Tom sets the bottle back down. In all these years he has never been asked not to drink for a better reason.

"Of course."

"How am I going to get rid of it all? I mean when I'm gone."

"I'll need to be appraised of the full aspect of your financial affairs, Dave. I mean everything. Then I can work out how it can be dissolved. It won't be a quick job."

"I know that. You'll be paid for your efforts as well. It's not without its risks for you." Tom is aware of this. He has never been shot at before.

"I don't want you to come round here anymore, Our Dave. My son lives here. You said someone is trying to kill you, I don't want them to try it here, not with my family." Our Dave's face winces:

"They don't want anyone else, Tom, I can promise you."

"They would have killed me as well this afternoon, if that container wasn't made of steel."

"I know, kid." Our Dave looks old. "I'm sorry I got you involved. If I'd have known they'd have been there, I wouldn't have asked you to come along. It might have been much easier if they'd done me in." Tom takes a deep breath. This is a difficult conversation. Our Dave is a complex man. Whatever issues Tom has with his little life - his wife leaving him, the drinking, the job; these pale into insignificance against this man who is preparing to be murdered by someone. Our Dave is beginning to pack his affairs up for when he is no longer here, and he does it, every day, with a breezy smile and light air to him because nobody at all knows what he is going through. Tom lays his hand flat on the table like he does when he is telling his students something serious.

"I'm here to help you, Our Dave. I'm not bothered so much about me, but I can't put my family at risk. Tomorrow, I'll come over to the taxi office and we'll go through the lot, top to bottom. You can tell me the whole thing and we'll see what we can work out."

"What's in it for you?" asks Our Dave.

"I don't have any friends," says Tom. "That's what's in it for me." The old man gives him a half smile. He picks up the glass of whiskey and takes another sniff before setting it down.

"I'm not much of a drinker, Tom." He gets up. "I best get back. I usually call Hazel on a Sunday evening." Tom gets up as well.

"There's no need for all that, Our Dave, not with me." The man nods and Tom can see the pain just behind his eyes.

"It's not for you, kid," he answers. Our Dave slides in his chair under the round kitchen table. "I'll see myself out." Tom hears the letter box jump softly as he leaves.

CHAPTER NINE
Dating apps

Turns out that Alex is staying with Inma at her mother's and so Tom has the full run of the huge, terraced house to himself. It's just got dark and Our Dave left a few hours ago. Tom looks out at the garden with the fallen down fence panel outside and notices in the security floodlight, that there are skids and marks where the kids from next door have been playing football. He smiles. Tom takes another big gulp on the whiskey. He's allowed to because he got shot at this afternoon. His feet still tingle, and when he shuts his eyes, he can still see the steady faces of the men in the blue van and hear the spitting and clanging of the bullets as they pinged off the steel container when he and Our Dave lay on the floor. Like the beating Tom got the other night, it doesn't feel as scary as he is sure it ought to. It feels thrilling somehow. He pours himself another drink.

As he is locking the front door, Tom gets a look at himself in the big ornate mirror that Inma bought. He has tried not to look at himself for so long – the hair and the beard were masks for it. The drinking is too. The burns that he has worn forever are a mess across his cheek and along his nose, they make his top lip look as if it's been folded in two and then unfolded again. In secondary school they called him Face. They called him Roadmap, Scars, Waxhead; they said he looked like he'd had his features melted off. Tom does not consider this abuse, this is how children are, the Chinese looking kid in one of the other classes suffered actual violence, he was just called names.

Tom runs his palm across the scars, he feels the bumps and the little valleys and ridges – if he is going to get anywhere, he is going to have to own this and not try to escape it. The name he hated the most was Face. There was a guy on the A-Team with the same name, he was handsome and charming, a confidence trickster. Face was the name they shouted at him as he walked down the corridors, it was the name the games teacher yelled at him, it was on the whispers of the kids at the bus stop and in assembly and in the darkness of the cinema. When he went away to university the name calling stopped but the stares didn't. Tom swallows. He remembers the words from his ghost father in the shed at the bottom of the garden. He has failed at being Tom. It's time to be someone else. What if that someone else has been there all along, looking back at him in the mirror, hidden under floppy hair and a beard with thick glasses, crouched terrified behind the booze, and drowned out by the clever talk of law and rules in university lecture halls? He is Face. Ever since that accident when he was a little boy. He says the name at himself in the mirror.

In the kitchen, he glugs down the rest of his drink, then takes the bottle to the backdoor, opens up and strides down the path to the end of the garden. He unlocks the shed and sets the half full bottle next to the old armchair. The paintings loom at him from the darkness. For the first time in forever he is stopping himself from getting any more drunk. It feels right.

"Not a word from you today, father," he whispers.

In the kitchen once more, he does the washing up, cleans the work surfaces down and wipes the cupboards with a cloth. His drunk brain is working things out as he goes. He is planning steps that he can take. First things first he has to prove something to himself. In the front room with a cup of cocoa, he sits on one of the comfy sofas and looks through the dating apps on his smartphone, the ones that Bev set up for him a week or so earlier. He has yet to set his profile to public on any of them. He scans through the photos that she filtered and alters then replaces the first one with a picture of him smiling from last week after Alex had cut off his beard and shaved off his hair. The scars are clear and bright across his features, it's not ugly, it's just his face. Tom uploads it and changes his profile information. 'I'm Tom, but my real names are either Face or Dad. I teach law. I don't really like ready salted crisps.' This will do. Like Bev says, 'funny first, big cock second'. He sets the profile to public on every one of them and puts the phone down, calls to the radio to turn it on and then listens to the smooth voice of the presenter and some light jazz. He's just going to sit there and sip his cocoa - nothing else. He's not going to be pulled into the drag of the news or his work or his face, just for a moment he's going to sit.

There's a light thud on the back of the sofa behind him and the blue grey house cat comes into view. The fur is puffed up like a teddy bear and the eyes are a light yellow. Galal pads down onto the seat next to Tom and sits upright looking at him, it's as if she is seeing him for the very first time.

"I don't imagine your mother will let you stay here," he says to her. The cat does not stop looking at him.

Alicja's father Pawel sometimes calls in the evening and Kasia usually has her phone on silent so she can't hear. There are many missed calls and a voice message she won't listen to. He has sent a text as well, it will only say the same as all the others – that he is desperate to see his daughter. She deletes it without bothering to look at the contents. It's too late for him to decide that he cares about Alicja. Kasia is unforgiving.

There's also a message on Kasia's Telegram app from someone called Ronny. It just reads 'job done'. She closes the message secure in the knowledge that it will be deleted as soon as she does. She puts the phone down on the kitchen counter and looks at the clock. It's half seven. Alicja is in bed already, it's school in the morning. Kasia hates these dark March nights. As soon as the weather begins to change, she'll make the most of it. Now she has the business with Our Dave sorted, there won't be anyone left who really knows who she is and what she does. She'll step back from the Dairycoates Inn and install a manager, someone she can trust, she'll make sure the business can run without her, and then, when there's enough money in the bank, she'll sell the lot and get out. Kasia has grown to like Hull and Hessle Road, she likes the no nonsense attitude of the old timers and thinks she understands the dry humour too, but it's not where she wants to be. Alicja is an English girl too much already, and Kasia does not want to go back to Poland after all this time, so she'll move out of the city to one of the leafy villages out west. She'll buy a semi-detached house with a big drive and do yoga at the church hall on Tuesday nights, she'll know other mums in the village and be best friends with her next-door neighbour as well. There's just one thing that she needs to complete the equation, she's been thinking about it ever since Alicja read that book about a mermaid.

Kasia takes her phone into the hall and sits down on the second to bottom step. She opens up the dating app and sees the reams of little electronic envelopes waiting for her to read against the pictures of the men who sent them. The Latvian photographer did a good job with the snaps he took – he digitally manipulated the images so that Kasia was smiling in the snow in her big jacket, riding her bike in the summer in a little dress and laughing while she held a white cup of expresso in the upstairs kitchen of the Dairycoates Inn. Kasia has ignored all the messages so far, she is not stupid, she knows what she wants, and she will know it when she sees it.

As a young woman back in Poland she used to hear the other girls talk about the kind of man they would like to marry, how they wanted him to have strong arms or blue eyes or big hands or deep pockets, but Kasia is more pragmatic. If you are a hunter in the forest you don't get to choose precisely what kind of boar you will kill, you weigh up the options you are given and take what you can get. Kasia scrolls through the pictures. There are men with tattoos and beards, strong gym types with short haircuts and tight trousers, and, as the algorithm delivers her less attractive sorts, she sees footballers, fisherman holding their giant catches, runners and men in suits giving speeches in conference rooms. She reads the bios, they like long country walks, someone to make them laugh, Sunday dinners, nights out but nights in, cooking and eating out, cars and motorbikes and music. It makes her usually cool head spin in confusion as she swipes left to reject them almost as soon as she gets the chance. She stops on one, a face looking at her out of the screen with a genuine smile, the man has scars on his face like he has lived through something terrible. Kasia is intrigued. She reads the bio: 'I'm Tom, but my real names are either Face or Dad. I teach law. I don't really like ready salted crisps'. Kasia does not see the humour. Her mind calculates. She likes lawyers. They are wealthy already. She goes back to look at his eyes and sees they are earnest and blue. His teeth are straight and well kept. Kasia likes ready salted crisps, in fact, they are the only sort she will eat. This could be a match. She swipes right on the picture and puts the phone down.

That'll do for tonight.

In the back of the red van behind the Adelphi music club on De Grey Street, Anita sits with her knees up to her chest and the phone in both hands. She almost wishes she had never been given it. She's read the news every day and found out that the world was more terrible than she had ever imagined and that the state of the environment is beyond repair. Clive lays next to her. The Adelphi will not be open tonight, so she's retired to bed already with the big dog and the phone for company.

She's used the dating apps as well. Anita is not afraid to get stuck into things and she's no wallflower either, so she has already been on two dates with men she met on the app. She doesn't go for materialistic stuff, so fellas with posh cars or smart suits are out straight away, lads with dogs score high but Clive doesn't get on well with other beasts. Anita met a guy in a pub round the corner who she chatted to for a couple of days, he said he was a musician but actually worked in an office in town. He was nice but dull. The other one was a hospital porter who looked thinner on his photos, they got on well and she liked him as a friend.

Anita does not have any expectation of what she will find, she is too wise to think that love will come her way, perhaps she has already loved and lost, so, the best she expects is a nice chat to someone on her wavelength, anything else would be a bonus. She is conscious too that she is getting old. At thirty-nine, she senses that her body is no longer as good at getting up or weathering the cold living in a van. When she looks at pictures of children she feels a sense of loneliness, she knows this is her hormones somehow controlling her. Anita puts her arm around Clive in the warmth of the van, she consoles herself with the knowledge that this is her way of life and not something that has been forced upon her – it's cold comfort.

She fires up the dating app she's been on, and the mobile glows yellow with the loading screen. She scrolls past men on beaches with their children, a man in front of a red sports car, someone with a traffic cone on his head, a man with a huge orange beard and someone riding a motorbike through a muddy puddle. She reads the bios and the men like Sunday dinners, nights in and out, films, music, football but not Chelsea, and F1 but not Max Verstappen, they live alone or with children, eat meat and drink socially.

She stops on one face, the man has scars across his cheek and under his eyes, across his top lip too. He hasn't tried to hide. Anita likes this. She reads the bio: "I'm Tom, but my real names are either Face or Dad. I teach law. I don't really like ready salted crisps'. She smiles in the yellow light from the screen. She doesn't eat ready salted crisps either and she likes that his real name is not the one given to him at birth – this second fact makes her look at his photos again. They are candid. One of him laughing and holding a bass guitar – the caption reads: 'I don't play'. The heroin addict Anita dated back in London was called Sol, not his given name, he explained that in some far-flung places in the world you give yourself your own name when you've earned it. She looks at his face again. She swipes right to match with him. That will do for tonight, she'll be up early in the morning to walk Clive.

Joanne is having a glass of wine. It's Sunday night and tomorrow she will be teaching. Mondays are good days because she has sixth formers, they are bright, savvy kids who don't wear uniforms or act like knobheads. It's actually a nice job.

Her legs are tight from the long cross-country run she did this morning and from Parkrun and a karate session on Saturday. She joined Cottingham Fitmums a few years back with a friend and they do Sunday runs through the countryside, they are a nice lot. Sometimes Joanne thinks about the big Welshman who left her all those years ago, she thinks back to his warm laugh and how gentle he was with her and her daughter. Perhaps that's all the love she'll get now, at forty-two, she is not going to get any prettier or smarter. She wishes for companionship sometimes when she comes home late from work and the house is cold. Joanne's friends envy her, of course, they complain about the unwanted sexual advances of their husbands, the mess the men and children leave, the petty squabbles and the noise. Joanne thinks a bit of noise might be nice sometimes. She did promise her mother she would start looking for a man. She ought to get at it. In a few more years she might sag even more than she does now. Jo grins at this.

She takes the glass of white wine over to the kitchen table and sits down on one of the faux brown leather chairs next to the radiator. There's the smell of washing up liquid and bleach from her downstairs toilet just faint enough so you know it's clean. She takes a delicate sip on the dry white wine from Aldi and powers up her phone in her right hand. The red of the dating app she uses lights up her face, she puts on her glasses and begins the scrolling dance of looking at men. There's a man on a yacht with his shirt off, another dancing with a blow-up doll, a singer doing karaoke in a crowded pub and a man in mid dive off a high board into a lake. She reads the bios, they like music, football, nights in but also nights out, cooking, tennis, watching films, the cinema, true-crime documentaries.

She stops on a face. The man has scars. He has pale blue eyes and is smiling, but not in a cocky way at all, more a kind of self-actualized sense. He could have taken a photo that didn't show the deep lines that crisscross his features, but here he is, baring himself for all to see. Joanne reasons that he must be confident enough to do so and at peace with himself, whoever he is. She reads the bio: "I'm Tom, but my real names are either Face or Dad. I teach law. I don't really like ready salted crisps'. Joanne smiles at this. The other bios are deadly serious with warnings they will not tolerate crazy ex-wives or smokers, here is someone who is off the cuff and fun. He teaches law. That means he will have money. Joanne doesn't want anyone else's cash, she has her own, but a man who can look after himself financially is attractive. She looks down his profile and sees that he has children, does not smoke, drinks infrequently and likes running. She cocks her head. There is no way this is the man of her dreams at all but he doesn't take himself too seriously and he lives nearby, why shouldn't she take a chance? If she were to meet him and if he did give her any trouble she could knock him out. She swipes right to match with him - if he decides to swipe right on her.

Joanne takes another sip on the wine – she doesn't actually enjoy it. She's had enough of the dating apps for one night anyway.

Tom looks at some of the photos on the dating app. He is still drunk from the whiskey to be honest, and the radio presenter has a soft Sunday night voice designed to put you to sleep. He looks at the ladies on offer. They are mostly smiling at the camera, there are blondes and redheads, ginger lasses with freckles, older withered looking women with heavy makeup, fresh faced mums cuddling their kids, there are women riding horses or running through muddy fields in Lycra. Tom reads a few bios, they like nights in or out, Sunday dinners, tennis, music, box sets. He can't be bothered to read. None of them will like him anyway, just like his cat and his wife. He runs his hand over his newly shaved hair and thinks about what the Face would do. He might let the universe do the work for him, after all, Tom does not know what he wants or needs. He does what he's heard lots of men do, you just swipe right on every girl until the app won't let you like anymore. This is what Tom will do, right or wrong. He opens the app with the yellow screen and swipes right till it asks him to pay, then he opens up the red one and does the same, he does the same again for two more and puts his phone into his top pocket.

That'll do for the night. He has to be up early tomorrow; it'll be time to find out what is going on with Our Dave and how he can help him. He's done enough.

CHAPTER TEN

Kasia says no, so does Inma

It's just after nine on Monday morning. The traffic on Hessle Road is light after the school run and the sky is a dull grey. Our Dave used to work on the docks back in the seventies as a fitter, he was fresh out of school and Hessle Road was a busy community back then. It's not the same anymore. The council have commissioned huge murals on the sides of buildings with images of fisherman mending nets and trawlers far out at sea, but in another generation the industry will be history, just like the whaling ships from a hundred years before. Our Dave has parked his grey Ford outside Maltby's next door to the Dairycoates Inn, and he walks up to the front door of the pub. He doesn't expect it to be open and so he goes round to the backdoor through a gate in a wall. Kasia's bike leans on the bricks just inside and Kasia herself is emptying a bucket of dirty water down the drain. She's been cleaning for the last hour; she likes to do it before anyone else gets in. She looks up at Our Dave and her expression does not change even though she had information that he had been executed the night before. She will have to get in touch with the scrap dealership straightaway and get the money back from them, she knew she should have handled the job herself.

"It's too early for a drink," she says. Kasia is wearing pink marigold rubber gloves and has a headscarf tied round her head to keep her hair clean, like her grandmother used to do.

"I'm not here for a drink," says Our Dave. "Can we have a chat?"

"I'm busy," she says.

"It wouldn't take a minute."

"Like I said, I'm busy. You'll have to come back another time. I prefer it if you make an appointment." This is true. She doesn't want to speak to this man without working out what she will say.

"I'm in a bit of trouble," says Our Dave. His eyes are earnest, and his face is creased with worry lines. He is a hard man not to like. "I don't need anything from you, just a chat, that's all." She flares her nostrils.

"Close the gate," she says. Our Dave steps back and does so. They stand facing each other in the little yard behind the Dairycoates Inn just off Hessle Road. This is the place where Kasia's predecessor, Leatherhead, would sell heroin to those that she knew well, it's now where Kasia shifts a lot of her gear too. She folds her arms as she stands beside the back door. Possibilities run through her mind. She is already dressed for the occasion in rubber gloves and her cleaning clothes, there is nobody else in the pub either, if she had the means she could get rid of Our Dave herself, right now. Maybe this is the opportunity she's been waiting for.

"Do you want to talk out here?" asks Our Dave.

"I don't want to talk at all," she answers. She could bring him into the kitchen and use one of the chef's knives on him. It would be too messy. Our Dave will not be a pushover either, she knows that he has done things in the past. He looks around him and takes a deep breath.

"I'll just come out with it then, shall I?"

"I guess so."

"Someone is trying to do me in, Kasia," he says. Her face does not give anything away at all and she does not respond. "There've been two attempts to kill me in the last few weeks. I don't know who it is. I've had no message from anyone. I think they'll try again."

"What's this got to do with me?" she asks.

"I wondered if you might know something."

"I don't have friends Dave, you should know that, and I don't know anything about your situation. You must have upset someone."

"I must have."

"Now I've told you I don't know anything, you can leave."

"I wondered if you'd like to buy me out."

"What?"

"Maybe you'd like to take over what I do. It's taken a good few years to build the business, but I could let you have it, all of it, for a reasonable price."

"What good would that do? Would that stop you getting threatened?"

"Look, if there is someone who wants me dead then they will get to it sooner or later. I know that. All I want to do now is make sure that all the loose ends of my affairs are tied up and finished so that when I'm not here everyone gets the best out of what I've got." She blinks her green eyes. Our Dave is wise and brave too. She likes him.

"I don't want your business," she says.

"You haven't even thought about it."

"I don't need to. I'm not interested in smuggling alcohol. I have my own products." Our Dave nods. She can see that he is worried. In other meetings, he has seemed intelligent and level-headed, now she can see that his eyes are red and tired. She does not like to think that she is responsible for his worries, it was easy for her to kill Leatherhead, the old woman was a monster and a bitch. It was easy for her to get rid of the crackheads up on the Bransholme Estate too because they were cheap and pitiful. Our Dave is not like that at all. He is self-aware and respectable. "Is that all?" she asks.

"I guess so."

"Thanks for coming here today then, Dave." Her voice is cold and metallic.

"You have got friends, haven't you, Kasia?" She can't help but wince at this.

"How is that important?"

"You just can't do it alone."

"Why not?"

"I used to have someone, you know. I was married and she's gone. Since then, I haven't had anyone to say goodnight or good morning to." Our Dave does not know why he is telling this frosty woman about life without Hazel, he has not even admitted it to himself. "You need someone to make it all normal." Kasia thinks of the red dating app she looked at last night while she sat on the stairs in the darkness, she remembers the couple who her daughter saw in the supermarket that were in love.

"I have someone," she says. Kasia doesn't have anyone, but she is sure she will find him.

"I guess that's good for you then. I probably won't be back around this way." She nods. She doesn't have anything else to say to him and if she had the opportunity, she would finish him off here and now. She no longer has the 3D printed pistols she used on the goons out at Bransholme, it was wise to have them melted down, but she can get more. She'll have to cancel any business with the scrap metal dealership and get this job sorted on her own. She's killed people before. It won't be any more difficult this time. She'll get onto it right away, as soon as he has gone.

"You take care of yourself then, Kasia."

"I will." It's graceless of her to answer this way. Her grandmother taught her better. "I'm sorry about your problems, Dave, I wish I could help." She manages to sound disingenuous when she says this.

"I wish you could as well."

"I've got work to do," she says. He nods. It's awkward. Our Dave steps back and opens the white gate.

"Good luck then," he says.

"You too." He closes the gate behind him and Kasia listens as his footsteps disappear along the front of the pub and back to his car.

The next time she sees him, she'll kill him.

Tom is getting used to running up and down Westbourne Ave. The front parts of his thighs still hurt but not as much as they did. He has even ordered a pair of running shoes online. They should be here tomorrow. He opens a letter from the university that comes through the front door, it confirms his two-week sickness leave will be over next Monday. There's another letter underneath explaining the terms of his redundancy, and, unlike his line manager explained, he is not required to go back to the university at all. After his period of sickness - his employment is terminated. He sits down on the bottom step of the stairs, he thought he would feel upset, but instead, Tom just feels relieved. That's that then, after more than twenty years teaching. His life is changing before his eyes. Tom was all set to meet Our Dave this morning, but the man sent him a message putting it off till tonight up at Avenue Cars.

Alex comes home from college in the afternoon with a guitar case, there's a bass guitar inside. He's joined a punk band, and the drummer has lent him the instrument to learn. Tom approves. In the mid-afternoon he hears the dull plunk of the fat strings unamplified from the front room as he cooks spaghetti. He is adapting quickly to his situation, his new face and his new way of being.

Later, the Iranian kids from next door sneak into the long back garden to play football on the lawn. It's a light drizzle. Tom fishes his raincoat and boots out of the cupboard under the stairs and Alex puts on his hoodie, they go out the back door and the two dark haired Iranian kids disappear through the fallen down fence as soon as they see them. It takes a few minutes to coax them back through.

Alex sets up a makeshift goal. One side is the trunk of the apple tree, and the other is a big pot with a posh bay tree. They are brothers these two Iranians, both with black hair and big smiles, their English is broken but passable and they play in the light drizzle first with Alex in goal and then Tom takes over. A shot hits the bay tree in the pot and flattens it; the grass gets cut up something rotten, and after half an hour their mum shouts at them from inside the house and they disappear after friendly handshakes and more of those big smiles.

In the kitchen Alex and Tom drink cocoa and leave their muddy boots outside. Alex explains about the punk band and that there are three of them, a drummer and a little guitarist with a shaved head and big earrings. They have been promised an opening slot at the Adelphi music club two weeks on Thursday and they have to come up with a name by the end of tomorrow. Tom thinks they should be called Loose Stools but Alex wants to go for Dogs on Leads. Tom gets a glimpse of himself in the glass from the cooker, sitting on his chair and laughing with his son. He smells the cocoa in his nostrils and listens to the teenage voice, feels the air in his lungs and the smooth tiles below his feet. He is living, for the first time in so long. This easy conversation, the light rain outside and the grey sky, the radiators heating as the boiler fires up on the wall behind. This is the simplicity of it.

There's a ping on Tom's phone and he fishes it out of his jacket pocket while Alex goes into the front room to practice on that bass. It's a notification from the dating app. He has matches and there's a message too. Her name is Helena, she is a curly-haired blonde from York. It reads, 'I only like ready-salted crisps'. Tom responds. 'I've got hundreds of packets here from those multipacks.' The conversation begins. He is light-hearted and fun. Helena is an art teacher from Fulford in York, a nice area to the south of the city. She has two grown up daughters and teaches art in a comprehensive three days a week. She is good at punctuation and witty too. She says she's been single for a year and has been on a few dates already, so she knows the ropes. They chat into the evening over the app. Tom drinks cocoa and, just like Bev advised him, he sets up a video call for the next day at three o'clock in the afternoon. In the shower upstairs Tom feels like a different man already.

At nine Inma enters the house. She finds Tom and Alex in the front room watching a TV show about samurai. She does not want to talk, particularly. Upstairs she rummages around in the loft where she keeps all her dresses and comes down with an armful of them that she takes out to a car waiting outside. She comes back to collect more. Tom offers to help but she says she is fine on her own and a friend is helping her move some of the stock. In the front room, Tom pauses their samurai film and opens two of the louver slats with his fingers to peer outside. There's a big range rover idling in the dark street and the driver's face is illuminated by the phone he's reading. Tom swallows. He's seen him before somewhere. This is the chiropractor that Inma visits on Chanterlands Avenue.

In the hall as Imna is going through the front door, Tom appears:

"Who's your driver?" he asks. Inma gives him a smile like she does when she is not comfortable.

"It's just a friend who's helping me out."

"Oh right," says Tom. His mouth is dry. He can see her swallow. She has altered her eye make-up and it makes her look younger.

"You've shaved off your beard," she states.

"Yeah. Are you still at your mum's?"

"I am. There's a place for Alex too if she wants to come and stay there with me. It might give you a break."

"I like having him here, this is where he lives." Tom is conscious that Alex is sitting in the front room and will be able to hear all of this. Inma has used the wrong pronoun again, but Tom is not going to dwell on it.

"Of course. We need to talk at some point, Tom, about what's going to happen moving forward, about the house and everything and our situation." He nods.

"I'm here all the time," he says.

"I'll be in touch then." Tom steps forward and his voice is a whisper, not threatening but quiet so that Alex can't hear.

"Is that man outside who you've left me for?" he asks. Tom

would never dare ask this kind of question because he would not want to hear the truth, but Face is not so afraid of it. He would like to know for his own well-being.

"I didn't leave you for anyone," she says. "He's just a friend." In truth, Inma left it late to visit the house because she thought Tom would be drunk and so wouldn't think to look who gave her a lift. He looks different without the hair and the beard and with his eyes clear and sober.

"Okay," Tom whispers. "I'm sorry to have said that." In all this, Tom still doesn't blame her, he more pities the man he has become.

"I'll be in touch," she repeats. Inma gathers the dresses up over her arms and goes to the door. "See you Alex," she shouts and there's a grunt from the front room in response. "I'll text you." Tom hears the car door slam and then drive off. He is going to have to accept what is happening to him, without judgement or blame.

Later, as he lays in bed in the darkness, Tom fires up his phone and looks through the dating app once again. He checks out the pictures of the York lady, Helena who he has arranged to video chat with. He writes:

'I'm looking forward to chatting to you tomorrow.' Tom puts his hands behind his head and looks up to the dark ceiling. He is a married man. He still has his wedding ring in the drawer of his bedside cabinet. Is it morally right for him to even talk to another woman? He thinks through the issue. Tom is a lawyer, and so he has never been so much concerned with morality more how it is interpreted in the law. He has taught ethics before and read essays where students wrestled with Kantian and utilitarian moral theory. What if he has this wrong and Inma has not left him for another man at all? When he closes his eyes, Tom can hear the rattle of gunfire from the day before. He is confused and frightened at the same time because events are moving faster than he can cope with.

Without the drink to shield him from reality, he is beginning to sense the world around him, both good and bad. He runs his hand over his nose and cheek and feels the rough burns. Perhaps this is all too much for Tom, like his dad used to tell him, he's not the toughest lad by any means. He should go out to the garden shed and grab a bottle of his father's whiskey.

That's not the answer.

All this is not too much for Face. He can cope with it. He can be many people at once and without contradiction, he can be a father and a friend at the same time, he can lose his wife to another man and his job too but that will not affect the core of him. He can chase women, he can run up and down Westbourne Ave without getting a stitch, he can understand complex and intricate details of European law, he can read Latin, he knows all about Pokémon. His grandfather was a trawler skipper on the open seas and a pirate as well, his great great grandfather descended from the invading Vikings, as did he. Truth is not a hard substance anymore, it melts and flows like treacle, and it can be one thing one day and quite another the next, so that an action Face makes today maybe good, and the same action tomorrow may be evil. He can use this.

He can be anything he wants.

What was it his grandfather used to say?

I like what I do, and I do what I like.

CHAPTER ELEVEN
A new job

It's Saturday morning and Tom has been clean for a week, again. He feels different as he cycles towards Chants Ave and over the speed bumps in the chill of an early March morning. He has done a lot this week, he emptied out all the kitchen cupboards and organised all his books and old-tech equipment. He cleaned the garage and moved all his father's paintings to one side so he could get his bike out and didn't hear the old man speak to him even once from his empty armchair either. He has been to the tip twice. He can feel the weight coming off him slowly, like he is shaking it free.

The girl he chatted to from York, Helena, decided after their video call, that they weren't suited. Tom has connected with others too. There's a punk looking Indian girl who says she lives in a van behind the Adelphi. She has a thin brindle lurcher dog, she's clever and self-aware. There's a teacher who works in the secondary school a few streets away, she's into karate and running – it was she who told Tom all about Parkrun, her name is Joanne and she's away this weekend. Then there's a redheaded Polish lass from near Hessle Road, she's kind of dry and doesn't message very much. According to Bev, Tom is doing very well to be talking to three ladies at once, her simple advice is to choose one and meet her. She explains that talking to three people at the same time will eventually lead to him making some sort of mistake and mixing up what he's written. Bev says this from experience. Tom thinks he can handle it.

Saturday morning without a hangover is still a new event to Tom, almost like a new day has been invented for doing stuff in. A spring sun tries to come up behind the roofs of the houses. He parks his bike behind Avenue Cars and opens up the back door.

"Are you there, Dave?" he calls through the galley kitchen

into the office. There's no answer so he pushes open the door a little more. He has tried to put the memory of the shooters from the last week at the back of his mind, but now he thinks back to the danger he was in. He calls again and his voice rings out into the office. There will be no school runs for the lady drivers on Saturday morning. Our Dave asked him to come so they could discuss what they were meant to a week or so earlier. Tom wonders, as he creeps into the office, if something has happened to the old man already. He thinks of the gun hidden in the tool bag in the cupboard in his hall.

Our Dave sits halfway up the stairs leading from the back office. This used to be a house, once upon a time in the seventies, and there are still bedrooms without beds upstairs. He watches as Tom walks into the office, he thought it might be someone else. He gets up. Our Dave will try to squeeze into a smile.

"Now then," he calls as he comes down the stairs.

"I thought you might have been bumped off," says Tom. You can take the piss out of Our Dave, he understands it.

"They will, sooner or later." He manages to say this with a lightness that may or may not be true. He goes to a metal document box on the table and puts his big hand on the top. "I'm not a young fella anymore, Tom. I can't see the future like I used to. I always thought it would be me and Hazel together, that was it." The speech is delivered with a comedy glint. This is the closest Our Dave will come to being candid. "You know you can back out of this now, if you want, Tom. I won't hold it against you, once you start going through what's in this box, you'll be a part of it."

"I'm a lawyer, mate. Don't you think I know that?"

"I'm just saying. Are you sure you want to do this?" Tom nods. He's thought about it. Ever since he got beaten up on the steps of the little cupola on Pearson Park his life has become sweeter. In any case, as soon as Tom found that gun in the tool bag, and failed to tell the police, he was in trouble.

By degrees, he has lowered himself into Our Dave's affairs like it's a hot bath. He likes it. Tom has been strapped up by rules his whole life, with his bully of a mum at home, a rigorous school, then uni, then the letter of the law and the rules of a university faculty. He feels free for the first time.

"I'm happy to help."

"Good. Once this is sorted, I can sit out the front of the office here till someone finishes me off." It's that Hull fatalism again. Tom's granddad was a skipper, he had it too, the sense that if your time is up then there is no use fighting. Tom narrows his eyes at this big earnest man in front of him. Everyone on this street knows him from the Kurdish barbers a few doors opposite to the owner of the huge petrol garage at the end of the street. He would rather something didn't happen to Our Dave for the simple reason that this older man has become something he has not had for some many years: A friend.

"Let's get started then," says Tom.

Every business lawyer knows about dirty tricks. There's tax avoidance, fraudulent accounting, money laundering and kickbacks. Our Dave's operation is startlingly clean even though it is illegal. The details are shocking but only in how much he is prepared to pay. The girls here in Avenue Cars make much better money than the company can afford to give them, there are painters and handymen at work on the properties he owns that charge a sweet fortune for their services. Those who rent out these properties don't pay enough, he makes donations here and there to charity, the cost of raw materials is too high, the profits are too low. You can see he is looking after people in the figures.

Our Dave explains that he has a wonderful accountant who actually works for the Inland Revenue in the computer department, and, for a simple fee and because he is Our Dave, his accounts sail through the automated service – they don't have enough people to check through everything, especially not for accounts below a certain threshold. They talk about the ins and outs of the booze business, how it's bought from big distilleries by mules who carry cash out there once a month, how he smuggles it through Holland on furniture lorries, how he distributes it all over the UK on these same trucks. Then there's the distillery he has recently bought up in Scotland, the used car lot he has next to the river Hull, and the factory in Louisiana that makes real moonshine, there's a farm he owns east of Hull and properties dotted around the north of the UK. It is a complex web. Tom is staggered the man can keep track of it all, but he seems to know. Our Dave is a much bigger fish than you would think for his easy smile and ready handshake. Now Tom is beginning to see the scale of Avenue Cars, it does not seem ridiculous that someone may want to take it all away from him, given how much he must be worth.

They break at just before twelve and go to the galley kitchen where Our Dave boils the kettle and fishes round in the cupboard for some biscuits. He seems back to his old self now he's busy. Tom can't help but get to the point as they stand looking out at the little carpark behind.

"What are you going to do with it, Our Dave?"

"I want you to shut it down." Tom takes a deep breath.

"How am I going to do that?"

"I don't know. Bit by bit I would imagine. Get rid of the assets first, properties and such. I'm not sure how you'd hide any money you made. It' would be hard to do, especially if you're not spending anything on product. I'm sure a man of your talents could find a way."

"How would I be able to do that? Those properties belong to you."

"Right now, they do, but when I'm gone, they'll go into the trust that you're going to set up for me. You'll be the only trustee. Can you do something like that?" Tom frowns for a moment. This is not some frivolous venture; he has already stepped onto the wrong side of the law. He did so when he first caught sight of the matt black Beretta pistol, so here he is wandering blind into even more criminality. He swallows. It actually feels like the right thing to do.

"I can, but it would take me months. It might even take years."

"You've lost your job, haven't you?"

"Aye."

"What do you say then?"

"I don't know."

"You could write your own pay cheque, Tom. You could help who you like. It would be all yours to fiddle with." The kettle rumbles and boils then switches itself off. Steam fills the little kitchen.

"When would I start?"

"You've started already."

"Why me?" Our Dave takes down two mugs from the cupboard and sets them right way up on the counter. He puts a tea bag in each one.

"You're smart, Tom. You need this as much as I do. You need something that's going to force you to work at the edge of what you can do. You drink because you're bored. You wouldn't be bored doing this. I never have been." He pours hot water in each one and replaces the kettle.

"This is your life, Dave. It's not a game of darts in the pub across the road, and you can't throw it away because you've been frightened off."

"You don't need to worry about me, Tom. Nobody does. That's the way I want it. That's the way I've always wanted it. Back in the past I thought I could do some good for people while I was on my way and I enjoyed it, don't get me wrong. Then when Hazel went, it soothed me because I didn't know what else to do. I'm tired of helping people out, Tom. Are you in?" The man turns to look at him. Our Dave has never seemed old before, but he is now, his eyes are earnest and calm, the laugh lines at the side of his head seem deep now he is not smiling. "Are you up for the job?" Tom gets a flashback of his father sitting in his old armchair with his yellow beard and knackered teeth, he can hear the old ghost explaining the failures of his youngest son. He sees the eyes of Inma as she stood opposite him in the kitchen before she left, eager to get away from the failure that he is. Then there's his boss at the university. Our Dave is giving him an opportunity. Tom would never be ready for this, but the secret man he is slowly becoming will take hold of it.

"Who else will know?"

"Nobody. Just like you're the only one who knows even half of what I get up to. Are you in?"

"I think I might just be the man for the job," says Face.

It's Sunday morning. Tom ordered a reasonably sized football goal from an online shop, and it was delivered early. He fixed it up with Alex and they set it at the back of the garden next to the apple tree. It doesn't take very long for the Iranian kids to come out to look, they slip through into the garden and the kick about begins.

The big one is Soheil and the little one is Majid, they speak Farsi and have educated feet but it takes fifteen minutes of play before they'll tackle Tom or Alex properly. They all take turns in goal and the grass gets more ripped up as they play. The sun doesn't manage to break through the drizzle until about eleven when there's a shout from the other house and a woman steps into view. She has dark hair that's dyed auburn and is young with heavy eyes and bags under them. This is their mother. She exchanges comments with her two sons and gives Tom a smile. They play for five minutes more before she returns with a Tupperware container – this she hands to Soheil who passes it to Tom.

"It's cakes," he says, "for you and him." He motions to Alex. The mother speaks in broken English.

"For you," she rolls her r sounds. "They are baclava." The th sound comes out more a ze. Tom nods in thanks. When she's gone they play for another ten minutes until Soheil kicks the ball into the next garden. Alex explains that they'll just have to wait for the old woman to throw it back over the fence. The two Iranian lads disappear back through the fallen down fence panel and Alex and Tom go down to the shed at the bottom of the garden. Tom opens up the lock and they go inside for a look at the space – Alex wonders if his band could practice in there, Tom wonders if the ghost of his father will still be sitting in the chair.

It's all as he left it last time, why wouldn't it be? There's his father's cream armchair and the half empty whiskey bottle next to it. Paintings line the far wall. Tom walks into the gloom first and Alex follows, he can sense that the old ghost is here but quiet. The paintings are landscapes with waterfalls, a trawler cresting a huge wave, a white lily on a black background, and all of them covered with dust in the light from the window at the far end. A spider web hangs down from the low ceiling.

"What will you do with all his pictures?" asks Alex.

"I don't know."

"You could sell them."

"The old man tried hard enough to do just that when he was alive. I don't know who'd have them." As well as the thirty or so on display, there are hundreds of them face down and stacked up in big piles in the darkness. Tom has thrown a few away already; even though his relationship with his father was not the best, he does not want to see the pictures tossed into a skip at the waste recycling plant near the Humber Bridge.

"They're a bit shit," says Alex. He's not afraid to speak his mind. It comes from his mother.

"He was doing what he loved to do. You can't fault him for that." Alex nods. He understands this and respects it too.

"I didn't know him very well," he says.

"Neither did I," says Tom. "I sometimes come in here to

talk to him, that's why I've kept the chair."

"Does he talk to you back?"

"He does, but it's not his voice." Alex knows that his father is a bit odd.

"Are you and mum finished, then?" he asks.

"I guess we are."

"What'll happen to me?"

"Nothing. You can live with me or your mum. It'll be up to you."

"Mum says you won't be able to keep this house. She says without her money you'll have to move, especially now you've lost your job."

"How does she know about that?"

"I told her." Tom nods. It wasn't a secret. "She says you'll end up living in a flat above a chip shop and drinking cheap cider. She thinks you'll be dead in five years."

"She's not often wrong, isn't your mum."

"I'll come with you, you know. I don't mind living above a chip shop. I don't even mind cider." Tom smiles. Alex is the best of him and his wife, brave and smart and honest too.

"Do you remember when you came to me and you said you realised that you were someone else?" Alex nods. He does remember, before that day he had a wardrobe full of dresses and bags full of make-up, he had pretty shoes and bright pink bedsheet with unicorn posters on his walls.

"I remember." Alex is not sure what his father will say here. His tone of voice is more serious than normal. His face is deadpan.

"I've been thinking about that day. I've been thinking about being someone else as well, or rather, going back to a version of me that I was many years ago."

"What were you?"

"It sounds stupid to say aloud."

"Go on. I did. You'll have to." Alex expects his father to say he's gay.

"The kids used to shout a name at me on the bus. They yelled it at me when I walked down the school corridors. Someone wrote it on my school bag. It's nothing like what you've been through, not at all, but it used to hurt me back in the day." Tom's eyes have begun to water. Perhaps it's the dust.

"There's a lot in a name," says Alex.

"There is."

"What was it?"

"It's like I want to be what I am, finally."

"You want me to call you it, is that it?"

"Yes."

"I will."

"It's such a stupid name."

"You just say it."

"Face." Alex frowns. In all honesty he has only noticed the burns when other people pointed them out. Friends Alex invited back after school would appear shocked to see his dad's face, people always stare as well, dogs bark at him sometimes, you get funny looks in the supermarket.

"Face," he repeats the name. The two men embrace in the gloom of the shed with the armchair looking up at them with a snarl. As Tom locks the door and Alex walks off towards the house he can hear the old ghost inside whisper to him:

"Stupid blood name."

CHAPTER TWELVE
Guns

Without the drink, Tom finds he has superior concentration, he doesn't suffer from distractions and he can work longer hours. He needs less sleep, and the weight is beginning to fall off him so he has to tighten his belt when he does up his trousers. The business that Our Dave explained to him has taken up much of his time in the last week and he does not miss the university, probably in much the same way as they do not miss him. Without the booze he feels bored in the evenings as he listens to Alex upstairs practicing the bass with a little amp that he borrowed. He also hears the Iranian kids next door as they wrestle with each other, and their mum yells at intervals. The noise is a comfort to him. He does yoga by following a Netflix show and, in the stretches, and deep breathing he finds relaxation, although the wine still calls to him from the case under the stairs.

Tom has been chatting to three women. It's nice. He's been dealing with words and essays all his life and so switching between them is not so much of a problem. He is mindful of Bev's advice however about cross messaging and takes care to read what he's written and checks who he is sending it to. He has not taken the time to consider whether it is ethical or not, he imagines they will be chatting to other men anyway.

The Polish one messages in the morning before she starts her cleaning job at the pub, and they chat back and forth about all sorts. She has a degree in economics and a dry sense of humour. It's playful somehow without actually being funny. She is called Kasia and has a glint in her green eye in one of the pictures, but otherwise she is straight-faced and serious. Tom likes this. She has mystery. Kasia says she has a daughter who is at primary school and is clear she does not want any more children. She has a bike with a basket on the front and she likes to ride out to Beverley on Sunday afternoons in the summer. Tom looks at maps on the internet to find a good place he can ask her to come for a bike ride with him – somewhere pretty but without too many hills – maybe they could ride down by the side of the river Humber. She says she's studying chemistry and needs the evening time when her daughter goes to bed to be without distraction, so he leaves her alone. That's nice too.

About six o'clock he messages the teacher, her name is Joanne. She's into fitness and says she can't be arsed to spell or punctuate properly. Her daughter is already off at university. Joanne is a second dan black belt at karate. In the photos on her profile, she looks fit with a plain but honest face, like someone you could put your trust in. There's a photo of her against a foreign sunset with a glass of wine, one of her pulling a face and pointing to a badge on her chest that reads 'twat', and another of her performing a mawashi geri front kick in the karate dojo. It is this Joanne who has talked him into trying Parkrun. She is funny and self-deprecating in her messages, and she drinks most nights but Tom imagines it will not be more than half a glass. She goes to bed about half nine because she runs in the morning and he says goodnight with a kiss. Tom is going to ask her to meet him after Parkrun on Saturday, they could have a drink in the café behind the car park. He has not got round to it yet, but he will.

At half eleven, tucked up under her military blankets in her big red van behind the Adelphi music club, Anita usually messages him. She sends pictures of her dog, Clive, and tells him about the bands that have played at the Adelphi that night. She is deep and thoughtful with semi-colons and long, well-constructed messages and insights that make Tom think. He has explained all about Alex and the change that he went through, not physically but spiritually, and Anita thinks that people should try to be who they need to be. Tom likes her spirit. He looks at the pictures on her dating profile again, she has a wiry strength to her arms in a cut off band t-shirt. He has told her that Alex has a gig at the Adelphi next week, albeit first on the bill with his brand-new punk band that they have called 'Dogs on Leads'. Tom and Anita discuss the deeper meaning for the band name for half an hour. She says she will get someone else to cover the bar so they can have a cup of coffee in her van – it's a youth gig so there won't be many drinkers there for her to look after. Tom likes her.

Tom goes to the tool bag that Our Dave lent him, and using a pair of soap yellow marigold gloves from under the sink, he collects the pistol that is therein. He will take the bag back to the man across the street and hide the weapon more effectively. With his phone for a torch, he goes down to the shed in the darkness of midnight. No doubt the ghost of his father will be loud in there at this time. He'll hide the weapon, and he'll be able to tell the old man that he is dragging himself out of the mess he has made of his life.

In the darkness he uses the torch to find the old light switch. The one bulb flickers and illuminates the corrugated iron roof and the lonely pale armchair that once belonged to his father, and still does. There's the stink of the old man in here, it's mildly sweet and musty, old people don't smell as horrible as people would have you think. At the back of the shed are stacks of the old man's paintings, and Tom goes down to the back of them and slides the pistol into a space between the canvasses and the wall.

"You'd be better off throwing it in the river, there's no sense keeping it, is there?" It's the faint whisper of the ghost in his ear. Like always there's no ghost. This is all Tom's making.

"That would be more dangerous. Then someone would find it for sure."

"Well… you're the lawyer. Too bloody clever for your own good, you are. Are you still not drinking?"

"I've had a couple, this week."

"You'll be back on it before long."

"I hope not."

"There's all this whiskey here, I'm not gonna bloody drink it, am I?"

"Neither am I."

"Let's have a look at this gun then, Tom. I mean, you haven't even had a good look at it yet, have you?" Tom goes back to the hiding place and draws the black weapon back out. "That's it," says the old man in his ear, "get it out, hold it up to the light so I can get a better look." The pistol is not as heavy as you might think, it's matt black and has the details written down the barrel in embossed letters. Tom pulls out the clip that slides into the handle, and sees a little tower of bullets stacked up and ready to go. He slips it back in and considers the weight in his hand. It doesn't feel like it's something that could kill. He levels it at his father's armchair and his finger, still in the soap yellow marigold glove, goes around the trigger.

"Don't bloody point it at me," whispers his father.

"You're already dead, you old sod."

"You wouldn't have said that to me if I was living, Tom. Now put that down."

"There won't be a bullet in the chamber, father, it'll be fine." Tom puts light pressure on the trigger and the gun kicks back and fires, a single shot with a loud snap sends a bullet through the back of the armchair and out the other side into the concrete. Tom stands shaken for a minute. It was so easy. Like a toy almost.

"You bloody fool," says his father. "What if someone heard that?"

"They won't have," answers Tom as he puts the gun back into the hiding place behind the paintings. He stands up.

"That make you feel like a man, did it?" Tom shrugs.

"You're going to have to move out," he whispers to the ghost who is not there.

"What do you mean?"

"The chair and all these paintings will have to go."

"Of course, who's going to want this armchair with a bloody great hole through the back of it?" It's much harder to talk to his father without being drunk. The sentences are forced and unnatural.

"When it's all gone, that'll be the end of it."

"You mean the end of me?"

"Aye."

"Your granddad used to say 'aye'. You're not a shadow of him. You've been brought up soft."

"I don't need to be anything like him, or you. I'm me, I'm Tom, that's who I am now."

"You've got that bloody stupid name you call yourself. You can cover it all up with lies, Tom, but you know the truth, deep down. You know that you're just a rich kid who got lucky with where he was born and the chances he was given. All this giving yourself a new name is middle-class shite." Tom is surprised how cruel he can be to himself without being hungover at the same time.

"You put that on me, father. You told me all that. I get to choose who I am now, and I'll be that stupid name if I want to be." The old man is not listening.

"It's your grandfather I blame, you wouldn't have a face like melted wax if it wasn't for that crash, and you wouldn't have had to go through all the shite you did, the name calling, the hospital visits, the self-doubt. It changed you, it made you feel guilty. Look at your brother, Julian. He's a success down in London with a good solid job and a tight family, and, more importantly, Julian doesn't feel guilty for being a rich, posh knob with a fancy job. He's proud of it."

"You don't know him at all, just like you don't know me. I'm becoming someone. I'm looking after Our Dave's business. Women are interested in me. I've got a son who's my friend. I'm getting fit. It's nothing to do with you or the burns on my face, it's just me getting it fixed. I wanted to tell you, that's why I brought the gun down here as an excuse."

Tom is getting worse at imagining how the old man might look, sitting in his chair.

"I just wanted what was best for you, Tom. The world's a horrible place, especially as you get older. I wanted you to know how hard it is and be strong against it."

"It's not your fault, dad. It's mine. Just like it's my job to fix it." Tom has spoken these words aloud into the darkness of the shed. The ghost is gone. He looks around and sees the paintings looking at him, smells the musty sweet smell from the armchair and light whiff of gunpowder.

"My name is Face," he says to the darkness.

Laura comes up the stairs of the Dairycoates Inn with the square blue delivery backpack on. Her hands are in thick gloves, and she wears a dark cycling helmet with a scarf across her face. She unhooks the bag and sets it on the kitchen counter. Alicja sits on one of the high stools at the table, she looks excited. Her mother has bought a takeaway. Kasia goes to her wallet and takes out a brown envelope while Laura removes the contents of her delivery bag. There are two square pizza boxes and another cardboard box.

"The little box here is from the Vietnamese, he says you will know what it is." By Vietnamese she doesn't mean takeaway. In the cold storage unit Kasia has just off the old docks, there's the same Vietnamese kid she has working in the computer lab there. He has 3D printed another item for her and this is inside. Alicja steps up to take one of the pizza boxes.

"Thank you," she says. She smiles. Kasia hands Laura the brown envelope. Inside there's a slip of paper with a piece of block chain code printed on it. With this, Laura can access crypto currency for payment and the sum will be far more than the cost of two fifteen-inch pizzas, one with extra cheese. She puts the square delivery bag over her shoulders to leave.

"The scrap metal people were not successful, again." Laura turns to her.

"Really?"

"Yes. I'm angry. I will ask for my money back. I'll have to do the job myself." It's hard to read Laura's facial expression with the scarf and helmet on.

"That's not a good idea."

"I don't have another option," says Kasia.

"I could do it for you." Laura and the Polish woman have done jobs like this before. Not so long ago they went up to the Bransholme Estate and cleaned up a house full of weed dealers and skag heads.

"It can't be you and me again," says Kasia. "It is too risky." Laura would rather not be working for her, but she is too far in already. At least the money is good. There's a sense that one day this will all go terribly wrong and there'll be a price for her to pay. Just as long as her family are well, she is okay with all of this, she tells herself.

When Laura has gone, Kasia opens the box and looks down at the pistol within. It's orange and just bigger than a mobile phone. Kasia knows the specs because she researched it herself – there are seven bullets in a clip in the handle. She asked for it to be tested thoroughly and bubble wrapped so it looks like a toy. When Kasia has finished with the thing, she'll take out any remaining bullets and burn it – it's just hard plastic. She did the same with the other pistols he made for her. Kasia has not thought where she will finish Our Dave. She could lure him somewhere easily, she knows where he works and where he lives. She'll have to plan. She closes the box and sits at the table opposite her daughter. The blonde girl is enjoying the pizza, she smiles at her mum because takeaways are a special treat.

"It's your birthday soon," says Kasia as she opens her own box. The smell of cheese and tomato waft into her face. "Did you decide on a gift?"

"I haven't chosen yet," she replies. Alicja speaks English with a Hull twang and her grasp of the language is instinctive.

"I also have some news," says Kasia. Alicja continues to chew.

"I have found a boyfriend." Alicja stops chewing. This is most unlike her mother. Her blue eyes blink. She goes back to chewing because the woman will only tell her more if she wants to. There is no point in asking. "He is a law lecturer at the university. He writes papers for academic journals and gives speeches at conferences." In many ways, Kasia is naïve. She has not been on a date with Tom, nor has she spoken to him face to face or even on the phone. To say he is her boyfriend is a lie, but, Kasia does not lie. In the time since she came to the UK, things have largely gone the way she wanted them to, she managed to get rid of her husband, and then Leatherhead as well, she runs the business her way and gets results. Why should it be any different with this man? If she wants him, she will take him. It's as simple as ordering a pizza from the takeaway around the corner.

"Do you love him?" asks Alicja. Kasia delicately picks up a slice of the pizza.

"I don't know yet," she answers.

"Does my father know?" Kasia freezes and her mean, green eyes fix on her daughter.

"Your father has gone, Alicja, and he is never coming back. I have told you this before."

"He said he would never leave me."

"How would you remember; you were a tiny little girl."

"I remember."

"You're a liar." Her words are cold. "Eat your pizza and keep your mouth shut. Your father is never coming back here and it's best if you forget all about him. Do you understand?" Alicja does not answer but keeps her eyes down as she chews.

CHAPTER THIRTEEN
First dates

De Grey Street is a long row of mid-range terraces built in the late nineteenth century and about halfway down you'll find the Adelphi. Since 1923 it's served beer and, in its time, has been a serviceman's club, a working man's watering hole and since 1984, a venue for original and live music. Tom and Alex stand at the side entrance. They've knocked at the door to no answer. In the far corner of the pot holed car park is the red, rotten and never-to-run-again van that Tom knows Anita stays in. His stomach churns, his hand carrying the mid-sized bass amp is sweaty. He is going to meet her tonight. It is his first date in more than twenty years, even though it's not quite a date. He's also going to watch the very first performance by Alex's band, 'Dogs on Leads'.

There's barking from within the club. It sounds like a big dog. At the side of the building, the double door opens, and the barking sound comes out. The dog is a brindle lurcher with a happy, wagging tail, this is Clive, and Anita comes out behind him. She's about five foot and is wearing dungarees with a vest top underneath that shows off her smooth brown arms. Her hair is a curly dark bob. She is much prettier than her pictures with a nose stud as well. Clive the dog dashes out to greet Tom and Alex with yips and friendly barks.

"The rest of the bands are already here, they're about to sound check," she says to Alex. He grabs the amp from Tom and makes his way through the doors at the side of the building leaving Tom standing opposite Anita. He smiles at her and she smiles back up at him. "Come in," she says.

A band is going through soundcheck as Tom steps into the main room at the Adelphi. It has been many years since he has been here and it's smaller than he remembers it. With the lights on he can see the red floor, band posters plaster the walls and the furniture is tatty and beaten. The band on the low stage are a teenage four piece with a blonde singer, their drummer is hitting the snare while the sound technician by the bar fiddles with knobs and wires on his sound desk.

"I've just got to set the bar up, and then we can have a coffee," she says. Tom smiles at this. It's as if she knows him already. She does, in a way. Tom stands with his back to the wall and watches the drummer sound check, Alex is in the corner with the rest of his band – they give Tom glances as they stand there. There is character here in these walls where musicians have come to play for more than forty years and whoever you are, it feels like home too. The blonde lead singer signals that he is happy with the sound and they step off stage to be replaced by Alex and his two mates. Anita appears.

"Do you want that cup of coffee?" she asks. Tom nods.

They sit in the green room at the front of the building. Tom remembers this used to be a little bar with a pool table and a TV where you could watch footie. Now it's where musicians dump their kit. Tom sits next to her on the bench that runs around the edge of the room with a cup of hot black coffee in his hands. He is nervous.

Tom has not come unprepared for this. He has viewed YouTube films on dating and consulted articles with advice for older men. As soon as they begin chatting, he reverts to type. The best defence is to ask questions. Anita chats well, she is not nervous because this is just a chat after all and she already knows that he's not a complete nutter. She tells him about her job and how she arrived here after playing drums with the Canadian singer who didn't need her anymore. Tom listens. He is interested in her but nervous still. She tells him about her life as Clive clambers up to sit between them on the bench. She explains her past and the squat in London. She has been single for a year. Tom is not a liar, but he is a lawyer and so there are details that he will leave out. He explains that he split up with his wife but not that it was two weeks ago. He likes Anita. She is warm and funny and seems carefree, she lives in a van and wants no more than she already has. Tom tells her about his burns and the accident, but not in a defeatist way. He explains too how he has lost his job at the university and how his relationship with Alex is the best thing in his life now he has cut back on the boozing. He has a cat called Galal who does not like him. Anita offers to let Clive come round to sort him out. The chat takes twenty minutes, but it feels like two.

At eight the Adelphi doors open, and a tiny crowd sprinkle the main room furniture with people. Anita goes back behind the bar. The big lights go off and the stage lights come on. The compare is a man with a beard and a woolly hat, and he introduces Dogs on Leads. They do a seven song set that is loud and tuneful. Alex plays well. The ten or so people watching clap and before he knows it, Tom has said goodbye to Anita and he and Alex are walking back down De Grey Street taking turns to carry the bass amp that they didn't need eventually. Alex is sweating and excited.

It was a privilege to watch.

Anita is perfect in every way.

It's Saturday morning. Tom has biked up to Parkrun. It's an organized three lap fun race round Pickering Park. It's nine o'clock and he is freezing. Tom would never have expected to be here.

He does not know if he is more frightened of the run or of meeting Joanne afterwards. In his tight running trousers, his legs feel scared as well as cold. His stomach turns over. A man who looks like Father Christmas addresses the crowd through a megaphone while standing on a picnic table. He details the milestones of the day, Rachel Greeves is running her one hundredth Parkrun today, Peter Philips is doing his fiftieth, runners should stay on the path and dogs should be on leads. Tom is conscious that somewhere among these runners stands the woman who is going to have a coffee with him when the run is over. Joanne said in her last message that she would say hello as she lapped him. Tom answered with a smiley face.

The race begins and the first lap is middling to difficult, the second is like finishing a marathon and the third is a form of torture. He has tried not to look at the other runners around him for fear of catching her eye but he at least makes it to the end and is thankful that she did not lap him. Tom collects his finishing token and takes it to the desk to scan it and his barcode, and after he has queued for a minute, a woman with long brown hair and a big smile takes his token.

"I didn't lap you then," she says. This is Joanne.

In the café behind the park, they have removed their shoes and sit in the far corner opposite each other at a square table. Tom has a cup of black coffee and Joanne has gone for a green tea. She has wonderful straight teeth and shapely legs with a fitted pink running jacket that shows off her figure. She did the race in twenty-five minutes thirty seconds. Tom was a lot slower at twenty-nine.

Tom reverts to his training again. He asks questions, it's his defence. Joanne tells him about her daughter and her teaching job, how her mum is in a care home and she visits on Saturday afternoons. Tom explains the scars on his face and that he split up with his wife recently, he tells too of how he has found a new job looking after a taxi and property business and how his relationship with his son is good. Tom knows how to tailor his conversation to a different audience, Joanne here is much more middle of the road than Anita, so he avoids talking about his drinking problems. Joanne is witty and self-aware, she has been single for many years, she misses her daughter who is at university, she does karate for fun, she's pescatarian, she likes watching period dramas on Sunday evenings with a glass of wine. Tom likes her.

The coffee goes down well, and she seems to smile a lot. Against his better judgement, Tom finds himself telling anecdotes from the university he has used on friends to good effect and she laughs, he finds himself telling her all about Alex's change and she nods in agreement. He seems to be winning her over. She explains the ins and out of karate to him and tells some of her stories about training and tournaments. She is well spoken and funny. In a million years Tom would not place himself here, talking to an attractive, intelligent woman over a cup of coffee and seeming to do well at it. It is hard to believe how far he has come.

It takes twenty minutes for them to finish their drinks. They walk out of the café together and into the car park, Joanne's car is on the street opposite and the park looks empty without the runners from before. They say goodbye and Tom walks back to his bike wondering quite how that went. His legs hurt from the run. He puts on the helmet he had locked to his bike earlier and swallows.

Joanne is perfect in every way.

It's Sunday afternoon. It's turned out to be sunny, but the wind is still cold, even for March. Tom is dressed in his big coat and boots with a colourful scarf. He said he would meet Kasia just before the Millennium footbridge that connects the Marina to the aquarium, they are going to walk down the side of the river and back, then get a coffee on Humber Street. Tom is five minutes early.

Once upon a time this was a working part of the city with the fruit market and the docks a mile or so away, nowadays it's home to swanky lawyer's offices, art galleries and gin bars. Tom checks his phone as he waits. Perhaps he shouldn't be doing this. He met Anita on Thursday, the runner Joanne yesterday and today he is meeting Kasia. This level of success is unprecedented, he thinks, for a man with a disfigured face, a drinking problem in remission and a broken marriage. He consulted Bev for her advice via text the night before and she was cautionary, her suggestion was to meet all three and then decide on one. This is what Tom will do.

Kasia arrives on time. Tom spots her walking down Humber Street towards him. She is short with dyed red wavy hair to her shoulders and wears tight jeans, white trainers and a black jacket. She smiles when she sees him and they kiss on each cheek, it's very European. Kasia has green eyes and is wearing light make-up, she smells of perfume and wears black leather gloves to cover her hands that are rough from so much manual work. They walk together over Millennium Bridge toward the aquarium and then out along the side of the river past the new build houses with the sun shining down from a clear but cold blue sky.

Tom adopts his usual tactic of questions and Kasia seems measured but complete with her answers. It turns out she cleans and runs the pub for a wealthy benefactress who was sick and since gone away leaving her in charge, she studied economics, she speaks German reasonably well and Russian to a high standard. She is pretty in a porcelain way with a refined petite nose, a small mouth and a delicate way of speaking. Tom likes her.

She has a no-nonsense way as they walk along the side of the river past the new housing estate. She has a daughter, Alicja, who is eight. Her husband left Hull to live in Peterborough just after she was born. Once she has explained herself to Tom, she expects the same in return. It's a business-like affair.

Tom explains his dealings up at the university without mentioning that he has already lost his job, he tells of his experience on the lecture circuit, his property on Westbourne Ave, his musical son who is his friend and the marriage that crumbled leaving him a single man. Kasia appeals to the rational side of Tom's brain that deals in facts and details, she is precise in her quick steps next to him. When they get as far as the ferry terminal they turn round and walk back. The wind is bracing but she does not seem bothered by it. Tom has always had a thing about cold women, it's what he liked about Inma in the later stages of their marriage. As they walk back towards the aquarium, she hooks her arm around his and they walk side by side. It's too soon to do this, he is aware, but the feeling is sweet as they stroll together – like they are a couple.

On Humber Street, they go into the art gallery cafe. It's quiet and sterile. They sit in front of a corrugated iron graffiti wall with the words 'dead bod' spray painted below a crude picture of an upturned bird. Tom has a black coffee. Kasia has a sparkling water. She takes delicate sips on her drink and Tom crosses his legs in the most middle-class way he knows. They are silent as they consider each other. Tom likes her, but only because he finds her attractive. There's nothing of the warmth he felt in the Adelphi club or at Parkrun, there's no heart to this woman with her cool and beautiful green eyes looking at him. They talk about how nice it is to be out of the wind, Polish writers, Slavic grammar, English food, why they like Hull. Kasia is intelligent and when she smiles it's like the sun shining. She is interested in him.

As they stand outside the art gallery on Humber Street, Kasia asks when they should meet again and Tom, without a single thought offers one evening next week. They decide on Tuesday, a dinner date near where Tom lives on Newland Avenue. They kiss on both cheeks as they did when they first met and as they do, Kasia takes hold of his hand and gives it a gentle squeeze. It's tender.

As he walks back towards town, Tom needs a minute. He is not supposed to be drinking by his own rules, but he walks down beside the covered market in the old town and goes into the Old Blue Bell Pub. At the bar he takes a seat and orders a pint of Sam Smith's bitter. It has been a strange few days. He looks at himself in the mirror behind the bottles, there's the same scarred face looking back at him. How is this possible? A man with a long coat and a ponytail stands next to him at the bar, Tom gives him a sideways glance.

"What happened to your face?" asks the man. Without hesitating, Tom responds.

"Roadside IED, Kandahar province, Afghanistan 2017. Do you have a problem with it?" He is not antagonistic as he lies, more perfunctory. He is surprised at how easily he gets away with it.

"You could have done with a better surgeon," says the man. "It looks terrible. I bet you frighten little kids." There's no malice in this conversation. It's just the cut and thrust of a civil old town drink.

"That's why they call me Face," answers Tom.

"Good name," comments the man.

CHAPTER FOURTEEN
Our Dave

The weather is a bit better on Wednesday afternoon. Alex and Tom take on the Iranian kids at football in their back garden, the rain from the day previous has turned the lawn into a muddy pit. When it starts to rain again, Tom invites the two lads into the kitchen and boils the kettle to make cocoa, they bring a lot of mud in. Galal hides in the space between the boiler and the wall watching with frightened eyes.

The four of them sit around the farmhouse table playing Uno. There's no need for small talk with these two or Alex. They eat biscuits and listen to the rain hammering the windows outside as they play. After ten minutes there's a knock at the front door, Tom goes to open up and it's the Iranian mother with her face worried and her eyes wide – he invites her in, and she looks relieved when she sees her boys are there. Now she's shown up, Tom feels like he has to make small talk and he offers her a coffee. The kids go back to playing Uno. Her name is Sawsan and she has bags under her eyes and pale skin tight against her cheekbones. Her English is poor and broken. She's been in the flat for six months but in the UK for a few years – the boys are doing well at school. Sawsan looks tired. She glances at the mud they have trailed into the kitchen and shakes her head with a tut. Tom grins back at her. She tries her best to chat as she sips her coffee, but it is difficult. It turns out that Iranian New Year is just around the corner on the twenty-first of March, Sawsan tries to explain but resorts to her big son to help translate. She has to tell him to stop playing Uno, she's not shy in her native language, Farsi. Soheil translates:

"It's Iranian new year," he explains. "It's called Nowruz. We're having a barbecue and a fire. We always do. She invites your family to come."

"It was new year in January," says Alex. Soheil shrugs his

shoulders and goes back to his game of Uno.

"I know it," says Tom. It's not just Iranians, Kurdish and Afghans celebrate it as well. It makes sense to start a new year at the beginning of spring. "We'd love to come," he tells Sawsan. She doesn't understand and Soheil translates. She nods and smiles when she hears this. The rain has died down outside and it's beginning to get dark, she says something to her children, and they complain back at her.

"We have to go," says the little one.

On his laptop, Tom searches up Nowruz. He reads the entry on the wiki page. 'Nowruz is new beginnings. It means 'new day, new year'. It's the arrival of spring and rebirth of nature and is celebrated by some 300 million people. It's a time to consider the past and make sense of the future that is to come. Tom reads it again. He looks at pictures of young men jumping over bonfires in celebration and reads the translation of what they say as they make the leap: 'My sickly yellow paleness is yours, and your fiery red colour is mine.' Tom looks down on his hands, they are pale from being inside all winter or typing at a laptop screen, they are sickly and yellow, like his eyes when he looks at them in the morning. March the twenty-first. That's three weeks. This fire will be his rebirth also.

Back in the eighties, Our Dave's Uncle Phil was diagnosed with a heart condition. According to the doctor, his heart could just stop at any minute, and he'd suffer a massive cardiac arrest and die. It was a weight for the man for a while. Every day he woke up he wondered if it would be his last. It's a bit like that for Our Dave these days. He checks the back door is locked, looks at the cars that park outside the taxi office and notices if anyone is walking behind him on Chanterlands Ave. It's not a nice feeling, like he's being watched, and Our Dave would rather whoever it was would just get on with it. He walks down Westbourne Avenue in the early morning and then onto Chants Ave. It's just after nine, he is late to the office, but nobody will care – the business runs without him, the drivers know who they are picking up and where they are taking them to. He will have to keep up appearances, today he's set up a viewing with the estate agent at a big building near Pearson Park, not far from here. It's had squatters in it who have moved on because the place is too run down even for them. Our Dave needs to carry on as normal, so he'll look at the place with a view to buying it.

Tom has been a big help with his will and his business affairs, the man is changing before his eyes, where previously there was a floppy haired, middle-aged tit, he is now thinner and fitter, and the work he does for Our Dave is complex and gives him focus. Although he can't be certain, Our Dave thinks the lawyer may be able to dissolve the business without too much trouble. It's important to leave things clean and sorted for when he goes. There have been the sleepless nights as always, but he has come to the realisation that the days he has enjoyed so much are over, and the pain he feels at losing his wife of so many years will be over as well. Just near the cheap supermarket before the library on Chants Ave, is Lilly. She's leaning with her back against the wall and her hood up while she smokes a cig and looks at her phone. The blue and yellow supermarket tabard hugs her figure and she's done her makeup to a medium standard. Our Dave stops when he gets close to her. She looks up and gives him a big smile to show the veneers.

"You alright?" she asks.

"All good," it's easy for Our Dave to lie, he's been doing it most of his life, especially to people who he likes. "How's the shop?"

"I get asked out all the time standing at that till," she answers with a grin. "It's murder on my feet as well." Our Dave looks down to see she is wearing shiny gold-coloured trainers. "I'm thinking about getting a job at the pub next door, the pay's a bit better and I won't have to stack shelves."

"You'll get asked out a lot more though," says Dave.

"I can deal with that. I've dealt with worse." She takes a pull on her cigarette. "I'm not supposed to be smoking this near the shop, but the manager doesn't mind, she smokes herself. She says it's company policy not to be smoking in our uniform. I said, I've covered mine up with my coat." Lilly is a chatterbox, beautifully so, you just wind her up and let her talk. Our Dave appreciates this at just after nine on Chanterlands Ave when the traffic is thin. She pauses to take another drag on her cig. A rare question forms:

"I tried to text Gaz but I didn't get a reply. Have you seen him?" she asks. This is the young man who looked after her a few months back. She asks Our Dave whenever she sees him.

"Up in Scotland still, last I heard," says Our Dave. "He's with that lass from the library, like I said before." Lilly will know all this information already. She has a soft spot for Gaz.

"How long have they been up there?"

"A couple of weeks. It's a holiday." Lilly narrows her eyes playfully.

"He said he used to drive up there for you."

"He does."

"In your van?"

"Aye." Our Dave finds himself grinning. He likes to think of Gaz and Kate together on the road somehow. Of course, he has Gaz drive up there to deliver money as always – this is one of the ways he launders so much of it, but he's also asked for another favour. Our Dave explained to Gaz that he might like to retire to Scotland when the day comes, and that the young man and Kate should drive across to Montrose on the coast to look at properties. The weather will be monstrous, and Our Dave has no plans to even visit the pretty little town on the coast, but he is pleased they are up there together.

"You'll ask him to message me when he gets back," says Lilly, "or he can pop in the shop here, I do mornings except

Saturday because we like a drink on a Friday night."

"I'll tell him," says Our Dave. "I'm going up to visit a house just outside Pearson Park that might be worth getting. When I'm done, I'll give him a ring and see how he is. He'll be alright, you know, Gaz is a pretty tough lad." Lilly's confidence drains for a moment as she looks at Our Dave. Gaz is very important to her.

"Make sure you do," she whispers.

At the estate agent on the corner of Newland Ave and Walgrave Street, Our Dave waits for the woman in a trouser suit who's on the phone. This is Julianne. She's been the acting manager here since Mr Westlock had his stroke in May last year. The stress of the office isn't too much for her, it's her two kids, her ex-husband, and her sick mother that make life harder than it should be. The nightly bottle of wine she drinks to cope with it doesn't help either. This has been arranged for a few weeks. Julianne has the key and she's to show Our Dave around the property.

"My mum's moving into a home today," says Julianne with the phone mouthpiece in her hand. Our Dave nods.

"Which one?"

"St Mary's." Our Dave nods. He knows it. Julianne goes back to listening on the phone.

"I've been on here an hour, Dave. It's the gas company to get her bill finalized. Are you okay to take a look at the place on your own?" It would have saved a lot of bother if they had arranged it like this in the first place. Julianne pulls open a drawer at the side of her desk and passes him an envelope. "The key's in there," she says. Our Dave takes the envelope and nods.

It's not far to walk to Pearson Park. He goes back down Westbourne Ave and onto the park itself. It's grand weather for the ducks that quack and waddle across the rainy grass. Our Dave grew up on these streets and they haven't changed too much. There are more cars and the people look different than they did back then, but the bricks and mortar are the same red. Just after Pearson Park, the houses are big and grandiose; built at the start of the century they're too roomy for normal families to want or be able to afford. Lots have been cut up into flats, but the one Dave stands in front of has been left to rot for many years – squatters moved in a while ago and now even they've abandoned it. He walks off the road and goes up the steps to the front where a new door has been fitted with a yale lock. With the estate agent's key, he opens up and steps inside.

Unlike most investors, Our Dave is not looking to make a killing on the property. Instead, it's a way to both get rid of his money and put something back into the city that built him. Our Dave steps down the hallway and looks up the stairs, he can see daylight through the rotten roof high above where the rain spits down on him. A project like this would keep more than a few people in work for a long time, it would launder a considerable amount of money too. In the hall the walls are crumbling and there are black plastic bin liners of rubbish, empty tin cans and beer bottles, there's a used condom coiled up on the floor – it stinks too.

In the big kitchen at the back of the house the windows have been boarded up so there's no natural light. There are more plastic bags full of rubbish. It's like being inside the apocalypse. He leans down to pick up a chair that's fallen on its side and sets it straight. Our Dave could get the place for a good price. It could be flats. It could be better than it is now. There's the smell of cigs and shit. Squatters were here not so long back – they're drug addicts, you wouldn't choose to live here if you didn't have a problem. Next to the kitchen through double doors is a dining room where there's a filthy double mattress on the floor with a sleeping bag at the bottom. The curtains are drawn across the French windows and Our Dave walks over to pull them apart. Grey freezing light floods the stinking room. He's suddenly conscious of someone behind him.

"How did you get in?" the voice is thin and nasal. Our Dave turns around and sees a ratty looking man with his hooded jacket up over his head and a thin, drawn face with the cheekbones showing above a patchy beard.

"I came to view the place," says Our Dave. He's spent his life talking to dangerous people. If you shit yourself, they'll know, and besides, Our Dave is a dangerous person, or maybe he was once upon a time.

"This is my place," says the man. He's not nearly as tall as Our Dave and has stooped shoulders.

"I'm not saying it isn't," answers Our Dave. "I'm from the council, part of the planning department, we're thinking about what to do with this place." This lie might make Our Dave seem less like a threat. He notices that the rat man is carrying a length of pipe in his right hand. Our Dave narrows his eyes and for some reason he doesn't feel afraid – this man isn't a hired killer, he's just a junkie who's prepared to defend himself.

"I've got twenty quid if you'll step out the way, and then I'll be off."

"I'll have everything you've got, ta," says the rat man. Our Dave shakes his head.

"My two mates are on their way, fella, builder types, they're big lads who don't mind having a go. I wouldn't have thought you'd last very long against them." The rat man seems to waver. You can't always reason with someone on skag. Our Dave knows this from experience, and they're still dangerous even if all their muscles have wasted away and their teeth have rotted in their face.

"Give us your wallet and you can piss off, you nonce. This is a squat – whatever you're after, you've come to the wrong place." Our Dave should have realised. If he was thinking straight, he would have walked around the back of the building to see if there was another way in, of course this won't be just a squat, other things will go on here because people will do all sorts when they're desperate. Men probably visit via the back door and pay for services. Our Dave thinks to the condom he saw on the floor in the other room.

"I'm not here for that, kid," says Our Dave. In his better days, he would have put this little man's head through the wall before he could move. He's not as quick anymore, and not as mean as he was either – that was Hazel's doing.

"You can hand over your wallet or I can batter you and take it myself." This has gone a bit too far. Dave can only do so much to help people, after that, they're just taking the piss.

"You need to learn some manners, kid," whispers Our Dave, not with any sort of real malice mind, more as a kind of sarcastic retort.

The pipe in the man's left-hand flashes out and catches Our Dave on the right knee. The rat man has had a bit of training obviously. He draws back the pipe again and smacks him around his bald head with a hollow thud. Our Dave crashes onto the filthy mattress on his side – his head spins. He feels the rat man on top of him going through his pockets and pulling out his mobile phone, then his wallet and car keys. This is how it is being old. You are not different, but your body is. Our Dave feels the sting of anger, but his fists aren't fast enough. The rat man stands above him looking down with a worried snarl.

"Can you get up, mate?" he asks. He feels remorse suddenly but not because of what he has done, it's what will happen to him when he gets caught. Our Dave opens his mouth, but words don't form from his lips; his eyes blink and his throat bobs as he tries to swallow. The rat man curses under his breath, he can see the blood coming from the side of the man's head and worries that he might have injured him fatally.

This is Browny – the same kid who kicked Tom in his jaw

the other night. Originally, he was brought up in Cottingham just down the road where he lived with his mother and father in an ex-council house near the park. Most would say Browny had every chance in the world, with a mum who liked baking and a dad who was into rugby and fitness. He was just too early on to be diagnosed with ADHD like he would be these days, he's twenty-eight, he was labelled a troublemaker and a bastard, so that's what he became. If this man is going to die, then Browny will be blamed for it, anyone on the street knows that he uses this house for the tricks he turns. He curses under his breath and fumbles in his pocket for his lighter.

You wouldn't like to say he was a bad kid as a little boy at primary school, but he really was. He was rude and angry, never a team player, violent, needy and all the rest. The drugs haven't made him calmer, and if his decision making was bad then, it is worse now, like he is spiralling out of control and one bad choice leads to another and so on and so on. It was a bad idea to hit the man, just like it's a bad idea to stand in the kitchen next door and light his empty cigarette packet. Browny angles the flame till it catches the paper and then when it's got going, he tosses it into a black plastic bag full of cardboard. He watches the fire take hold and for a moment is transfixed by the flickering, it doesn't take a minute for the flames to get bigger.

Browny goes out the backdoor in the kitchen, the one he used a crowbar to open a few months before and pushes it closed when he's outside. He pulls up a plastic garden chair and jams it under the handle so it will be harder for the man inside to get out, if he can even get up. 'Let the fucker burn,' he thinks.

Our Dave hasn't been knocked out, but he's been dumbstruck for a few minutes. He lays on his back on the mattress and he can feel the pattern of the material on the back of his head. His hand goes to his temple, and he feels sticky blood on his fingers.

If someone is going to kill him, he wishes they would do it properly. Our Dave tries to bend his leg. It's painful. The rat man hit him just above his knee and it hurts to put pressure on it. The smell of the squat fills his nostrils. It's going to be a struggle to get out of this one. Our Dave rests before he tries to stand up and he notices smoke seeping in under the door of the backroom where he lays. The smell of burning stings his eyes. He gives a weak grin.

There might not be any point getting up at all, if the rat man thinks he's killed Our Dave, it might be as well to set the place alight to cover his tracks. He looks to the French window behind the curtains – he could smash the glass – then catches himself. Why rush? What's the need for him to get out of this situation? There's someone after Our Dave anyway, and they will catch up with him sooner or later. What's wrong with here, on the floor of a squat? He'll be suffocated by the smoke quick enough and then that will be it. He has tied the loose ends he needed to, there's Tom with his melted-up face working on the business. Perhaps this is how it's meant to be after all. Smoke begins to billow into the room.

Our Dave is calm. He has missed Hazel. It was she who helped him become the man he is, and without her, he would have ended up in jail or dead many years ago. At least with the time he's had, he put one in the eye for some and helped out others. When he's gone there should still be some good done as well with what he's left. Our Dave is not sorry to go, not even a bit, he has had more than his fair share of everything; friends, money, happiness, love too. Things come to an end, and so will he. He lays backwards on the stinking mattress and feels the smoke roll over him like a shroud. There are figures in the grey curls, memories and shouts from friends, sunny days and winter walks, autumn rain, cold spring mornings, his mother's face, Hazel and he walking down the beach on Christmas Eve at Scarborough all those years ago.

There are two loud crashes from the front of the house and

Our Dave opens up one of his eyes as if he's been woken from a beautiful dream. Someone is shouting his name.

"Dave!" The door to the backroom flies open, and a figure dressed in black steps in, sees him laid there and mutters swearwords under his breath. Then strong hands grab Our Dave and haul him up, two arms go around him and clasp at his chest as he gets dragged out through the door. The smoke is thick and the figure that pulls him coughs and splutters as he works to get the body down the hall towards the front door that has been kicked off its hinges. He manoeuvres Our Dave through the doorway and down the steps to the little path and the drizzle of a late Thursday morning just outside Pearson Park. The figure sets Our Dave down and gasps in the fresh air outside - smoke is pouring out of the front door from where they emerged and there's the flicker of flames coming from the kitchen.

"Another minute and you'd have been cooked," says the man as he squats down. Our Dave tries to say something but all he can do is grab at the sleeve of the figure that has just saved him.

It's a familiar face.

It's Gaz.

CHAPTER FIFTEEN
Second date

This is the vegan deli on Newland Ave. There are black iron chairs outside and a little table but it's too cold to sit out still. It won't be in a few weeks. Anita is not a vegan, but she likes the people here. A woman with glasses and short hair serves them up a black coffee and a lemonade for Anita. They lean against the wall in the corner next to a counter fixed against the wall. It's got that shabby, trendy feel to it.

"How's the drinking?" asks Anita as she sips her lemonade. They've walked and talked all the way down from the Adelphi car park and covered all the important things, work for each of them, Tom's son Alex, Anita's dog Clive (she would never call a dog Clive!), some aspects of the news and interesting things they have heard on the radio. With that out the way, they can crack on with difficult stuff. Tom hasn't been drinking very much at all. He tells her how he bought four cans of Guiness and drank one but didn't fancy the others. She explains that she was all about getting off her face once upon a time and that's why she was either going to die or stop. Anita tells him about the heroin addict she loved down in the London squat, and how he died. She is not afraid to show her emotions but does not over dramatise them either. Tom likes this.

They walk back down Newland Avenue and, just after the second-hand furniture shop and the Caribbean restaurant they somehow reach out and take each other's hand. Tom is not sure how it happened. It's tender. They walk like this all the way down the busy, cosmopolitan street, past Newland Tap Brewery, the Piper Club, Oxfam and Admiral Casino Slots Experience and then up De Grey Street to the car park of the Adelphi. The light touch of her hand is gentle on Tom's, she smiles back at him and the sun breaks through the clouds when they get back to her van. They sit together on a rickety bench behind the red Mercedes and hold hands some more, like teenagers. Anita explains the ins and outs of the van's engine and how she hopes to get it running some day while Tom listens. He feels big and rude and dumb next to her. He tells her about the Iranian kids who they play football with next door, and about the Nowruz festival in a few weeks. Tom thinks he might go to the fire next door and maybe have drinks with friends – he's not sure if he has any friends to invite, at least there will be Alex if he is lucky, and the two Iranian kids from next door. Anita likes this. She has a good and clean smile with bright eyes that sparkle in the new spring sun. His heart beats tight in his chest. Tom leans down and they kiss on the lips. He pulls back. He does not remember kissing a woman when he was sober – it is thrilling. She puts her hand on his face as she looks up at him. They kiss again.

The last time Tom was at King George Park, Cottingham was when Alex was little. They used to walk round the outside and into the woods at the back. Tom has parked up in the car park in front and there, waiting at the gate for him in a figure-hugging windcheater is Joanne. She's got a wide smile under light make-up and her black hair is swept into a ponytail. They are going for a walk into the woods out at the back of the main park. Tom suggested going for a run, but Joanne said she'd like to chat rather than get all sweaty. She says she has a hangover anyway; as a big drinker, Tom doesn't believe this is true at all.

They walk across the wide and open field frequented by dog walkers and to the corner of the park with the turnstile that leads to the woodland area. They go over all the most important things, work, Tom's son Alex and his band, Joanne's job, things they've cooked over the week. With that out of the way they can get onto the more interesting stuff, Joanne explains about her ex-husband who was a big Welshman and how he left her to join the army many years ago, how training has given her space to relax and how lonely the house feels without her daughter. She is humorous with it and although Tom can sense there is hurt behind the self-depreciating comments, there is no desire to complain. Tom explains about Alex's journey and his own with Inma's leaving. He details his newfound role as a portfolio manager for a local businessman, Tom adds sprinkles of humour and dashes of modesty just as she did. It's not just for show, Tom really doesn't know what he is doing with all the business affairs that Our Dave has his fingers in.

They walk through the woods and to the fields where the sun struggles to break through the grey clouds. It's been dry for the last few days so the going is good as they walk into what will be a cornfield when the autumn comes. Tom explains about the festival of Nowruz and tells Joanne about the two Iranian kids who play football with him and Alex in the back garden. He knows he has told this before. Joanne likes it.

On a fallen tree at the side of one of the fields, they sit next to each other. Tom has brought a flask of green tea in his backpack that once upon a time he used for sherry. Joanne gets the nice cup from the top and he has the little one. They sit, with their cups of green tea and the grey, nearly spring sky above them. Birds tweet in the trees behind, there's scurrying from the bushes, and the peaceful rustle of the wind over the grass in front. They talk again. Tom tells her about the accident he had all those years back and the burns that cover his arms and his chest. He doesn't add any drama, that's all in the past. He explains that he doesn't like to show his arms or take his top off because it frightens little kids. Joanne smiles. She tells him about her mother's death and how she never thought she'd miss the old cow, but she does. It feels like they have known each other for a long time somehow.

They walk back through the fields towards the park itself where Tom has left his car, and Joanne follows him over the little wooden bridge. As they walk across the open, wild meadow, Joanne steps closer to him and hooks her arm around his so they are walking together – Tom likes this, it makes him feel warm. They go at the same speed and her legs are shapely in tight jeans with black walking trainers on her feet. He likes her. She has the light smell of perfume.

They sit in the front seat of her car to get out of the wind with the wall next to the tennis courts for a view. She asks if he wants to meet again. Tom says he would. He turns to her and smiles. She smiles back, and before he knows it, they are leaning together, over the space between the two front seats, over the hand brake and the hollow where she keeps her loose change, he is close to her and she to him. They kiss. It's delicate. Just as before with Anita, Tom feels his sobriety and tingles of pleasure go across his head and down his shoulders.

In the car driving back to Hull, Tom clutches onto the wheel as he drives. His mouth is dry. This is impossible. His body is covered by burn scars, he is an ugly drunk, Imna said so herself. His rude appearance frightens dogs in the street. How can he have lightly kissed two women in the space of three days? Bev told him to see all three of these women and choose one, but so far that has not been possible and now, with the memory of both at the front of his head he cannot select one. He feels guilt and pride at the same time. He is becoming someone else he reasons. It is happening, and Tom tells himself that these meetings are just steps towards that person.

He finds a car parking spot down Westbourne Ave just a few doors away from his front door and parks his car. His phone buzzes on the passenger's seat. The name reads Kasia.

The Deep opened in 2002 and stands at the edge of the river Hull and with its point looking out over the Humber Estuary. It was designed to look like a crystalline rock formation rising to the sky. It's a place where you can look at loads of fish. Tom's friend, Leo, works there, and if you go round along the side, you can sometimes see him smoking a fag outside the big air vents. It's Leo that got Tom the free tickets for today – the aquarium isn't really a great place for a date, but it was Kasia's idea. Tom doesn't mind going along with it.

They meet at the statue of the big shark and kiss on each cheek in greeting. Kasia has ridden here on her shopper bike with a basket on the front and locked it in the bike racks. She's wearing a sensible padded black jacket and a plum-coloured beanie hat over her red hair, her green eyes sparkle. She has a pretty smile. In the queue they go over the usual stuff, cleaning at the Dairycoates Inn, Tom's knowledge of European Law, bringing up kids, why bike lanes are such a good idea, which law journals Tom has written for, and the best points about British weather – Kasia likes the grey skies.

In the aquarium they wander through the computer displays to the main tanks. There are silent, deep-sea crabs in the darkness of a fake boat wreckage below white eerie cod. Warm tropical waters in the next tank display coral with colourful shoals of fish weaving in and out of the rock, and a fat mummy shark resting and breathing through wide gills that look like slits in a home-made pie. Kasia wants to know why the sharks don't eat the other fish, and Tom explains that they are well fed enough not to bother. They pause in the tunnel under the water and look at the ice wall, but they have both been here before and it's nothing new. The café is packed so they go outside and walk along the other way towards the Marina. In front of the Minerva pub, they lean against the wall looking at the flat cold water of the Humber. Tom takes out his flask of green tea, Kasia gets the top cup, and he gets the little one.

They talk of recent business court cases, the essential differences between European and British law, quick evening meals, the benefits of cycling, American politics. Kasia tells him about her blond Polish ex-husband and how he was dull and unambitious, she tells of the jobs she has had over her time in the UK, Tom explains his estranged wife Inma and how she went from eighteen stone to twelve and started a successful Instagram business in the loft. Kasia is measured and attentive with striking intelligence that shines from her green eyes. She reaches out as they lean there and takes hold of his hand, it's warm and soft. Tom gives it a squeeze. He is getting good at this.

They walk back to the deep where she locked her bike and the wind is stronger than it was. They share a chaste kiss after she has removed the D-lock, and he watches her cycle off down Humber Street.

"I was actually alright you know, Gaz," says Our Dave. They are in the office at Avenue Cars. It's after six and all the other drivers are done for the day. Gaz sits in front of Our Dave at the round table.

"You were about to be cooked." Our Dave gives a light cough that hurts his chest, but he doesn't show it. The blow to his head turned out to be just a scratch and his leg is bruised but better. Gaz got back to Hull that morning and was coming to drop the van off at Avenue Cars, he heard from Lilly at the supermarket where Our Dave was going so he followed him to the house, as a surprise. He booted the door down when he saw the smoke and managed to get Our Dave to his van parked on the street round the corner. Gaz called the fire brigade from the burner phone in the glove box in the van and gave a false name. It's much better if they keep themselves out of these things. Official people like to ask questions that are best avoided. Gaz and Our Dave sat in the van till they saw the flash of blue lights down Beverley Road, then drove away. Gaz has made the old fella a cup of tea. He looks worse than he has ever seen him before. Our Dave explained about the skag head squatter with the iron bar.

"You're looking well," says Gaz. This is the kind of thing people say around here. Our Dave manages a grin.

"I didn't expect you back till next week. What about that place in Montrose?"

"It rained for three days solid, Dave. We didn't see anything. My advice would be to stay in Hull. I saw Bev when I came here earlier."

"Oh aye."

"She says you've got some sort of lawyer fella working here. Tom."

"That's right. He's putting the business into shape."

"Wasn't it in shape before?"

"Not like it should be, to be honest, Gaz. There are all sorts of loose ends that need tying up, papers that need to be sorted, just to make it all right. He's a quick lad, ugly looking, with burn marks all up his neck and face, but he knows his stuff." Gaz narrows his eyes.

"Can you trust him?"

"I think so. We know a bit about each other, me and him, things that it's wise we don't let anyone else find out. He's been helping me out." Gaz does a big sigh. He feels protective over this man.

"You know if you ever need me, Dave, then I'm here. I could have helped you out as well." It was not so very long ago that Gaz took a beating to stop Dave getting one, the man is the closest thing to a father he has ever had. Our Dave sits forward and puts his big hands on the table in front. His face is washed out and cold.

"I know, Gaz. This Tom has got skills that we don't have. He's not a street kid like we are, and I have to put this place in order. I'm not gonna mess about, Gaz, I feel old. I feel tired too." He licks his lips. This is difficult. Gaz is a good kid and with that Kate who went with him to Scotland, he is on a positive road. Our Dave does not want him involved in the upside-down world he's created here, he doesn't want him in on the deals or the brown paper envelopes or the violence or driving a body up to Cleveland Street furnace wrapped in an old carpet. Our Dave wants Gaz kept out of it. "I don't know how long I'll be around, kid." In the will that Tom set up, Kate will get the house that she lives in, and Gaz here will get the van and fifty grand. It should be enough to start something legitimate up. He has had it tough already.

"I didn't know," says Gaz.

"You do now. This place is on its last legs, kid. Like me."

"Maybe I should come with you when you go places then. Like today. Maybe you need someone to look after you, not like a lawyer."

"Like a bodyguard?"

"I'm trained for it." Our Dave smiles. He couldn't have a minder; it would only put off what is going to happen anyway and put Gaz in danger as well.

"If I need you, I'll call." The conversation has become serious and unnecessarily dark. Our Dave has to turn it into something light, partly so he can hide his predicament from this earnest young man. "How's Kate?" Gaz's eyes light up.

"She's well, thank you. She loved Scotland but she's got a lot of work on at the uni."

"How about you, are you going back to nightclub doors?"

"I'm saving up for my own van, Dave. I know someone who needs drivers to do airport runs, you know, taking families on holiday and picking them up." Our Dave nods. This is legitimate and solid.

"Good."

"I'll keep an eye out for you, Dave."

"There's no need." Gaz takes a deep breath and finishes the glass of water. He senses that Our Dave is not telling him the full story.

"You just call me if you need me."

"I will, Gaz. I'll be fine. You'll see. I always am."

CHAPTER SIXTEEN
Inma and Kasia

Alex has a bigger bass amp now and he practices a lot more. The glass doors on the cabinet in the front room buzz when he hits the lower notes and Galal hides in the space between the old armchair and the wall in fear. Tom likes the noise. It feels like home. In the kitchen he listens to the radio and drinks alcohol free beer but today the house is quiet. Alex is off skateboarding this afternoon and Tom is in the kitchen washing up.

The front door opens and slams and there's the clacking of square heels down the hallway towards the kitchen. This is still Inma's house, so she can just walk in. She appears at the doorway and her face is serious and perfectly made up under her black pixie cut.

"My friend saw you on a dating app," she says. Tom wipes his hands dry with a tea towel. She is starting to lose whatever power she had over him. He is calm. "Is it true?"

"Yeah."

"We're married."

"You're sleeping with your chiropractor." Tom blinks back at her. He has not really admitted this to himself. She swallows.

"You can tell whatever lies you want if they make you feel better about what you're doing." She is going to deny it. It's much easier than being heartless.

"It's kind of common knowledge." Tom's mouth is dry as he says this, his chest is tight, he has skirted around the truth for so long. It hurts him to say it aloud to her. Inma gives him one of her withering looks. She wonders how he found out.

"I'm here to talk about things," she says. Tom walks over to the table where there's a yellow cardboard file. He opens it up and removes a booklet of printed documents stapled together. He passes it to her.

"These are the details of all our assets," he says. "I've

divided them up in monetary terms, and proposed a couple of scenarios for us to untangle our finances. I can buy you out of this place, or we can put it on the market. I'd suggest that you get a professional to look through those papers just to make sure I'm being fair with you. As for a divorce, that will take a little longer depending on which avenue we take. I'd suggest separation for the time being." Imna forgets that he is a lawyer.

"You won't be able to buy me out. Alex says you lost your job."

"I have another one." There's a look of disgust on her smooth face. She hasn't noticed him for so long and only now sees that he is visibly thinner and looks better than he did. She does not like to see him doing well. She wants to hurt him.

"You can see all the scars and burns without your hair, Tom. It's not a good look on you." Imna is effective at making people feel small.

"It's not meant to be a good look, it's just me."

"I shouldn't imagine you'll have much luck finding anyone online – it's all about appearance on there."

"I was good enough for you once upon a time."

"Not anymore." It's not good to argue with Inma, she is sharp and nasty. Tom cannot think of intelligent things to say quick enough, being an effective lawyer means preparation; the cut and thrust of a common verbal row is not something he can plan for.

"You just get someone to check through those documents as quickly as you can, and we'll be able to straighten this out."

"Is there anything about Alex in here?"

"Like what?"

"Like where she's going to live."

"I think Alex can make that choice."

"She's fifteen."

"Sixteen soon. Alex can choose for himself."

"She's a girl for God's sake." Tom looks down at the expensive laminate floor. He might as well be straight with her.

"I don't want to have this conversation. It's all Alex's choice, all of it. It's got nothing to do with you and I."

"I want what is best for my daughter, and if she's in an environment that's inappropriate for her then I need to do something about it. I don't think it's good for her to be here. How much are you drinking?"

"What's that got to do with it?"

"You're not a capable person, Tom. You've been drunk for the last ten years. I think she should live with me, at my mother's."

"You were never bothered how drunk I was, you were always fine to leave Alex with me while you did whatever you did."

"I want her away from you, Tom." Inma did not know she would say this. The fact that he is aware of her relationship with the chiropractor has blindsided her, so she is grasping at something to beat him with. In truth, Inma would rather Alex stay out of her way so she can get on with her life.

"I'm not going to fight you, Inma."

"You're dangerous," she whispers. Tom thinks about the matt black Baretta pistol that he has in the shed at the bottom of the garden. Perhaps he is dangerous. His grandfather was a pirate after all and of course, there comes a time in every person's life when they must raise the black flag – metaphorically. He does not want to say what he is about to:

"How could you go with that man, after all these years? We were married."

"I haven't done anything unreasonable, Tom. You're a wreck, overweight, drinking all the time, always at work, I moved on, I changed my life and you didn't come with me. You didn't grow."

"You didn't give me a chance. We were in it together. You could have told me how you felt."

"I tried to. You didn't want to listen. I outgrew you, Tom. You'll just have to accept that." The words are harsh and true.

She is ready for war. Tom nods and he regains his composure.

"I knew you were changing. Now I am as well." They stand facing each other in a house that was always too big for them and cost too much money as well. It was a journey they started on together, and they do not know how they got here, but it is the end.

"Most of the stuff here is mine, you know," she says.

"Take what you want. Come anytime. There's nothing here I need. You could start with the cat." Imna cocks her head.

"You know my mother is allergic to them." He shrugs his shoulders. "I'm going to have to talk to a solicitor about our situation, Tom."

"That is my advice," he says with steel.

"I'll get this house, and I'll get Alex too, I'll make sure of it. I'll screw you down for everything I can get." Inma says this with bitterness. She is angry at herself and her decision to be with this man all those years ago. His calm demeanour ignites her anger. "The chiropractor is called Deano. He's a better lover than you ever were. He looks after himself and he looks after me. I regret the time I spent here, and I regret our marriage." Tom hears the words, and they make perfect sense to him. Now the storm of her full hatred is here, he feels much better about it. Like the bullets from the machine gun pinging from the outside of the container or the boot to his jaw from the rat man as Tom lay on Pearson Park, they are meant to hurt him, but they don't. He smiles. Turns out Face is much stronger than he thought he was. "He's a better man than you are," she adds, "and I wish I had met him twenty years ago. We laugh about you when we're together."

"I hope he'll make you happy," says Face. "Next time you visit, I'll need notice so I can make sure I'm out."

He hears the door slam after she has clacked down the hall in her high heeled boots.

It's Monday afternoon just after twelve. Alicja is at school and the Dairycoates Inn is almost dead. Kasia is upstairs in the kitchen, she has ringed a date on the kitchen calendar, it's the twentieth of March. It's Thursday. There's no need for more explanation because the mark is just for her. She's made a decision. This is when it will be. She has the weapon and she's chosen the way to proceed. It will just need a bit of setting up. There's a Woman's Institute group off Ella Street, she's been to one session and will attend a further three. Our Dave doesn't live too far away so, she'll cycle up on her bike and take the route down the alley behind his house. She'll leave the cycle in the darkness against his back fence and pay him a visit. There are angles she hasn't quite worked out yet, like how she'll get through his back door if it's locked, and how to make sure he is in. These details will come in the few weeks left till then. No one will suspect her anyway, she'll be at the WI meeting till late. They won't even find his body for a few days.

She pours herself a cup of tea and her phone buzzes from inside her handbag. She reaches inside and, next to the orange gun that looks like a toy, there's a message from Tom. It reads: 'I'm here'. She smiles. Kasia has invited him to the pub for a cup of coffee. She will also kiss him. Kasia understands that men are often controlled by what's in their pants.

Down in the barroom, Tom is waiting inside the front door. He's wearing a colourful scarf with a smile. Kasia is pleased to see him. They kiss on each cheek as they have done before and then she takes him upstairs to the sleek kitchen where he sits down on one of the stools. He is dressed in a tweed style jacket and a checked shirt that has the top two buttons open to show his chest. He has good cologne. The burns on his face don't look too bad at all and he has a nice smile. Kasia is dressed in her running gear – it's spandex pants and new trainers without socks, and a tight black top that shows off her petite figure.

She fixes him a black coffee and they make light conversation. It turns out that Kasia runs the pub as well as cleans it. The landlady has gone on a permanent holiday to Florida and so she handles every aspect of the pub these days, for now Kasia knows that she likes Tom, she wishes to impress. She is keen to show him that she is not just a pub cleaner, she is also rich enough to be independent.

She sits opposite him, and they cover plenty of ground, current business tax levels, challenges still facing the UK judicial system now it has left the EU, how to clean carpets effectively. Kasia tells him about how her grandmother raised her in Poland and taught her to be thankful and thrifty. Tom explains about his brother Julian down in London with his glittering career and two perfect children who go to private school.

When they have finished their drinks, Kasia offers to give him a tour of the place and he accepts. She starts downstairs in the pump room where beer barrels are connected by plastic pipes up to the bar. She shows him the near deserted pub and the smoking courtyard, upstairs they stand and look out onto the main road leading off Hessle Road, Kasia tells him that she will buy her own pub one day in the near future when she has saved enough.

In the spare bedroom, the bed has been freshly made up and there is the light smell of lavender. At the window, Kasia stands opposite him and looks up into his eyes with a playful smile. Tom's heart beats in his chest, his palms are tacky and his mouth is dry. He did not expect this so soon. Images flash through his brain as he looks down on her – what about the girl from the Adelphi? He likes her more. What about Joanne from the school who he kissed the other day, he likes her too. What is he doing moving towards this attractive Polish woman with petite features and piercing green eyes? He remembers Inma too, perhaps right now she is in the chiropractor's strong arms in his clinic above Chanterlands Avenue. Why shouldn't Tom do this?

They kiss with passion. It is awkward. It has been so long

since Tom did this kind of thing that he feels panicked by it. She is tender and skilful; her hands cup his face, and she can feel the scars on her palms, but they don't bother her – it is the man she requires not the burns on his body. She will let him take the lead even though it was her decision to bring him into this room, and her choice to change the bedsheets on the double bed, and to wear a tight top that shows off her petite boobs. As she kisses him, she sees the future – she will move on from the Dairycoates Inn and be with him, she won't clean toilets, deal with heroin, carry a plastic gun in her handbag or have to eliminate threats; she will be a normal woman with a life and a respectable man. Kasia knows a lot about Tom already, she's researched him online, looked at the speeches he's given as a visiting lecturer, seen his wedding photos on his wife's Instagram page. She knows where he lives. Through the dark web she's seen his finance history and bank details, the loan he took out to buy his estate car, how many years he has left on the mortgage of the big house on Westbourne Avenue, where he spends his money and on what.

Tom pulls back from the kiss.

"It's too soon for me," he says. Kasia smiles back at him. She thinks this is the perfect thing to say. "I'd rather get to know you more."

"I agree," she answers. They are both lying. Tom is worried that he doesn't know how to do it anymore, or that his bits and bobs won't work properly, he is concerned about her seeing his arms and his chest with the burns all over them, he has not had chance to prepare himself. Kasia thinks that his reticence means he likes her more than he does, it is her experience that men want to fumble first and chat later. They fall back to kissing and it is more relaxed than it was.

On the way home in his long estate car, Tom waits at the railway crossing on Hawthrone Ave. His phone buzzes on the seat next to him. It's a message from Anita.

'What are you up to tonight?' it reads.

'Nothing planned,' he answers. 'Shall we go for a drink?"

Tom has a bath with the radio on. He scrubs his chest and washes his short, shaved hair. He knows what he is doing is wrong, but the world has been cruel to him, why shouldn't he be cruel back? He's not a murderer or a thief, he has not lied so much as not told the full truth, he has not physically hurt anyone, nobody has been caused any harm at all. He has arranged to meet Anita that evening in the St John's pub near the Adelphi. Joanne has been in touch as well. He has arranged to go for a walk with her in the early evening tomorrow out at Skidby where there is a windmill and a quaint pub. It's all set.

It's never been like this. Noone has been interested in Tom in this way. Rejection has been the only currency he has known for so long. That does not make seeing three women at once right, but it is success that he has never known. There must be a mistake in the universe somewhere, a ripple that is out of line with how it should be, for ugly Tom Williams to see three women is insane and unimaginable.

At the bar in the St John's pub there's a pot of snuff in a metal dish attached to a heavy rock – this stops it from getting nicked. It's not that the people who drink here are bad sorts, it's just that some folks will steal anything just because they can. Tom is at the hatch bar, he orders a Guiness for himself and a lime and soda for Anita. Then, they sit opposite each other at a little round table in the backroom and talk about music, vegetarian cooking, how often Clive has to be wormed, Tom tells of his holidays in Greece many years ago, how he is slowly coming off the booze (apart from now) and how his scars have affected his life. Anita explains her troubled past and violent father that she ran away from in the nineties. It's real talk. Anita has weathered a good deal of life, she is a survivor and beautiful and intelligent with it. Tom likes her thumb ring and the smooth skin on her arms, he likes the curve where her neck meets her shoulders.

They walk back to her van in the car park of the Adelphi where she has left Clive. The dog fusses Tom and they sit at the back, on the bench behind the van with the back doors open holding hands like they were teenagers, again. Anita says she likes him. He says he likes her. There's no suggestion of anything sexy like there was with Kasia, but a connection between them is forming. She likes his lack of arrogance and that he listens well.

"On your dating profile you said your real name was Face or Dad," she says. "It's one of the reasons I swiped right on you." Tom is surprised she remembered. "Where did you get the name?"

"The kids used to call me it at school, but I guess it's a name I've chosen for myself." Anita likes this. It reminds her of the heroin addict she loved in that squat in London. His name was Sol.

"What does it mean?" Tom has not considered such a question. "There must be more to it than the burns."

"It means I'm not hiding anymore." Anita takes her hand away from his. She is serious.

"It will take me a long time for me to reveal myself to you, Face," she explains, "if I ever do at all. I lost the man I loved and I'm not sure if I can love again." He feels close to her and that this is privileged information.

"We could just spend time together."

"As soon as I get too close to anyone, I run. I just want to be honest with you. That's why I spent so much time on the road. This is the longest I've stayed anywhere for a few years."

"Let's just take this slowly then," says Tom, "I'm happy just to chat."

It's Tuesday. Tom has driven up to the village of Skidby and parked opposite the windmill and the posh restaurant. The sky is brooding and there's a chilly wind. Sitting on a bench is Joanne – she's come on her push bike. Her black hair is smooth and sleek over her shoulders, and she has a wide and bright smile as she greets him. They cross the road and walk through the deserted playground next to the windmill, the big red sails creak in the light wind. It's easy to walk and natter as they go out along the side of the field. They cover healthy breakfasts, where to get cheap but good trainers, holidays in Scotland. Joanne is warm and friendly. Although she does not say so directly, she is looking for someone to share her life with, someone who will visit Greece with her to look at the ancient temples, someone who will come on walking holidays to the Lake District and who will accompany her to gigs to see early nineties bands that are making a comeback. Tom tells her about his father and about how the man's ghost lives in the shed at the bottom of the garden along with his old armchair and all the pictures he painted. She smiles at this.

They sit in Tom's estate car out of the wind. She smells of perfume and her eyes are a smoky, rich blue. She puts her hand on his leg, and they kiss, as if they are teenagers. It is tender.

"What are you looking for?" she asks him.

"I don't know," he answers. This is the truth.

As he drives back to Hull through Cottingham, Tom thinks about her perfect teeth and the curve of her body under her cycling jacket. He thinks of Anita as well, and of Kasia too. Like the drink, these girls are a distraction to what is really happening to him.

This cannot go on.

CHAPTER SEVENTEEN
Our Dave needs someone

Our Dave doesn't like being at home. He should have got rid of all of Hazel's stuff a long time ago. It has been more than eighteen months. In the wardrobe in the double bedroom at the front of his house, her clothes hang yet; shoes are neatly lined up next to each other, her knicker drawer is full and her dressing gown hangs on the back of the door as if she is going to arrive home at any minute. Whatever happens to him, someone else is going to have to pack up his stuff – it will be one of these house clearance firms anyway and all these memories and pictures that detail Our Dave and Hazel's life together will be nothing more than charity shop tat. It's easier to busy himself with other things – the Iranian family from across the road have bought a new carpet for the front room and Tom has offered to take the old one to the tip in his battered long estate car. Our Dave said he'd help too.

There's a tap on his door. He opens up and Tom stands on the doorstep. He looks a lot better than he did a few weeks ago. Our Dave has got used to the burn scars on his face and notices that the man is fitter and thinner. He seems to have more confidence as well.

"Are you ready?" Our Dave nods.

Tom has parked his estate car on the other side of the road outside his house. He's put the seats down. It's a good car for going to the tip. They walk the steps to the front door of the Iranian house and press the bottom buzzer for flat one. There are footsteps and Sawsan opens the door with a big smile. She invites them in, and they walk down the corridor to where there are three rolls of old carpet on the floor. Tom and Our Dave move them out into the street and into the back of his long estate car. Once they have them in, Sawsan invites them back up to the house, at the door of the flat she points to their shoes. Soheil appears to translate:

"You'll have to take your shoes off to come in," he says. He has a thick and rich Hull accent. "My mum wants you to have some tea," he answers. Tom looks back at the old man and raises his eyebrows.

In the front room of the flat, Tom and Our Dave sit cross-legged on the floor. Soheil and Majid sit on either side of them. There's a big red rug with an ornate pattern in the centre and cushions around the outside against the wall. It smells of pomegranates and perfume. Sawsan walks through from the kitchen with a golden tray which she sets down on the floor, there are cups and a plate full of sweet treats. Tom and Dave are not quite sure what is happening.

Sawsan goes down on her knees, then leans forward to begin pouring from the big ornate pot. Our Dave has seen the kids and the woman in the street before but never stopped for a chat. He wouldn't know what to say. She passes the men cups of the bitter coffee and then offers them some of the pistachio baclava. It's very sweet.

"Where's your dad?" asks Our Dave.

"He died," comes the answer. Soheil is matter of fact with this information. Our Dave is sorry he asked. He sips his bitter drink and swallows it down even though he doesn't like it.

"Sorry to hear that," says Tom.

"It's okay. We never really met him." Our Dave knows how to turn a conversation round:

"Which football team do you support?"

"Liverpool," says Soheil with a wide smile. Our Dave wrinkles his nose at this.

"What about Hull City? They only play around the corner." Soheil kind of shrugs.

"Could you say thank you to your mum for us?" asks Tom. Soheil translates and Sawsan smiles. She has heavy bags under her eyes and her skin is yellow. Tom feels sad thinking about her husband. Sawsan makes them eat more of the baclava which is too sweet and runny with treacle. It's awkward sitting there on the floor. Tom would much rather be out playing football in his backyard. Probably Dave would too. Sawsan explains something to the men sitting there. Soheil translates:

"She says we're having a party on Thursday night. She's going to make a fire in the garden. It's for new year." Tom remembers this. "She wants you to come, both of you." Sawsan says something to Soheil, and he shakes his head as if he doesn't want to translate. She forces him. It's embarrassing.

"My mum says she doesn't have anyone else to invite, and if nobody comes then it will be unlucky for us."

"I'll come," says Dave.

"I already said I would," says Tom.

"You have to bring your family too. My mum says she'll cook. There'll be food. Just as long as you come." The young lad looks apologetic as he asks. Tom only has Alex.

"Will you tell your mum that my wife is away, but I'll be there." Soheil translates. Tom casts a sideways glance at the old man – the familiar lie that is always on his lips, that his wife is away and not gone for good.

"Thursday," says Sawsan. Her pronunciation is poor.

"We'll be here," says Our Dave.

Outside, and standing next to Tom's estate car, Our Dave and Tom pause now they are out of earshot of the little family. They loaded the carpet into Tom's yellow estate car already.

"I'll see you tomorrow then," says Tom. He means up at the taxi office.

"How long till you've got it all sorted?"

"A couple of days. It needs managing all the time if it's going to run properly. What about Thursday night, will you go?" asks Tom.

"I said I would."

"You're gonna have to stop lying about your wife as well, Dave." Tom is learning to straight talk. The older man's face frowns back at him.

"What's that supposed to mean?"

"You might as well be honest with people."

"It's my business, Tom."

"I know, but it's worse the longer you keep it up." Our Dave could flash with anger at this, but he has learned over so many years to keep any fire deep down within him – cool emotions lead to better decisions in the long run.

"I keep my own business to myself, kid. I'd suggest you do the same."

"I know pretty much everything about your business already, Our Dave. It's very much in my interest to make sure it's secure and well managed and that includes you. I think you need to talk to someone about what's going on. Not me. I mean a professional." Again, Our Dave keeps his chest cool although fury begins within.

"I don't need to speak to anyone. I'm coming to terms with this in my own way. Do you understand that? Not everyone needs to talk about how they're feeling, so, I don't want you to mention it to me again." Our Dave's jaw tightens, his nostrils flare. "I know she's gone, Tom, I don't need reminding of it."

"You spend so long looking after everyone else that you haven't got any time to look after yourself." Tom would never have said this, but Face will. "It's a cover story, Our Dave, all the deals and the charity donations, the extra payments to workmen, charging too little rent, all the odd jobs you do for people up and down these streets. They're a cover up. Like the booze is for me. They keep you busy and stop you looking at the problem that's staring you in the face." Our Dave knew there was something sharp about this man when he first heard him speak about matters concerning the law, now it seems this has bled through into the rest of him. He is keen and quick. Tom has cut Our Dave to the bone with his clarity. It's the kind of thing Hazel would have said to him.

"Who are you to tell me that?" he asks.

"I want to be a friend, Our Dave. That's what you've been for me. I don't mean someone who's on your payroll, I mean someone you can rely on, and not just as your lawyer." Perhaps Tom is the only person who has the knowledge and the balls to say this to him. It's harder to take help from someone than it is to give it, Our Dave has been rock solid for so many years. It's him who you can turn to if you have a water leak and nobody else will help, or if you need money in a hurry, it's Our Dave who knows a fella who knows a fella.

"Don't preach to me, kid," he tells Tom. "Why don't you take a bit of time off from the office?"

"What do you mean?"

"You said yourself you've nearly got the job wrapped up."

"I have."

"Take some time for yourself, then." Our Dave's voice has a ring of menace in it. Perhaps Tom has overstepped the mark. He watches Our Dave walk across the road to his house opposite, Tom gets into the driver's side of the estate car and closes the door. Someone at the tip will help him with the carpet. He wishes he hadn't said all that to Our Dave.

It's half nine. Bev picks up the phone. The name on the screen reads Our Dave.

"What's up?" she asks into the speaker with it held against her blonde hair.

"It's Dave. Have you got a minute to chat there, Bev?"

"What is it? I've got Chloe home from uni and I've just put a dye on her hair. If I don't get it washed off it'll go blue. What is it? I can ring you back."

"It's nothing, Bev, just something about the office, I'll ask you tomorrow. You have a good night with Chloe, I didn't realise she was home."

"She turned up out the blue. You sure you're okay, Dave? It's not like you to ring."

"I'm fine lass, I'll sort it out with you tomorrow.

It's twenty-five to ten. Liz gets to her phone after it has rung quite a few times. It's Our Dave.

"Hiya Dave," she sounds breathless. "Are you ok?"

"Aye."

"How can I help?"

"Are you free for a quick word?"

"I am, Dave, but I've got the girls from the kids' group here. We're just finishing up, we'll be done about half ten, or maybe later. Can I call you back then?"

"I'll be okay, Liz. It was nothing really."

"Are you sure? Are you okay?"

"Yeah, I'm fine. It's just a quick thing about your taxi, it can wait till tomorrow, it'll be okay. I'll talk to you then."

"Are you sure?" Our Dave can hear voices on the other side of the line, like she's in a crowded room. Liz is a busy woman now she runs the parent's group. It's a place for families such as she who have severely disabled kids. She's good at it.

"Aye, it's all ok. You have a good night now."

"I will call back, Our Dave." He can hear her moving somewhere quieter. "You've helped me in the past."

"Don't be daft, lass, I'm okay. It really was a thing about your taxi." Our Dave is a good liar.

"See you tomorrow then," she says. Liz's voice sounds bright and happy.

It's quarter to ten. Lilly answers. It's Our Dave.

"What you up to, Dave?" she asks. It sounds like she's in a small room.

"Not much lass, have you got a minute?"

"I've got about thirty seconds, Our Dave."

"Where are you?"

"I'm on a date. I'm in the lav. It's just outside town. It's called Lazzat – a Moroccan place. He's nice, he owns a garage."

"It isn't Barry, is it?"

"Barry from Richmond Street? It's not him. He's nice, Dave." Lilly's voice is raised. He can tell she is slightly pissed. "Not like most blokes. I've just come to powder my nose." Our Dave smiles on the other end. You can't help but like Lilly. "Are you okay?"

"It's alright, I'll catch you another time?"

"It's not about Gaz, is it?"

"No, it's not about him. I just wanted to have a chat about something."

"I can call you tomorrow, Our Dave. I promise."

"No need, Lilly, I'll be fine. I've got someone else who can help me out with it."

It's ten to ten. Gaz will be asleep; he and Kate go to bed early and Our Dave doesn't want to bother them. There are a million people who would talk to him. There's Brian from the chip shop, Mahmoud from Maya Spice restaurant, the girls from the tanning studio, the priest from St Vincent de Paul Catholic church, Steve from Steve's Cycles. There are the people in the address book on his phone, tenants who rent his properties, workmen who maintain them, the truck drivers who deliver the goods he brings in through the docks. Then there are the other contacts, the people from way back, the man who runs the night clubs in Leeds, the strip club owner in Manchester, the Scots brewers, the Americans who make moonshine in the deep south of Louisiana.

Anyone would talk to him, but nobody knows who he is at all. Nobody would talk to that Dave. Only Hazel.

He sets his phone on the side of the bath as he sits on the toilet in the darkness with the lid down and his pants up. He holds his hand in front of his face, over his eyes and weeps silent, wet tears into his wrinkled fingers.

Everything Tom said is right.

The quicker someone comes to kill him, the better.

CHAPTER EIGHTEEN
Third dates

Tom has never done this before. Not ever. It isn't something he ever imagined he'd have to do. It's Friday afternoon, an hour or so before Kasia has to pick up Alicja from primary school. Tom is alone and he is waiting for her to arrive. This is the Sailmaker's pub on the edge of the river Humber just a stone's throw away from Hessle Road and the Dairycoates Inn where Kasia works. Tom has arrived early before her and sits in a booth on his own. He has got the drinks in already. He has a black coffee and she's having a tea – like last time. This is an eating pub. They have two-for-one deals, and it's packed on Sundays because of the big shopping parks nearby. There's a soulless feel to it. Tom could do this by text or over the phone, but he's heard that isn't the way to do it. He's been dumped before, through friends and by email in his university days, he has also just been ignored. In fact, it hasn't happened as many times as he might like to think because he hasn't had that many relationships. Rejection in general however, this is an area in which Tom excels. Face on the other hand; he doesn't give a toss.

Kasia comes into the pub through the double front doors. She's wearing a plum-coloured beret, and her makeup is heavier than it was previously with red lips and more foundation. She's opted for a red coat that goes down to her waist and she's in thick tights with sensible shoes. Tom stands from the booth as she enters. He feels his stomach gurgle. He is not sure why he is worried, she's not anything to him but a woman he has kissed and held hands with. He meets her at the deserted bar and they exchange a kiss on both cheeks in the European way. Her hand clasps his forearm and gives it a squeeze. They sit down. Kasia smiles up at him and Tom returns it with a weaker and disingenuous grin. He's looked up how to finish with your girlfriend online, the first one of the bullet points was 'don't put it off'.

They exchange small talk about the weather, the traffic on Hessle Road, the teachers at Alicja's school, English traffic rules – it's all going as it should go and Tom finds the talk easy and diverting. Kasia is intelligent and her observations are keen. He has to remember why he is here. It is the right thing to do. There's a pause in the conversation and Kasia reaches out her hand and places it on his, it's soft and warm.

"I have some time before I need to be at the school," she says. "You could come back to the pub, and we could go upstairs." Her green eyes twinkle. Tom swallows – he thinks back to the bullet point list of advice on the website, number two read: 'say it clearly and directly'.

"It's too soon for me, Kasia." Tom pulls his hand back from hers. She cocks her head.

"Too soon for what?" she asks. They both know what she meant, but now she has altered the context, she can claim it didn't mean that at all. Tom sees the opportunity.

"For a relationship," he answers. He is inwardly pleased. He has got the information out clearly. Kasia withdraws her hand. She lifts her teacup to her lips and takes a sip. She is comfortable in silence.

"Do you need more time?" she asks.

"Yes." He knows he should be more direct, but he doesn't want to offend. Tom prefers the other two girls he's met. He prefers Anita.

"I like that about you, Tom. I like that you say what you want. I do that as well." She sets down her teacup and her hand is calm and level. "I know we only met a few times. I already like you. I want to take this slowly as well. If I come on too fast, it's because I am new to this kind of thing." Her use of the zero conditional is perfect. This is not going quite as Tom planned. In his mind, at the first suggestion of his cold feet, Kasia would have left or laughed or both, as if he had the arrogance to dump someone, with a face like his.

"I've just come out of a marriage, Kasia," he explains. "It's been about a month since she left me. I thought I was ready to meet someone but now it seems that I'm wrong. I feel like I am not ready for a relationship with anyone." This is a good lie for her to believe. It makes it seem like Tom is not ready rather than he doesn't like her. Kasia considers him with her now cool green eyes.

"I understand. I know you have seen other women." Tom blinks. She takes another measured sip of her tea.

"What do you mean?" Tom is confused.

"I've got friends in this city, Tom. I know that you visited a woman who lives in a van in a car park. I know that you have seen a black-haired woman twice."

Tom swallows. It's his turn to cock his head in confusion.

"Have you been following me?"

"Like I said, I have friends in this city." This is another business deal for Kasia. She already knows everything about him, and she has those who deliver products all over East Yorkshire. It wasn't hard to get one of her drivers to find out where Tom went and what he got up to. They're savvy lads who deal with the police, they know how to follow without being seen. They work for money and so they'll do whatever Kasia wants them to do.

Tom's mouth is suddenly dry. This has not gone as planned at all. He realises, suddenly, that he doesn't really know anything about this slight, red-headed woman who sits opposite him in a deserted pub on Friday afternoon. He will have to be more direct.

"I'm sorry that your friends told you that. Either way, I'm not in the market for a relationship. I enjoyed meeting you, Kasia, but I need time to work on myself." She nods.

"I can give you that time. Like I said, I'm new to this. I haven't been with anyone since my husband. I'd rather take it slowly as well." Tom looks down at the black coffee that he hasn't touched. He takes a breath. Who'd have thought he'd ever be in a situation like this. The information she has about Anita and Joanne must be from someone she knows, he will have to put his best lawyer foot forward and explain.

"I don't want a relationship with you," he says. Her green eyes look back at him:

"You are making a mistake." Her words are clear and cold.

"I am sorry." He swallows. "I'm not really the man you think I am, Kasia. I drink. I have unresolved issues with my past. You are an attractive, intelligent woman. You deserve better than me, you really do." It's funny how the truth comes out in clear words when we least expect it.

"I'll give you time to think about it. You might change your mind. I have a lot to offer you, Tom. More than you think. I'm not just a pub manager who cleans the toilets as well."

"I know there's a lot more to you." Tom does not know this, at all. He doesn't know that Kasia murdered the fat woman whose pub she now runs. She shot Leatherhead in the back of her skull while she was dying her hair. Kasia took over the drug business and has liquidated others who stood in her way – she gets what she wants. She wants Tom. In a few days she will kill the only other player that she does not control, Our Dave.

"This has been awkward," she says.

"We can agree on that."

"I'll call you."

"I'm sorry. I'd rather you didn't."

"I'll call anyway. You might have changed your mind." Tom nods. He has said all he can, if she wants to ring him, he'll be polite. "Until then." She slides off the pew in the little booth and stands in front of him as she puts her handbag over her shoulder. Even now, between her phone and her purse is that orange handgun. Tom stands as well.

"Goodbye, Kasia," he says.

"See you soon," she answers. They kiss on both cheeks. He watches her walk to the door. She doesn't look back.

Tom sits in his car and does not feel the sense of relief that he thought he would. He looks at his phone and there's a message from Anita.

'There's a right good band on tonight, you should come down and see them.'

'Ta! I will,' he texts back.

In the kitchen of the big house on Westbourne Ave, Tom looks at the case of wine on the floor in the corner. There will be six bottles inside. He could just have one glass and then walk down to the Adelphi to meet Anita. He wouldn't be drunk, and he's had a bad day with that Kasia woman. Galal hops onto the kitchen table and meows at him, he's already been fed so Tom doesn't know what he wants. Perhaps he's missing his mum. Tom has given up trying to say anything at all to the beast. He thinks about the case of wine again.

There's a tap on the front door. Tom goes down the hall and sees the tall figure of Our Dave through the frosted glass. He opens up. It's raining and the sky is a dull grey as the late afternoon creeps into evening. He has his collars turned up. His face is grey and thin. The familiar smile returns.

"I'm sorry about the other day," he says. Our Dave is only sorry that he revealed too much of himself to Tom. Now he has things straight in his head, he feels a lot better.

"I meant to come and apologise to you, Dave, I mean, I am sorry for what I said. It is your business and not mine." Tom is genuine when he says this.

"Can I come in?"

Our Dave sits at the farmhouse table and looks out of the window to the long garden. He's wearing his red checked shirt with the sleeves rolled up to the elbows. Tom boils the kettle.

"You've lost a fence panel," says Our Dave.

"I know. The kids from next door come and play football with me and Alex." Our Dave nods.

"They've made a right mess of your grass."

"Grass is for playing football on, not looking at."

"You've got that right," says Our Dave. They are more alike than they think, these two. Tom pours water out to make two black cups of coffee. He brings them over to the table.

"Where's Alex tonight?"

"At his grandmother's with his mum."

"How are you getting on with your misses now?"

"It's the end of it, Dave. It's done." Tom looks over at the case of wine in the corner of the room with a sigh.

"You sure?"

"Yeah. How did you and Hazel keep it together for so long?"

"I was lucky, Tom, she was a special lass. She knew me better than anyone. It wasn't always easy. There was none of the distraction you have these days." Galal jumps onto the table and Our Dave puts his hand out for the cat like he's been doing it forever, the animal goes straight to him and rubs her head against his leathery palm as he plays with her ears. Tom wishes he had this natural, steady charm.

"I had to finish it with a girl this afternoon," he says. Our Dave raises an eyebrow.

"Finish what?"

"When Inma left, I went onto those dating apps. You know the ones, they're soulless places where people upload pictures of themselves. I thought it would be a bit of fun. It was Bev that put me onto them." Our Dave looks concerned. "Anyway, I got talking to a few people and the next minute I'm having a coffee with them. It's too soon for me. She was a red headed Polish lass, worked in a pub off Hessle Road. She had green eyes, she was kind of cold. I only saw her a few times, but I got a bad feeling. I called it off. It was horrible. I mean you can see the state of me, Our Dave, I've never had to tell a woman I'm not interested in her in my life." It feels good to be able to explain to someone how he feels. Dave has stopped petting the cat.

"Was it the Dairycoates Inn?" he asks.

"Yeah. She took me upstairs. We had a kiss and a cuddle in the kitchen there." Our Dave has raised his eyebrows. Very gently he lifts Galal and sets her on the floor.

"Was her name Kasia?"

"Do you know her?" Our Dave puts his face into one of his big hands like he does. He couldn't make this up if he tried. He doesn't answer the question.

"You dumped her?"

"We were never really going out. Is she someone you know?"

"Just a bit," says Our Dave.

Our Dave stands in his nineties style oak panelled kitchen. The glow from the lights under the cabinets is a soft orange. He boils the kettle. Now he has made up his mind that he is going, he feels a lot calmer. He has accepted it. It's not something to be afraid of. It's a way out.

His phone buzzes in his pocket and he takes it out. It's a number he does not recognise. He thinks about hanging up, it might be a sales call but at least whoever it is will be someone to chat to. He clicks the green button and holds it to his ear.

"Are you, Our Dave?" The voice on the other end is foreign sounding. At least he knows the name everyone else calls him round here.

"Aye. Who's this."

"You don't know me," says the foreign voice. "My name's Pawel. I lived in Hull a long time ago. I'm looking for someone and I hope you can help me find them."

"How did you get my number?" asks Dave.

"A woman called Lilly gave me your details. I put a message on Facebook. I'm looking for my daughter. She contacted me and passed on your number. She said it was best I call because you never look at social media." This much is true. Lilly is a sucker for lost causes. This guy has clean and no-nonsense

English. He could be a nutter. Our Dave will see.

"Why does she think I'll know anything?"

"She says you know a lot of people."

"What's your daughter's name?"

"Alicja, she's seven." Our Dave winces in thought.

"Off hand, I don't think I can help you, mate. Have you thought about going to the police or something?"

"I was with her mother for a long time, and she won't answer my calls. I don't know if my daughter is safe. I don't know if she is still in Hull even." Our Dave can hear the worry on the man's voice on the other end.

"I'm sorry," says Dave. "I don't know her."

"Maybe you know her mother. She's a Polish woman called Kasia. She's short with red hair. She's not nice." Our Dave closes his eyes when he hears this. He can't get involved. It's none of his business. Kasia is a powerful woman, ruthless as well. Our Dave knows that she murdered her predecessor, Leatherhead, and he knows that she has done the same to associates who she does not see eye to eye with. He heard about a lad in Peterborough who got chucked off a multistorey car park. "Do you know her?" asks the man on the other end of the line. Our Dave does know her now he thinks about it, he knows that Kasia has a young, blonde daughter.

"I'm sorry, mate. I do know a lot of people in this town but I don't know her." Our Dave does not like to lie. It doesn't come easily to him, but the prospect of war with Kasia and her business is dangerous for him and more importantly the people he knows. Our Dave swallows. He has walked through into the front room where there's a brown leather sofa and two armchairs. Nothing has been touched since Hazel left, he rarely comes in here. If Our Dave is going to get finished off, then what problem does he have helping this man out? "Have you tried to get in touch?" he asks.

"Of course. The mother does not answer my calls or messages. She has a court order. I can't go near her. I am in

London. I just want to speak to my daughter and know she's okay. That is all." The man sounds earnest, his voice is a few moments away from cracking.

"Would you leave it with me, mate?" asks Our Dave.

"What do you mean?"

"I mean I'll ask around. I'll see what I can do. Can you text me all the details? Your daughter's name and date of birth, a photo if you have one."

"I will," says Pawel. "You know the woman who gave me your number, this Lilly, she says you help people out. She says there's nobody better." Our Dave has walked towards the window and is looking back at the sofa where he and Hazel spend nights together watching the TV. This is how it is. He can do right by people, that's what he enjoys.

"You leave it with me. I'll see what I can find out."

"I'll text you the details now," says Pawel on the other end of the phone. He sounds happy.

"I'll be in touch," says Our Dave. He is not sure how, but he will try and work something out for this man.

He knows what it's like to lose someone you love.

It's dark already. There's still a light drizzle. Tom uses the torch on his phone to light his way as he goes down to the shed at the bottom of the garden. Our Dave has told him a number of gruesome stories about Kasia. As he unlocks the iron door to the shed he can smell his father already.

Inside he feels for the light switch and the single bulb hanging from a wire flickers on. His father's chair looks eerie in the shadows now Tom is not drunk. Like always, the paintings looking out from the wall opposite loom over him. The shapes seem angry and brooding.

"I've come for my gun," he says to the armchair. He wonders if his father is still here without drink in him.

"What for?" comes a silent voice.

"Turns out the lass I went out with and said I didn't want

to see anymore is someone dangerous, according to Our Dave."

"She'll be happy to see the back of you," whispers his father.

"That's what I thought. Turns out she's vindictive."

"How come she's dangerous?"

"Our Dave reckons she's responsible for most of the hard drugs that come into Hull."

"He'll be talking shite," comes the whispered answer. Tom shakes his head as he goes over to where he left the pistol.

"That's just it, father, Our Dave doesn't talk shite. That's why you can trust him."

"What's the gun going to do?"

"I dunno."

"You might as well sit yourself down now you're here. Pour yourself a whiskey while you're at it." Tom takes out the matt black Beretta from the hiding place and holds it up to the light. It's the same as it was.

"I'm off the booze, dad, but you know, I might just have one." Tom fishes out the glass he used the last time he had a drink with the ghost of his father. It's underneath the chair where he left it. Tom finds a whiskey bottle too, and then listens to the glug as he pours himself a good half glass. He sits on the stack of tyres and takes a swallow. It dulls and soothes his senses right away.

"The first one's always the best," whispers his father. Tom looks at the glass in his hand and the clear copper coloured liquid within. He really will just have one.

"Who'd have thought you'd finish it with a lass, with the state of you." These are Tom's own words after all, he can be as cruel as he likes, the old man was never this overtly mean to him. "These lasses you've been seeing, Tom, it doesn't mean you're a better man, you know. It doesn't mean you're worth anything more, the attention just feeds your vanity, like the drink feeds your greed. You're still that ugly kid with burns all over his face and a wife that's left him for another bloke – that's the truth of it. Does it make you feel more like a man to have rejected that poor lass?"

"She's not a poor lass, Father, she's some sort of criminal."

"That'll be bollocks. She's a pub cleaner, you've seen it yourself with your own eyes, you're not in a bloody gangster film. The best thing you can do is get rid of that gun before someone gets hurt. Just like them lasses you've been messaging, get rid of them too. Someone will get hurt, Tom, and it'll be you." Tom's father was not verbose or insightful enough in life to be as nasty as this. There's cold comfort in these cruel truths like the burn of the whiskey down his throat. It makes him feel like a kid again.

"You've always had it too easy, Tom. I blame your mother. You have to start standing up for yourself. It's all well and good you galivanting off to meet that lass at the Adelphi club, but at the same time, your wife, the father of your child, is round the corner with her legs in the air and that bloke on top of her." Tom does not like to think of this.

"You've got to think of the here and now, kid. When you and her divorce, she'll try and take this house off you, and she'll screw you for money as well. She'll get Alex you know, and she'll poison their mind against you. You need to start thinking about how you can protect that because without that university job, you'll be on your arse. And don't go relying on Our bloody Dave across the road." This is actually sense. "How are you going to look after Alex when you haven't got anywhere to live? All these years you've grafted at that uni and now your wife is going to diddle you out of the lot. You are a shit husband, and a drunk, and you do have a face that looks like it's been cooked in a frying pan, but you have to stand up for yourself." Tom imagines that his father would be pleased to get off a rant such as this. There was no warmth in the man, and little eloquence either. Tom paints the old man's memory with more colour than he actually had. Like his paintings, he was a lost and watery man who lived under the shadow of his own seafaring father. "You'll have to try and get her back, Tom. She's the one you're after. It's her you want really." Tom looks down at the gun that he has set on the floor. It's the simplest advice.

"I'm sorry, Dad," says Tom.

"What for?"

"That we never got to chat properly. I'm sorry that I never got to know you."

"What's there to know? That's all your books and education talking, Tom. I was just a working-class lad who grafted and drank and watched telly. There wasn't anything more than that."

"Maybe you're right."

"You'll have to do better, Tom. You'll have to speak to Inma and see what you can do about sorting this mess out. She's had a bit of fun, and so have you, now maybe it's time to try and put this thing back together. You've lost weight, you've cut back on the boozing too, see if you can give it, one more go." He finishes the whiskey in a straight gulp, sets the glass on the floor and picks up the gun before he stands up. "You're not going to need that, kid.," says the ghost.

"It's just for protection."

"Someone will get hurt, Tom, and in the end, it'll be you." He turns out the light and the shed floods with darkness once more, the armchair is silent, and the paintings loom from the walls. He uses his phone to go back to the house and carries the pistol loose in the other hand. The conversation with his dead father has given him food for thought – Inma is savvy enough to get her hands on the house and mean enough to get her claws into Alex as well. Tom has to defend the lad. When he gets to the back door, he opens up his messages and scrolls to Anita.

'I've got something important on,' he types. 'I'm sorry. Can we do it some other time?"

CHAPTER NINETEEN
Kasia goes visiting

It's Saturday morning. Kasia has left Alicja with the family down the street who have a daughter of a similar age. She's told them she's expecting a delivery at the pub and whilst this is true, she gets the staff to handle trivial matters such as these. She's going for a ride on her bike.

She goes down Hawthrone Ave and over the railway tracks towards Anlaby Road, waits at the traffic lights before cycling down Albert Ave and then over another set of railway tracks until she is on Chants Ave itself. She doesn't look as she passes Avenue Cars, it's not time for Our Dave yet. She has other people she is looking into.

At the end of Chants Ave, she turns left and cycles past the primary school and into a little street off the side where she stops her bike and gets off. In the wicker basket with fake flowers around it sits her handbag, and within, between her phone and her purse as always, is the orange handgun that she had 3D printed by her gifted Vietnamese associate.

There's no car in the little drive, so Kasia assumes Joanne must be out. It wasn't hard to find out the details of who Tom has been talking to. It took a couple of conversations with that same, very talented Vietnamese man for her to get everything she needed. He hacked the red dating app in under half an hour, found Tom and then downloaded every message he ever sent, it took him a little longer to crack the yellow dating app, but he did that too. Kasia looked through everything Tom sent, and he was a busy little bee, but there were, in the end, only three who he had any major contact with. Joanne here exchanged her number with Tom, and it was easy to find her mobile contract through the dark web, and then her address and her credit rating, her medical notes, and her Facebook page. Kasia hacked that too and read all the messages between her and her sister. She feels a little sorry for the woman. Kasia is going to have a word with her, about Tom. That should be enough to make her back off for good, and if she doesn't, there are other things Kasia can do to the woman – she'd rather not go down this route though.

Kasia wheels her bike up to the front door and taps on the glass. The house is quiet. She peers in through the bay window and sees an ordered and well cleaned living room. There is nobody home. She's got someone else to see, she can pop back later.

Kasia rides down to Newland Avenue and the traffic is thicker and more manic between the busy shops and people. At the corner with the karaoke place she turns left into De Grey Street and cycles up to the Adelphi. She'd never heard of it until she read the messages between Anita and Tom – it's not really the sort of place she'd come. The white building has the words 'You've come a long way, baby,' written on the side in big letters. Anita doesn't get the reference. At this time, the side door is closed and locked, she can spot the big red van parked up in the far corner – you can even see the thing on Google maps it's been there that long. She wheels her bike closer to get a better look.

As she did with Joanne, Kasia found all of Anita's records in the end, she discovered her criminal record including assault on a police officer, drunk and disorderly, and vagrancy. Anita has had a difficult life and Kasia feels for her, she read her Facebook messages too. Anita's mother died but her page now shows the word 'remembering' above her name, and every year on her birthday, Anita messages her with a long letter that the dead woman will never read. Kasia knows she is looking for a life partner, even if she pretends that she is not. It felt wrong somehow to read such personal material, but Kasia comforted herself that it was for the best. She leans her bike on the side of the building and holds her palm over her eyes against the sunshine to get a better look. The red van is deserted. She wants to have a word with Anita about Tom, she'll explain that he has been seeing her as well and that they have slept together and have a relationship. Although Anita has an assault conviction, Kasia is not afraid, she has that orange pistol in her bag if anything gets nasty. She knows that Anita has a dog called Clive, and that he's friendly as long as you are. As she approaches the van, she hears sharp dog barks from within and the beast moving around inside. She is sorry to do this. Anita seems like a good person who has not had much luck. The dog barks and the red truck wobbles as he jumps around inside but there's no sign of anyone.

Kasia gets back on her bike. She looks up and down De Grey Street. She'll have to come back later for both these women. Maybe tomorrow. She could call of course, but she knows from experience that if you really want something doing properly, you have to do it face to face. She sets off down De Grey Street and then turns left onto the busy traffic of Newland Ave.

"They're divorce papers," says Inma. She let herself in while Tom was out running. She's sitting at the farmhouse table but hasn't taken her leather jacket off. In front of her is a white envelope. Tom is red faced and sweating. He goes to the sink and fills a pint glass with water.

"Where's Alex?" he asks after he's drunk a gulp.

"At my mother's with me."

"I haven't seen him for a few days."

"We've been talking a lot. I think it's best Alex stays with me. I'm her mother. We need to discuss the settlement, Tom, so we can both go about our business and get on with our lives." He pulls out a chair and sits down in front of her. The scars and burns on his face seem redder when he has been exercising.

"You look terrible," she whispers. He picks up the envelope, takes out the documents inside and unfolds them to have a look.

"I'm happy to sign all this, but the mediation will take me time to complete. Do you have a list of everything you want?"

"It's all there. I had a friend advise me."

"Good." Tom looks at the documents again.

"You want the house?"

"Yes. Alex and I need a place to live." He looks down the list and there is a figure that is a lot lower than half of the price.

"It's not enough," he says.

"Yes, it is. I think you'll find I need this place more than you do."

"I don't need it at all. I just want to get a fair price for something I have worked hard for."

"Please – most of the money came from your father." Tom looks across at the woman he once loved. He is not sure he can heed his dead father's advice; he does not want her back and now they have come this far, he cannot imagine ever being with her again.

"Why do you hate me so much?" This is a genuine question; Tom expects an answer.

"We've been through this, Tom. I changed and you didn't. I moved on and you haven't."

"You never gave me the chance to." Tom is sad to hear himself say such a sentence. He is better than this. The man who is called Face doesn't plead.

"The woman you married isn't the woman sitting here. I was eighteen stone, Tom. I married you because I thought nobody else would have me. I married a monster because that's what I thought I was, but I'm not anymore. I'm sorry to say this, but you'll just have to deal with it."

"Have you told Alex all this?"

"Yes. I explained it all. I told her about the drinking, she already knew. I explained how you won't last more than another few years before you keel over and die. I don't want my daughter to turn out like you." Tom sighs and looks out of the window at the long garden.

"Alex is too strong to be like I was," he says. "How long has it been going on?"

"What?" Inma knows what he is getting at.

"The affair you've been having with that man. Is it ever since you had your back problems?"

"Does it matter, Tom? Really? It's not going to make any difference how long it's been going on. The result is the same."

"I'd just like to know."

"You wouldn't."

"So, it was when you went to his studio with your back." She doesn't want to tell him, but maybe this is the only way.

"A few months after, yes." Tom still looks out the window.

"That's two years, nearly. Were you going behind my back for two years?" This information would have crushed Tom previously. Now he's stopped drinking so much, got fitter and been shot at with a semi-automatic weapon, he doesn't seem so bothered, even though he is.

"It wasn't like that, Tom. You didn't even notice me for so long. You were always at the bloody wine, or work." He's not angry. He would have done the same in her position. He hated himself too.

"You made a promise in church. You've got a cross around your neck. Don't you feel the least bit of remorse? What will it teach Alex to be like when he sees his mum is as loose and easy as a block of butter on a summer day." He delivers this deadpan without looking at her.

"You hurt me. You did. You didn't try and now you're blaming me because you're a scarred and troubled man." Tom sighs again and looks at her.

"This isn't getting us anywhere – make me a better offer on the house and we can get this sorted. You can go your way and I'll go mine."

"That is my best offer." Imna is stubborn. She says it's her Spanish blood.

"Then we'll have a bit of a fight on our hands."

"You'll lose. You know that."

"I'm not the same man as I was, you know."

"Just because you've stopped drinking two bottles of wine a day doesn't mean you're a new man."

"A few things have happened to me."

"It's never been the burns, Tom, it's always been the way you've dealt with it. They made you self-conscious. They made you afraid of what people think. I mean it's admirable that you're not trying to hide any more, but it's still the same old you underneath."

"Without you to remind me what I look like, I feel a lot better. Even the cat doesn't mind me so much. I'm done with worrying about how I come across, Inma. I'm glad I lost the job, I'm glad you started sleeping with your chiropractor. I'm glad I can get on with the job of finally being me." This is the pirate in him talking.

"I don't want Alex to visit you anymore, Tom."

"You can't stop him."

"I think you're a bad influence. I think you're dangerous."

"He's fifteen, he can do what he likes."

"Not legally."

The conversation is stale. They are beginning to knock chips off each other like they would routinely do. Inma stands up and the farmhouse chair from the expensive furniture shop scrapes against the equally expensive floor tiles.

"I hate you, Tom," her words are whispered. "I hate you because just looking at your face reminds me of who I used to be. I thought you were the best I could get once upon a time."

"I'm not interested anymore," says Tom.

"Why don't you do all of us a favour and keep at the drink? You could move out of here into the homeless refuge at the end of the street and in six months someone will find you dead in a ditch." This is what she expected him to do. These words will not be lies. It would be easier for her if Tom were dead. "The next time I come into this house, it will all be mine," she says. "My solicitor will be in touch with you, and that will cost you thirty-five quid a letter."

"Crack on," says Tom.

Tom looks at himself in the bathroom mirror. He needed to get washed after his run. There's only one spotlight bulb left working in the bathroom, and it gives the little room an eerie feel. Tom is a shite name, he thinks. It's just posh enough not to be working class but not quite smart enough to be anything else – that would be Thomas. He's been christened Tom. He looks at the burns that crisscross his face and neck, sees the patchy beard growing back and that his skin is flushed red after his shower. It's like Tom Thumb, or the cat from Tom and Jerry, he is Tom Nook from Animal Crossing, he's Tom Robinson from To Kill A Mockingbird, he's the mousey little guy who plays spiderman, he's the pisshead singer Tom Waits. This is a name someone else gave him. He did not choose it.

He lays in the double bed under the thin duvet in just his pants. His phone buzzes on the bedside table. It's Joanne.

'How are you doing?" it reads. He puts the phone down and it buzzes again. He picks it up. This time it's Anita:

'Turns out the band were shit. Did you get your stuff sorted?' He puts it face down on the cabinet. It buzzes again. He picks it up. It's Kasia.

'Night xx,' it reads.

All this being someone else is not quite working.

He still feels like Tom.

CHAPTER TWENTY
A visit to see Dave

It's the twentieth of March today. The first day of spring. Tom has tried to text Alex but has had no reply – this isn't strange because teenagers don't get back to you straight away, but it has been a few days since he has heard from him. He gets out of bed and stands in the shower – his hips hurt and like always, he is sure he can feel his liver expanding in his chest from the booze, even though he hasn't been drinking as much as normal. In the kitchen he looks up at the grey sky and then drinks a black coffee.

He texts Anita, 'Sorry to hear the band were bad, I had something to sort for work.'

He texts Joanne, 'All good, hope you are as well. What have you got planned for the holidays?' Like Bev told him, he will have to choose one of these two, and it will have to be quick. He laces up his running trainers and thinks that probably the best thing would be if neither of them got back to him at all, and they met other, more reasonable and more attractive men on the dating app.

At ten o'clock he runs down Westbourne Ave towards Princes Ave, crosses the road and does a lap of the park before running back up Spring Bank west alongside the cemetery. It's not quite the Easter holidays yet, so anyone with something to do is trapped in an office or a classroom. He passes a spice head asleep on a bench but sitting upright, there's an old man in a suit and tie walking at a clip and two twagging school kids on mountain bikes with almost identical black and grey outfits, one is smoking an e-cig. You can feel spring creeping in, it's not all sunshine and daffodils, but it's warm enough for the spice head to sleep outside and for the school kids to be out on their bikes rather than in a warm classroom.

Tom runs around the top of Spring Bank onto Chants and stops to walk at the Ainsdale's sign on the side of one of the houses. It's from the thirties maybe, and it's been repainted. It's been a good two mile run at least for Tom, so he will take it easy along this street. He passes the expensive supermarket, the library, which is usually closed, the Avenues pub, the cheap supermarket with Lilly standing outside smoking, then the flower shop, a wedding dress place and somewhere that sells crystals. Tom stops jogging when he gets to the lights. Opposite the Greek café is the white chiropractor studio where his wife went for a course of treatment two years ago, outside and dressed in white trousers and a white t-shirt is the man she has been sleeping with while married to Tom. He's chatting to a delivery driver who hands him a white box of what look like chemical ingredients. They have a little chat as Tom approaches and then the delivery driver goes back to his van idling just at the side of the road. The chiropractor looks up and sees Tom, his expression is dead pan. Tom is not sure what he is going to say. He hadn't planned to see this man but the side of him that is Face can't help speaking out.

"Can I have a quick word?"

"I'm a bit busy at the moment," says the chiropractor. He is called Deano Wilson. He has jet black hair and smooth well-defined shoulders, he manages to sneer at Tom as he says the words. It's the look Tom is used to because of his facial disfigurement.

"It wouldn't take a minute."

"If you want to make a booking, mate, you can step inside." He doesn't even know who Tom is as he holds the box in his hands.

"It's about my wife," says Tom.

"Go on." Deano still doesn't know.

"Her name is Inma. She's half Spanish. Did you know she was married when you started sleeping with her?" Deano swallows as he realises who he is talking to. "It's a genuine question," says Tom.

"I don't want any trouble," says the chiropractor. He steps

forward and his voice becomes a whisper. "This is my business and my home as well."

"I'm not going to give you any trouble. I just wondered if you knew."

"What difference does it make?"

"It would make me feel better if you didn't know, I suppose." Tom is not confrontational but there is the sense that he could be. He does have a matt black Beretta pistol hidden on top of his kitchen cabinet.

"In that case, I did know. She told me all about you." The chiropractor is a little taller than Tom, in much better shape, he has his teeth whitened every six months and says that his grandfather was Italian to account for his attractive mediterranean looks. Inma did tell him all about poor Tom here, she went through, in the finest of detail, his failures as a lover, a man and a father. Deano's opinion of this man is lower even than Inma's.

"You thought it was okay to sleep with another man's wife?"

"Not any other man, but someone like you, yes. I thought it was okay. You neglected her and yourself. This is what happens. If you can't keep your woman, someone else will take her." Tom blinks. The chiropractor is full of himself.

"I hope you're happy with that."

"I am, friend," he replies. "I have to get on, some of us have got jobs." Inma will have told him also, that Tom lost his position up at the university. Deano steps up to the door of his shop and pushes it open with his shoulder leaving Tom out on the street.

He runs home. The man's words echo in his ears. It's painful to what little pride he has. In the downstairs toilet he washes his face in the sink but doesn't look at himself in the mirror, he knows what's there. He's not anyone else. He thought he might be able to get a new name but here he is, just the same. His grandfather said he would have been a pirate if he wasn't a trawler skipper. He said all that and made Tom think that he could be a pirate too. Then, when he was drunk, he drove himself off a bridge and his little six-year-old grandson as well. That's what kind of a man he was. It would be so easy for Tom to open a bottle of wine from the case in the corner of the kitchen, but he reasons, he is not the man that his grandfather or his father expected him to be.

They called him Tom.

Maybe that really is his name after all.

It's all set. Kasia has asked her friend Laura to come over. They have known each other for a few years and Kasia is certain this is a woman she can trust, not least because she's been paid very well. Like every Thursday, Kasia is going off to the Woman's Institute on Ella Street, they have a local writer coming to talk tonight. Kasia was sent the link to the books by email, but she hasn't really had time to check them out – they look so boring anyway. She's got more on her mind. This business with Tom's girlfriends will have to wait a couple more days, perhaps she won't have to say anything.

It's just getting dark as she sets off on her bike. She goes the same way as she did before over the railway tracks, down Albert Ave and across over more railway tracks again. She cycles past Avenue Cars, and the lights are off. This is a good sign. She turns right into Marlborough Ave and then goes into a snicket that leads to the ten foot behind our Dave's house. She turns off her bike lights as she gets to the tall fence behind his property on Westbourne Ave.

It will be easy. She has planned it over and over again. From her handbag in the basket in front, she removes and puts on rubber gloves. Under her dress, Kasia is wearing a pair of old, thick tights which will help her with what she has to do next, she'll get rid of them when she's done, just like she will the gloves and the orange gun she has in the pocket of her denim jacket. She steadies the bike and puts her foot on the seat, gives a hop up and grabs onto the lip of the tall fence. In a few fluid movements she is on the other side. The tights stopped any chaffing.

She picks her way through the garden and sees there are lights on in the house. This is good as well. Kasia had to be sure that the old man would be in at this time, so she sent him a text as one of the councillors in his phone book and asked him to be at home for one of those survey things. Our Dave is a community sort, that's why Kasia knows he will be here. She walks down the garden keeping low, so the neighbours don't see her. As she gets closer to the kitchen, she sees him inside illuminated by orange lamp light and sitting at the square table with a mug in front of him.

Like the girls she visited the other day, Kasia feels remorse for him. She hacked his social media accounts a long time ago, his bank accounts too, she knows where he spends his money if he does so electronically, and she knows what he buys. Kasia knows too that his wife died a year and a half ago – there was a payment to the crematorium up at Willerby and a payment for flowers, she checked the births and deaths on the council archive website. She died of bone cancer. It must have been painful. Kasia moves to the back door and removes the pistol. It's not that she doesn't like him, or respect him even, it's just that she can sense what will happen. Our Dave knows who she is and what she does, this cannot stand, if Kasia is going to make a go of her life as a normal person with a daughter and a lawyer boyfriend then she is going to have to tie up all loose ends. Anyone who knows what sort of operation she runs will have to disappear, and that includes Lithuanian Laura who even now is making a cup of cocoa for Alicja while she is watching cartoons. Kasia has to get it all clean, like she always does.

She taps on the glass of the back door with the barrel of the orange gun, hears footsteps behind and the door opens to reveal Our Dave wearing a blue checked shirt. The orange lamp light bleeds out into the new darkness.

"It's you," he says. She shows him the pistol in her hand.

"Inside," she commands in a whisper.

Our Dave sits at the table facing away from the window. Kasia stands behind him next to the cooker. It smells of bleach and air freshener. She didn't think he would put up much of a fight due to his age, but she's surprised that he just went back to his chair and sat down.

"I didn't figure on it being you," he says.

"On what being me?" It's obvious what he means.

"The someone who wants to have me killed."

"You know too much about me, Our Dave."

"I think you'll find I don't know anything at all."

"You know enough for me to be uncomfortable." She's methodical in her thought process. Kasia should have been a government advisor or in logistics, but she has no sense of morality or empathy.

"You might as well get on with it," he says. His voice has none of the musical quality that it normally does.

"I will. There are just a few things I need to set up. This has to look like a gangland hit."

"Isn't that what it is?"

"I'm hardly a crime boss, am I?" Our Dave shrugs his shoulders because this is exactly what she is. She tosses a thick cable tie over his shoulder, and it lands on the table. "I'd like you to put this on over both wrists and pull it tight with your teeth."

"Why should I help you if you're going to shoot me anyway?" he asks.

"It means I'll be nicer to the people who work for you. There will be a hole in the market when you are gone."

"I'm one step ahead of you, love," says Our Dave. "I've had someone working on the business for the last few weeks. A lawyer, a good sort. I know I'm on my way out, and so he wrapped it all up watertight for me." Kasia steps forward.

"Good. I hope you didn't tell him anything about me." Dave is glad he is not looking at her as she asks him this. He did tell Tom about her. He shouldn't have.

"Why would I say anything about you. As far as he knows, my property interests are legit, just like the furniture imports." She levels the gun to the back of his head.

"Put the cable tie on please, Dave. It'll make it look more professional."

"I don't see how."

"If I'm implicated the police will guess that I'm not strong enough to put those on a big man like you with any force." Our Dave sighs.

"Can't you just get on with it. I'm ready."

"I don't want to have to threaten the people who work for you Dave, but if you don't do as I ask, I will."

"How would you threaten them? They can look after themselves."

"I've been through their lives on the internet, I can see their social media accounts, health records and all the bank statements. It would only take a minute to have an accident happen to any of them. The girls who drive for you are sweet enough, and that long distance driver you have, the tough one who's a bouncer, it wouldn't be nice for his girlfriend if the police found him face down in the river. The blonde one could lose her daughter. The little handicapped boy could lose his mother. That Kurdish girl could have both her children kidnapped with no trouble at all." Kasia's voice is husky and quiet, as if she is explaining a recipe to her mother, without emotion or sentiment.

Our Dave complies. He fits the thick cable over one of his wrists and then the other, he pulls it tight with his teeth and his hands come together and are locked in place.

"I'm ready to go, lass," he says. Our Dave thought he might cry here. He thought that all the emotion he's kept pent up in his chest for the last year and a half might come out, but it doesn't. Just like he's been taught all his life, Our Dave keeps it all in and after tonight there will be nobody left to hear him ever again. He's not a religious man but he knows somehow that he will be with Hazel, even if it is just to not exist at all anymore. Without her, these months have been the hardest of his days. He looks down at his chest.

"Have you got an alibi sorted?" he asks.

"Of course. I'm just about to cycle down to the talk at the women's institute meeting on Ella Street."

"Ballistics?"

"This is a 3D printed gun. I'll burn it. I had the bullets made in a lab."

"They'll need to find a killer," says Our Dave. "That's how the coppers work. Even if they don't know who did it, they'll pin it on someone."

"Exactly. I thought about that." Our Dave looks up.

"What do you mean?"

"I've got someone coming round to take the blame already. I got into your messages a long while ago, Our Dave. I can send anyone a text to tell them what to do, and they'll think I'm you. He'll be here in a minute or two after I'm gone. The bank records show you transferred a lot of money to him already. It'll be easy for the police to join the dots and he'll take the wrap." Our Dave swallows. Perhaps he has not concluded his affairs as well as he thought.

"Who?"

"You know him well. His name is Gaz.'

CHAPTER TWENTY-ONE
Raise the black flag

It's just getting dark outside. Tom has tried ringing Alex but there is no answer on the other end. This is odd. He misses the lad; he misses the noise of the bass from upstairs and the chats they have about all sorts of nonsense. Galal pads into the kitchen and whines. Tom has fed him already. Even the cat is missing the noise and the chatter.

The last few days have been bad for Tom. He is beginning to lose his way. He is slipping back into the old world where he lets his father and Inma bully him, and he is reminded of his failure at every turn. The case of wine in the corner calls to him. Just one glass. All that nonsense about becoming someone different, about giving himself a different name, that was just the release of his body losing a few kilos and the solidity of being straight after being hammered every day for the last ten years. Tom is not anyone special. He goes to the corner of the room and rips open the mail order wine case, there are the tops of six bottles of expensive red looking up at him. He bends down and takes one out. From the cupboard he grabs a big wine glass and fills it halfway. There's the satisfying glug sound. He holds it up to the light and sees the heavy viscous liquid inside, then takes a sip. It is divine. He sits down and sets it on the table in front of him. Everyone drinks after all – it's not like everyone's an alcoholic. He swallows the rest of the wine in two more gulps and pours himself another. It is a step backwards.

Tom is not an evil drinker, that's why he's been able to get away with it for so long. He doesn't start fights or make nasty comments, he doesn't even fall over. Tom is a reasonably sober sort of drunk. At times when he is depressed, the chemicals in his brain sway, especially when he is alone. At least if he is going to drink, he should walk down to the German beer house so that he can be around other people.

Tom thinks back over the days. He sees Inma sitting in the chair he sits in now with her face dark and cold as she explains what a bad husband and father he is. He sees the snarl on the chiropractor's face as he delivered his comments the other day. He sees the disapproving look in Alex's eyes as he staggers to bed on a Saturday evening. He stands and reaches up to the top of the cabinet. Where he left it, is the matt black Beretta pistol he got from Our Dave. He looks at the letters embossed on the barrel, feels the weight of the cold steel and the dots that make up the grip of the handle. He wonders if Inma and the chiropractor are at it now, upstairs in his little shop on Chants Ave up the road. How they must have laughed at him. How they must laugh at him still, and when he is gone and Inma has this house, the chiropractor will move in upstairs into the double bed. He will become Alex's father and they will go on family holidays to Ibiza and people will not point and look at his ugly face and burns as they do Tom. Inma can have a normal life without him. Alex can be normal as well. They can be an everyday, regular family.

Tom goes over to the wine bottle and picks it up. He takes a swig on it like a gunfighter and his mind mists. He looks back into the past all the way to his grandfather's house on Hessle Road before they had the accident. At the kitchen table the old man taught him to play pontoon while he smoked cigarettes. They gambled for one and two p coins and Tom drank lemonade from a dirty pint glass.

"We're pirates, you and me," said the old man. The drink has given Tom focus. "If I wasn't a skipper out on the open sea, Tom, I'd be a pirate. I do what I like, and I like what I do. I work hard and look after my friends because it makes me happy, and if you get in my way, I'll run you through." The old man waggled one of his crooked yellowing fingers towards Tom as if he was stabbing him with a cutlass.

Tom sees himself in the reflection of the big kitchen window. Even in the blurred image he can see the grotesque burns on his face from where they crashed. Perhaps he is a pirate after all – he looks like one. Tom takes the pistol, makes sure the safety catch is on, and slips it into the back of his belt. He walks to the farmhouse table and takes his teacher's jacket off the chair – the one with leather elbow patches, he puts it on. Just for a moment, his brain flickers – this is madness.

It's not madness. He's going to walk up to Chants Ave and have a quick word with the chiropractor, with the gun if necessary and he isn't going to shoot him or anything stupid, he's just going to have a word, that's all. He needs to show to himself more than anyone that he's capable, he's a man, like his grandfather and he does what he likes because he likes what he does.

Outside, Tom slams the door shut behind him. It's just getting dark properly as he steps down the front path to the gate and goes through. Westbourne Ave is deserted in both directions. The gun feels heavy in his belt. It's probably safer for Tom to go up to Chants Ave behind all the big houses so he crosses the road and goes down the tenfoot by the side of Our Dave's house. The lights are on inside. He wonders what the old man will be doing, maybe he'll stop in on his way back.

Tom walks further down the track and the darkness engulfs him. Away from the streetlights and the road he can suddenly hear the crunch of his boots on the ground and the sound of his breath. His phone buzzes in his pocket and he takes it out to check the message in case it's from Alex. It's from Joanne. It reads:

'I just got back from Wales this morning. It was a great few days. How's your week been?' He puts it back in his pocket as he turns the corner and walks on into the darkness of the tenfoot. On either side of him is the glow from the houses and gardens in the night sky. It's peaceful. The cold has sobered him, even though he is not so drunk. He stops when he gets fully into the darkness. Whatever he is about to do to the chiropractor is a bad idea, and like the ghost of his father explained, in the long run it will be Tom who is hurt by it all. He notices a bike leaning against the fence behind Our Dave's garden and it feels like he's seen it before, there's a basket on the front with fake white flowers around the rim. He blinks in the darkness. This is Kasia's bike.

He swallows as he remembers what Our Dave told him about her, and his lips are dry. What is she doing here? Maybe someone has stolen her bike. He steps back a few paces and looks down the tenfoot along the side of the big fence. His stomach gurgles. Something is not right. He may be a lawyer of sorts but there is still intuition in him, especially as he has only had half a bottle of overly expensive wine. He walks to the gate in the side of Dave's tall fence and looks down at the latch in the darkness. He tries the handle, and the door opens up. Kasia assumed it would be locked. There's nothing to steal in the garden, and those who know wouldn't steal from Our Dave anyway.

Tom creeps through the fence door and into the garden proper. There's orange lamp light coming from the kitchen window, he can hear himself breathe and he can feel his elevated heartbeat in his chest. He walks closer to the house and peeps in over the sink. Facing away from the kitchen window he sees Kasia's red hair loose to her shoulders as she stands looking down on something. Tom edges closer.

There's Our Dave sitting at the table in front of her facing away. Kasia is holding something. Tom can't be sure what. He moves out of sight of the window and presses himself up against the wall. His heart rate has gone up even more. He is suddenly sober. He needs a wee. He peers through a corner of the kitchen window again to get a better look, he sees what Kasia is holding. In her hand is an orange pistol pointed towards the back of Our Dave's bald head. It looks more like a toy than an actual weapon but the gravity with which she holds it suggests that it is real, as does the stillness of Our Dave. Tom can hear them talking. He moves out of sight and feels the rough brick of the wall under his palms as he presses against it.

This is ridiculous. All of it. He has stumbled on something, and the best policy is to double back through the gate and to his kitchen and the bottle of red wine on his clean counter. He would never have got as far as the chiropractor, sense would have prevailed, as it should now. Tom has Alex to support, he has bills to pay, he must preserve himself. He swallows. There is moonlight above and behind the dark clouds, and the glow from nearby houses and streetlights is soft. A raven calls somewhere far off. There's the swoosh of a passing car on Westbourne Ave in front of the house. Tom flares his nostrils. He has not stumbled upon this – he is meant to be here. He is meant to have the gun tucked in the back of his trousers and his choice hereon in will decide who he is from now on.

So much of his life has not been a choice, more so now he looks back on it. He didn't choose his name, or his angry, unemotional father or his middle-class upbringing, the merits of which have been drilled into him. He did not really choose Inma, rather she chose him, and he went along with it, who else was going to look at him twice with his face like a road map and his confidence on the absolute floor. Six-year-old Tom did not choose to sit in the passenger seat of his drunk grandfather's Jaguar that Sunday afternoon, he didn't choose for the old bastard to show off how fast he could go and then drive the car off a flyover, he didn't choose to have the face he has either. He takes a breath. This isn't the story. There's no sense in him whinging about everything that's happened to him, so many more people have had worse and better too. The story is where this man is going to place his right foot next.

He can either do something or run away.

"Goodbye, Dave," whispers Kasia as she levels the orange pistol to the back of his head. The splatter will be all over the kitchen table and the closed door in front, there may be some splash back, but Kasia will wash everything she's wearing. In any case, Gaz will be over here in ten minutes after she's unlocked the front door and he'll leave his fingerprints all over the place like a schoolboy. She can't predict how the young man will react, if he calls the police that's fine, if he doesn't that's better – they'll catch him quicker.

She readies her finger over the trigger and her nostrils flare. She loves this. The explosion of the bullet and the release of all that tension. It's like popping a big zit.

There's a light cough behind her. She does not lower the pistol from the old man's head. She senses that someone has stepped in the back door but does not see who it is. If it's that Gaz then he's come far too soon, the bloody fool, Our Dave's fake text message instructed him to be here at seven on the dot, and to knock at the front door, then come in if there was no answer.

"I'm going to shoot him," she announces. She takes a deep breath in through her nose. Her plan has taken a wrong turn. Whoever this is will have to die as well, and it will all have to be done and dusted before Our Dave's little friend Gaz shows up, if this isn't him. Kasia does the maths in her head. The old man has his hands tied so doesn't pose much of a threat - unlike whoever has just entered. When she does turn, she will have to shoot whoever it is without hesitation and then, just as quickly, turn and shoot Our Dave. She will have to keep her head.

She steps her left foot back and swings her body round so the outstretched gun is facing the other way. She will need to aim. There are six shots in the pistol, she'll shoot at least four bullets into this person and save two for Our Dave. She sees the scarred face and the black pistol pointing back at her, sees the tweed teacher's jacket that he wore when he visited the pub a few days before, smells his aftershave and the light notes of red wine on the air.

"Tom," she whispers, and here is the hesitation that she

did not want to fall prey to. She should have just fired the pistol. He looks different somehow, out of context in an unfamiliar, nineties style clean kitchen bathed in orange light. Where did he get the gun? How is he here? What is he to Our Dave? Has she been played?

"Did you set me up?" she whispers. It's not that she would be surprised anyone would do this, rather that she is shocked at her own naivety and that she did not see it. They stand staring with the pistols pointed at each other's heads. Tom is taller than she is, and his matt black Beretta looms as she aims the orange 3D printed weapon that the Vietnamese man made for her at her storage facility off Hessle Road. She'll have to shoot him. What about the detached house in a leafy West Hull village where she was going to live with this man, what about the Christmases and the holidays, what about her growing old with him and Alicja's children coming to visit at the weekend? She hesitates. She will have to shoot him.

Tom calculates too with the academic side of his brain. He sees her green eyes flash, remembers what Our Dave told him, that she's a killer, that she cuts the heroin she sells with fentanyl, that she had a man executed down in Peterborough. Kasia gets jobs done. He understands her no nonsense, humourless attitude. He'll have to shoot her and not just because she might shoot him first.

Tom thinks faster than she can.

There's the flash of light and a clicking sound as Tom's gun recoils backwards. A single bullet shell pops out the back and lands on the kitchen counter. Kasia staggers against the American style fridge and the orange pistol falls from her hands. The bullet hit her just below the neck and she struggles to breathe, a line of blood rolls down her chin from the side of her mouth. Tom looks across at Our Dave who has turned around. His eyes are bloodshot and wide with fear.

"Bloody hell, Tom," he whispers.

"Not Tom anymore, Dave. Not after this." The older man

stands up and his hands are tied in front of him, he watches as Kasia slides down the fridge leaving a thick line of blood as she does. She gurgles from her throat and her eyes swim.

"She would have done worse to you, Tom," says Our Dave. "How did you know?"

"I went out with her, I told you. I saw her bike leaning on the fence behind your garden. I'm not Tom anymore, Dave, I mean it." Dave sighs. It's typical for someone to say something stupid after they've had a near death experience.

"Who are you then?" Our Dave has to humour him, for in his action he has just changed the future significantly for the old man. Now there will be nobody out to kill him he will have to alter his plans. He sees that Tom is looking down on the woman he has just killed, who, only a few days before was in his arms. Our Dave pushes him on his shoulder to turn him around so he can look into his eyes – not everyone is made to shoot someone in the chest and come away from it. Our Dave should know. "Who are you then?" he asks again.

"My name's Face." Tom's eyes water. He is earnest and worried at the same time, unsure of himself too. He has murdered a person, and he will see punishment for it. Our Dave can see him beginning to spiral into panic – this is not how it works, he must defuse the seriousness of their situation with the only real emotion he knows how to control.

"I bet it took you a while to come up with that," he says. There is no situation where taking the piss does not help calm the mood. Tom gives him a weak grin. He knows this pirate humour from his grandfather, it feels like home.

There's a knock on the front door of the house behind. Our Dave steps back. He holds his finger up to quieten the man.

"You just wait here, kid. Don't move and don't touch anything. I'll deal with this." Tom nods. Our Dave goes to the front door and his hands are still stuck together with cable ties – he hopes it's Gaz just as Kasia explained. He unlocks the door and pulls it open as he puts his head around. There he is, dressed in a black donkey jacket. It's Gaz. Bang on seven.

"What it is, Dave?" he asks.

"You'd better come in." Gaz steps through and closes the door behind him.

"It's been a bit of a wild night," says Our Dave

In the kitchen, Tom has not moved. He still has the Beretta in his hand, held loose by his side now, and his burned, melted face looks pale. Opposite him sitting upright against the fridge with her legs splayed out in front of her, is Kasia, lifeless. Our Dave explains as he steps through the door:

"It's not as bad as it looks, Gaz. We have a body and two weapons to get rid of, but I've dealt with worse before." The young man looks at him with his eyes wide. Gaz has stepped into a scene from a gangster film complete with the characters. Our Dave is the old fella you didn't expect to be involved in this sort of thing, the man holding the gun with scars across his face looks like he's been melted with acid. "I didn't want you to be part of anything like this, kid," says Our Dave, "but here you are. First things first I need you to get some scissors out the kitchen drawer under the microwave and cut this off me," he motions to the cable tie on his wrists.

"Who's this?" he asks as he looks at Tom.

"A friend of mine. He just saved my life, he saved yours as well. His name's Face." Gaz looks at the man holding the matt black Beretta by his side.

"Pretty name," he says as he sees the burns all over his cheeks and forehead. Tom couldn't have shot anyone. He wouldn't have dared.

"If we're going to get out of this," explains Dave to the room, "then we'll have to do it together."

It's just getting dark outside. Alex has let himself into the big house on Westbourne Avenue. He's been staying with his mother and the constant bad mouthing of his old man has been grating. His father is out. He's fed that blue, shorthaired cat, Galal and it whines to go out, then whines to come in again. Alex worries about his father and despite the teenage sense that his parents are nothing to do with him, Alex feels a protective over the man. It wasn't so very long ago that Alex needed him, and when he did, Tom had been the only one who would listen. Alex stands in the kitchen dressed in his baggy jeans and big coat. The front door open and closes with the letterbox banging. His father walks down the hall into the kitchen, the burns look bright against his pale skin, but he grins wide when he sees his son.

"Where've you been?" asks Alex.

"I've just been out." Tom's not quick enough to lie and he still feels shivery after shooting a woman in the neck. "I haven't seen you for days."

"I dropped my phone in the toilet," says Alex, "it's knackered." Tom steps forward and goes in for a hug. They embrace. It's warm. This is family.

"I'm here for the fire, what time's it on?"

"What fire?"

"Next door are having a fire, it's that New Year festival. It's tonight. You said you'd go." Tom remembers.

"Your mum told me she didn't want you coming her anymore."

"She can piss off," says Alex. This is exactly the kind of thing his mother would say. She's taught him well.

"I've had a bit of a busy evening so far." Tom has been busy. He and Gaz got some tarpaulin from Our Dave's shed and wrapped the body in it. They cleaned down the kitchen as best they could with towels and old bedsheets. Blood is sticky stuff. Our Dave made them wear marigold gloves as they worked. He removed the bike from behind his house, it's better that it doesn't get nicked and end up with the coppers.

Our Dave assured Tom and Gaz that he needed a new kitchen anyway, so the place would be ripped out and refitted, and he'd get rid of both the guns as well. He said that Kasia would not be missed, not at all, perhaps not even as much as her predecessor, Leatherhead. He reminded Tom, once again, that she would have killed him if he hadn't her, and Our Dave too, and young Gaz would have got the blame. It was a difficult hour. Tom is surprised how resilient Our Dave is to it all, as if this kind of thing has happened before. Young Gaz appears to be as hard as stone with a dry humour. They feel like good company for the man he has become. As he walked across the street, Tom remembered that Kasia had a daughter.

Alex goes to the back window in the kitchen and sees that there's a bonfire through the gap in the fence, he points to the flames licking up into the trees and the bits of glowing ash drifting up into the night sky.

"They've started already," he says.

In the darkness, Tom and Alex step through the fallen fence panel and onto next door's garden. It's a not a crowd by any means. There's the hippy couple from the second floor flat, the biker type with a leather jacket and his long hair in a ponytail. The bonfire isn't very big. Alex goes over to help Soheil and Majid drag a wooden a palette onto little bonfire.

Standing on his own and looking into the flames in the nearly dark March evening is Our Dave. He would have remembered about this even when Tom didn't. The few residents chat behind and the two men have a moment alone.

"I'm glad you stopped by at mine before," says Our Dave. "Did you go back home for the gun?" There's no need to lie, not with all that has gone on between them.

"I already had it tucked into my belt, Dave. I was on my way to see that chiropractor that my wife's been sleeping with." Our Dave examines him in the flickering light from the fire.

"Looks like I did you a favour then."

"You did."

"There's no going back to what you were before, Face." Tom likes the ease with which the man slipped in his name. It makes him feel safe.

"Good. What will you do with her body?"

"Same as always, Cleveland Street incinerator. I'll chuck the bike in there as well."

"She's got a child, Our Dave. I only just thought about it as I came home. She's got a kid at primary school."

"I know. Turns out, there's someone looking for her." Our Dave thinks back to the earnest man who called him the other night, the one who was looking for his daughter. It's like Brian from Dundee Street Fisheries says – funny how things work out.

"What about you, Our Dave? There's nobody out to finish you off now, is there?" The taller man nods in the firelight. He has not considered what he will do now there is a future, but he will have to step into it.

"I might just copy you, Face. I might just become someone new." The words are sarcastic.

"It is New Year's Eve, after all, in March."

Sawsan circulates with a tray of plastic cups filled with some sort of soup, it smells sweet and salty in the cold night air. She gives Face and Our Dave a smile as they take a cup each.

The bonfire is not very big or exciting. There's a wooden palette nearly burned away and the fence panel that blew down and snapped in half is on there as well. It's a far cry from great fires Sawsan might have seen where the young men jump the flames in celebration. Face takes a gulp on his soup.

"I've got some stuff in my shed we could burn," he says. "I'll get Alex to help me bring it across."

With his phone for a torch, Face goes back through the fence and down to his shed at the bottom of the garden in the darkness. Alex follows. He unlocks the door and wonders if his father will still be in there, there's the smell of the old man straight away. Inside he feels the paintings loom at him from the far wall as he goes to the light switch.

The bulb flickers on and there's the empty chair. Face stares at it for a minute to see if he can hear the old man, and just before the voice comes to him, Alex cuts through the musty silence.

"What have you got to burn?" he asks. Face is sorry to do this, somehow. The old man has become a confidant of sorts, even though he is not there, and even though he is not particularly friendly either.

"Granddad's chair," says Face. Alex stands next to him.

"That's granddad's chair."

"I know. He doesn't need it anymore."

"You said you come in here sometimes to speak to him."

"I did. That's got to stop. Things have to change, Alex. That includes me more than anything." The young man gets this.

"Mum doesn't think you'll manage it. She says you'll be a sorry old drunk till you die."

"Well, I can't promise I'll win," says Face.

"You just remember that I'm on your side, dad."

Face knows that he is lucky to have Alex.

The two of them lift the heavy chair through the shed door, each carrying one end, and in the next garden, they set the armchair into the fire upright. It looks majestic there surrounded by the flames in the darkness, like a throne almost. The cream white material doesn't catch right away, but soon enough the fire takes hold of the sponge material in the seat and the yellow flames turn a pale blue colour in the darkness, the smoke is oily black as it climbs into the night sky.

"Goodnight, Dad," whispers Tom. He feels a hand on his shoulder and turns. It's Alex. He's glad the lad is here.

CHAPTER TWENTY-TWO
Wrap up

It's Good Friday and there's a queue of punters out of Dundee Fisheries. Tom stands outside Steve's cycles with his hands in his jacket pockets. He didn't sleep very well last night after everything that happened. Joanne is inside dropping her bike off to get a service and Tom suggested they meet up to have a coffee in the Greek place two minutes' walk away. She didn't seem as chatty on her texts as she normally does.

She comes outside and wears a wide smile as she greets him. Tom gets a flashback of shooting Kasia in the space between her neck and her chest, and watching the shock on her face when he did so. He sees it every time he blinks.

"Are you ok?" asks Joanne as she stands in front of him.

"All good," answers Tom, but he isn't. They walk to the café, and they don't have that easy chat that they did before. Something's changed. Tom orders a lemonade and Joanne goes for a tea. The conversation begins with Wales, and moves onto the weather, why people eat fish on Good Friday, religion, the reason Joanne dislikes flip-flops, it stalls on current affairs and Tom finds himself metaphorically grabbing at the air around him for a question that will make Joanne talk. He should be better at all this by now. He keeps thinking about his father's armchair that they burned and wonders if his memory of the old man is unfair, perhaps he wasn't that bad after all. The lack of booze is making him question everything. Joanne is silent opposite. Her hands are crossed on her lap as she looks him in the eye.

"I think you're too soon out of your relationship, Tom," she says. Maybe she can see he's distracted. It has taken her a while to work up to this, but she delivers it with aplomb. This is what he needs. Calm seas never made a decent sailor. Face can tell himself he was going to say the same thing to her but what would be the point. He's made his mind up already.

"Are you dumping me?" he asks. He is playful with this.

"Kind of," she answers. "We were never really going out. I'm sorry, Tom."

"I think it's for the best," he answers and means it.

It's a Sunday afternoon. In the carpark of the Adelphi, there is a big, empty patch in the far corner that looks much cleaner than the rest of the tarmac. It takes Tom a minute or so to work out that the red van is not there. He's messaged Anita many times and called her too, but there was no reply. It worried him, so he came down to the Adelphi to see for himself. The side doors to the building are open even though the club isn't and just inside the door is a man with light brown hair and a goatee beard mopping the floor. He's broken a sweat. This is Carlos, the bar manager.

"Can I help?" he asks.

"Have you seen Anita?" Carlos puts his mop into the bucket and stands up straight.

"She's gone."

"Where?"

"I dunno," Carlos shrugs his shoulders. "Are you Face?" he asks, and immediately regrets it when he sees the scars that Tom wears across his cheeks and down his neck. "She said you might come looking for her."

"Here I am."

"Barry from Richmond Street Garage fixed the van yesterday, it was a miracle he got it going and then, Anita and Clive just jumped in and drove away."

"Where to?" asks Tom.

"Like I said, I don't know. Maybe she wanted a change. You know how it is with some people, they don't stay anywhere long. She even gave Paul his mobile phone back and he was happy for her to take the van too, it'll save him from scrapping it. She said to say goodbye." Tom looks at the clean corner of the Adelphi car park where the red van sat for so long. He'd made his choice, just like Bev told him he had to.

Tom walks back down De Grey Street and wonders where Anita and Clive will end up. He thinks about her smooth shoulders and calm smile, she did say she would run if she got too close to anyone. The old Tom would have been angry at how cruel the world is, but Face is just glad he met her, Clive too. He wishes them well, genuinely and can only hope in the future that he'll meet her again.

When Kasia does not come back that evening, Laura takes Alicja home with her, and when she can't contact the Polish woman the next day or the next, she is reluctant to get in touch with the police. Laura worked with the Lithuanian army in her past life before she came to the UK, she has done things for Kasia that used those skills she learned all those years ago. Laura would rather the authorities did not look into any business that could connect the two. Kasia's daughter Alicja does not look as worried as she should considering her mother has disappeared.

Laura hears on the grape vine that there is an investigation at the Dairycoates Inn. It's kept out of the papers and off the internet, but the pub is closed down while the coppers take it apart bit by bit. Kasia was very careful, but the breadcrumbs will lead to Laura in the end, and she regrets the easy money she was offered for simple, but nasty jobs just because she is a woman with military skills. Laura will have to pack it all up, she has two young children and a big blonde unsuspecting Lithuanian husband. They will have to go back to Vilnius as soon as is feasible without looking like they are running away. Then there is the problem of little Alicja whose mother has disappeared, and Laura knows will be dead. She can take the little girl and pretend she is her own, but there will be questions at the border, and what about Alicja herself.

On the third day, there's a tap on her front door of her newbuild, red house on the Kingswood Estate just north of

Hull proper. She opens up and there's a blonde man with a crew cut and wonky teeth.

"I'm looking for Laura," he says and pronounces her name in the right way so she knows he's not English. There's something familiar in his blue eyes.

"That's me. Who are you?"

"My name's Pawel," he says. "A friend of mine told me about Kasia." Laura invites him to come in before he says anything more in the street and he closes the door behind him. They stand in front of each other in the little hallway that Laura wallpapered last year. It smells of evening primrose from the diffuser plugged in the socket.

"What about her?"

"She's gone away, that's all I know." Laura considers this foreign man in front of her. He'll be Polish like Kasia.

"How did you find me here, and what do you want?"

"There's this guy called Dave, he runs a taxi office in town. He told me about you. He says you have something of mine." Laura trained at the military academy of Belarus, she was Lithuanian special forces from 2007 to 2013 and learned a mix of karate and the Russian martial art they call Sambo, it's all headbutts and elbow strikes. This blonde man Pawel is a few seconds from being knocked out.

"What do I have that is yours?" she whispers. He can see her hand curl into a fist by her side.

"I was Kasia's husband," he answers. "I've come for my daughter." Laura does not alter her stance. She is afraid. The man does not seem threatening, but the information that he has about her is unnerving. He may know more. "This Dave wanted me to tell you that Kasia has gone away and won't be coming back again and if the police haven't got in touch with you already, they'll leave you alone. They think it's a Vietnamese gang." Laura's mind links the information she has heard.

"Why should I believe you?" she asks. Alicja heard the

door and the voices in the hallway from upstairs. She was told to stay in her room if anyone came but she is curious and wilful like her mother. At the top of the stairs, she listens, and she knows the man's voice, so she comes down about halfway. The man notices the little girl, and his hand goes over his face as tears form in his eyes. He said he wouldn't forget her.

This is Avenue Cars. It's Friday afternoon. Deano Wilson runs the chiropractic clinic across the road from the Greek restaurant and over the last three years business has been good, he's just moved in with someone new. Our Dave has made him a coffee and he sits easy as the two of them chat in the back office, the old man has called him to talk about the rent that he pays on the shop. They've always had a good relationship, especially since Our Dave charges such a small fee for the two-storey shop. Turns out that the old man is having trouble with his finances, he's very apologetic, he's having to move with market forces. Normally it's just a handshake and a bank transfer every month.

"I'm having to change the way I do things, Deano," he explains. "I just can't operate like I used to, the tax man will clobber me." Deano nods. He thinks the taxman clobbers him as well.

"The clinic is on its knees to be honest, Our Dave. I only make enough to get by as a single man." In truth, Deano has a lucrative contract with the NHS and routinely manages to see people for half an hour when he is paid to see them for two. He has a crêpe van business that his brother runs for him, and he is just about to move in with his girlfriend to a sleek flat in the posh part of Hessle. She's a pixie haired, half Spanish woman called Inma with a successful dress business and a sideline as an Instagram influencer. "I'm not sure how much I can afford." Our Dave nods.

"I'm sorry things aren't going to stay the same, Deano. My wife died, you see." Our Dave says this as if it were a broken boiler or a flat tyre. In truth, the words get easier to say every time, and the grief has started to come out, bit by bit in conversations with those he can trust. To someone like Deano here, he will make light of it but at least he will admit that it happened. Our Dave can't do counselling. He won't talk to the girls in the taxi office about it at all, but Gaz will listen without saying anything. The man he calls Face talks to him too, and slowly, Our Dave is coming to terms with Hazel's death, even if he never really will.

"I've got someone else looking after the business now," says Our Dave, "he's upstairs. It's him you'll have to chat to." Deano gives a kind of grimace and sets down his mug of coffee.

Tom has set up his office in the front bedroom. Avenue Cars was a terraced house once upon a time. He likes the noise from the street and the sunshine in the morning. Deano Wilson sits opposite at the big table looking at him. Our Dave has explained that Face ought to be careful not to become an arsehole. Face is mindful of this advice.

"I'm the business director here," says Tom. "My friends call me Face, but you can call me Tom. It doesn't look like you've got any formal contract with Our Dave." Deano swallows. It's this dickhead again.

"It was always just verbal, you know," says Deano.

"Well, I'm afraid that's going to have to change. We can draw up a contract here and now and get it all sorted within the hour. Does that sound ok? It's only the same as Dave has had me do with the other properties down Chants Ave." Deano better come clean or this fella with the burned up face is going to screw him. He means about the fact that he was sleeping with Tom's wife for so long and he has pinched her away from him. He regrets speaking to this disfigured man the way he did in the street a week or so earlier.

"I didn't know you were married. I just said all that stuff to scare you off. It's real with us two you know, me and Inma, it's for real." Tom locks his fingers together on the desk in front of him.

"I can assure you that the business with my wife has got nothing to do with your rent increase. In fact, without you, I might not be here at all." He doesn't just mean sitting behind this desk. "I have a lot to thank you for, in fact, Mr Wilson. So does my ex-wife." Face is earnest. Deano sighs and gives a nod. He heard from Inma that her ex-husband has changed a bit, and he knew he worked for a local businessman, but he didn't know it was Our Dave. The burns on his face no longer look like something the man is ashamed of, he made a cash offer for the family house and bought Inma out. Deano had hoped he could move in there, but it's not all bad, the kid that Inma pretends to care about spends all his time with his old man these days, he's got some sort of noisy band. The music sounds like shite to Deano.

"So, the rent isn't going to go up by much then?"

Face gives him a great big smile.

#

Avenue Cars 4 will be out in 2025. It's the last one. Promise. Head over to www.chrisspeck.co.uk to sign up for the mailing list.

Printed in Great Britain
by Amazon